JAMES HENDRICKS

D1606555

AUGUSTUS
PUBLISHING

Copyright 2007 James Hendircks
ISBN: 09759453

Edited by Anthony Whyte
Design/Photogaphy: Jason Claiborne
Graph Art: Kel1st.com

First printing Augustus Publishing paperback May 2007

AugustusPublishing.com
info@augustuspublishng.com

IN MEMORY OF'
ERNESTINE "BIG TINA" MORRIS
FRAND and ESTELLA CASTER
LENARD "LEN G." GARNETT
ALONZO "ZOE" MURPHY

Gone but definitely not forgotten.
Through your loved ones your memory lives on.

LOVE!!!

ACKNOWLEDGEMENTS

First and foremost I want to give praise to my Lord, Allah, who has truly blessed me. Next in line is the love of my life, my strength and support, my wife, Lisa L. Barnes. I want to say "I love you" to my children: Marvell Barnes, Marcus Barnes, Markel Barnes and my stepson, MarJuan Barnes. Thank all of you for loving me unconditionally.

I want to thank my uncles: Steve Emmons, Samuel Smith, David Caster and Anthony Caster for giving me the game from a male perspective. My lil' cousin Leekemia "Deon" Caster for always being there, Love.

My grandmother, Ruth Brown, I love you. My favorite aunt, Rhonda L. Campbell. My other aunt, Oletha "Lisa" Campbell, Tira Seals and Toni Seals. Thank all of you for giving me the female side of the game. I love you all.

I want to say "what up?" to all of my little cousins because it is too many of ya'll to name at this present time. Tasheka Russell, Precious Seals, Steven Rice and Alisa Alexander, you four could always make me smile.

I want to say "thank you" and "I love you" to both of my godmothers whom were there for me at different and difficult times in my life. Brenda D. Smith-Cooper and Diane "Mama J" Johnson.

My god kids, Sarai and Sammie Johnson. I love you both. My god brothers, Wiley "Waldo" Johnson and Benjamin "Bobo" Johnson. My god father, Eddie "Gingerbread" Fryer who's still too smooth and young in heart. The coolest mother-in-law I could ever have, Marlene Barnes. I love you all.

My brother who has always preached to me, especially when I didn't want to hear it, Thelonious Hobdy. I'm ready to listen. The truest friend I ever had, Odell Arnold. Be patient because I got you. My adopted lil' brother, Timothy "T" Pierce, who believed in me and this book more than anyone, including myself. A person who has helped me out a lot, Christian "O.J." Riley. Some real men: Karlos "Pudgey" Mayhew, Terrance "Boolash" Stokely, Brock "Bookie" Spaulding, Dontarion "Don-Don" Nolan, Randy "Ray-Ray" McNeil and Marko "Tabu" McGee. Jessica Randolph for helping me out when I really needed help. Despite our differences, you still my girl.

Some brothers who really got fucked in the game like myself, CCA: Bobby "B.O." Suggs, Seantae "P-Long" Suggs, Terrance "T" Dilworth, Columbus "Nate" Malone, last but definitely not least, Terraun "Boo Rock" Price. Bronx member Jason "J-Boo" Best. As long as we're still breathing we got hope and hope can be very powerful when believed in. Our day will come but until it does, practice patience and stay strong, focused and true to y'all principles. We gone make it!!

Finally, I want to send thank you's to Anthony Whyte, Jason Claiborne and the whole Augustus Publishing Family (The Dream Team). Thanks for giving me the opportunity to tell the world my stories. The slogan: Go Hard or go home, is for real.

A note to all Vice Lords, Gangster Disciples, Latin Kings, Bloods, Crips and every other organization influencing our youth, it's time to get away from the gang-bang mentality that was instilled within us and put our focus back on uplifting our communities as it is supposed to be. It's time to guide our youth back to the proper path. We are their leaders and they are the leaders of the generation.

Peace and Love,
BayBay

PROLOGUE

Los Angeles, California has the Crips and Bloods. The Midwest has Vice Lords and Gangster Disciples. They were established in Illinois and have their signs and colors. Take a journey into this world.

From the mid-eighties continuing into the early nineties, Washington D.C. was not only known as the Nation's capital, but also as the murder capital. This all changed in 1993 when on a cold January night in a small city called Gary, Indiana, two thirteen year olds took an oath that would change their lives forever.

1

"Man we did it," Don said.

"Yeah brother, we did it," Jon said trying to sound as enthusiastic as his twin brother. The twins were tall for their age, five-foot nine and rising. They were identical in every physical aspect; high yellow, skinny and often teased that their heads were too big for their bodies. They were considered to be pretty boys because they had hazel eyes and corn rolls hanging pass proud shoulders. Neither liked being called pretty boys.

At the initiation were Twon, Antwon Jones a five-foot wanna-be. Zoe, Alphonso Jackson, an albino who thought every girl was in love with him. Kory Kay Smith was five-foot seven cute and chocolate.

"We not leaving here until we come up with another name for ourselves," Don said letting everyone know he was in charge.

"Y'all lil' brothers get up with me tomorrow," the man who had just blessed them in said. "I got something for y'all."

"All right," the boys said and went back to thinking about a name.

"I got it!" Jon shouted after an hour. "Since you Conservative Vice Lords, we gone be SCC-Straight Conservative. Keep our shit tight, ya know?"

"I think we got a winner," Don said putting his arm around Jon's neck and smiling. "Plus I'm freezing my balls off. We'll meet in the Dungeon tomorrow."

Saturday morning, the crew sat in the twin's basement. It was known as the Dungeon. After a while they agreed the Boys Club on Fifth Ave was the spot to be. They made their way upstairs.

"Y'all bet not get ya'll asses in no trouble." Tina Jenkins shouted. Five-foot ten, with cocoa butter complexion and long black wavy hair down her lower back, she was the twin's mother. She had hazel eyes and the perfect figure, she was a beautiful woman. Tina Jenkins was a nurse at a nursing home in Skokie. The boys' father walked out on her. For the past two years, Tina was not only mother but also father to the household. She worked twelve hour shifts and had a fiery temper.

"Ma, we just going to the Boys Club to shoot some ball," Don said.

"Ma, can you give us a ride because you know that it is freezing out there," Jon said.

"Sure baby," she said extending her arms to give Jon a hug. "Just let me grab my coat and keys."

Don knew that she favored Jon. He didn't understand if they were identical twins how she had a favorite. He always said that when he got older he'd ask her.

The boys piled into Tina's 1991 GMC Safari. Jon sat up front with his mother. Pulling in front of the Boys Club, Tina looked at all of the boys and said, "Don't forget what I told y'all." Then she kissed all the boys as they made their way out.

The Boys Club was packed. Kids from everywhere were up in there. The boys went straight to the basketball area where Don called next game. The game ended and the boys stepped on the court and won onto the court. Since Don, Jon, Kay, Zoe, and Twon had played together since fifth grade their chemistry was picture perfect. Jon who was the better of the boys had been embarrassing Tyrone all game. Tyrone finally had enough and pushed Jon out of the air when he went up for a lay-up.

"Man what the fuck's your problem?"

Don stepped up to protect his brother.

"Shut the fuck up and mind ya BI!" Tyrone snapped.

"My brother is my bizness, bitch!"

Don swung with all he had sending Tyrone flat on his ass. Jon and Kay started kicking him wherever there was an opening. Security rushed over and snatched the boys off of Tyrone. He looked like he had just gone twelve rounds with Lennox Lewis. He could barely stand up.

"This ain't over you little punks." Tyrone managed to say as they walked away.

The boys were outside laughing and talking shit about what they had just done when Don interrupted.

"We need to get to Bay Bro's before we miss him."

Bay Bro stayed four blocks from the twins which meant they didn't have to walk far in order to get back home after seeing him. They reached Bay Bro's house and Don knocked on the door.

Lynette answered the door looking fine. Jon was in all her classes and had a huge crush on her.

"Where ya daddy at?" Don asked.

"He's in the living room," she said with too much attitude.

The boys walked in. Jon tried to kick it to Lynette. She just glared at him as he walked by.

"What's up old man?" Don asked.

Bay Bro was thirty-four, stood six-foot four with walnut complexion. He had short wavy hair and his body was ripped from a three-year bid at Joilet State Prison.

"What up lil soldiers," he smiled at the new members.

"We just had to stomp out this dude at the Boys Club." Don said nonchalantly.

"He was bigger and older, but it wasn't nothing." Twon added.

"That's right little men," Bay Bro said. He got up from the living sofa. "Don't take no shit from none of these niggas out here. Sit down and let me explain some things to y'all."

The twins and Kay sat down on the living room sofa and Twon and Zoe sat on the love seat.

"Lil' brothers, y'all part a something now, something big. Now, not only do y'all have y'all selves to look out for, but y'all got a whole nation of brothers to look out for." Bay Bro was really getting into his speech. "Do y'all know why I was in Joilet?" He asked.

"No," the boys answered in unison.

"I broke this G.D's. nose, jaw and collarbone for picking on one of the young Lords. I don't give a damn if you like the brother or not. You're obligated to assist that brother. If you're round and do nothing, then you'll be dealt with. There's no looking the other way or running. I don't care if it's one or one hundred. Do I make myself clear?"

"Yeah," the boys, with the exception of Twon answered.

"I got something for y'all," Bay Bro said and walked to a China cabinet in the dining room. He returned carrying a brown paper bag. "These are for y'all." He emptied the bag and five black six-shot .32 hand guns were on the table.

"These are for us?" Don asked jumping up.

Bay Bro flashed a smile. "Yeah little brother, these are for y'all. But don't go turning this city into the Wild-Wild West because these are for protection purposes only."

"We not old-timer," Don said smiling now that they had heat. "You know we responsible."

The weekend flew by. Monday morning came and it was time to get back to school. With the exception of Jon, the boys hated school. The morning went as it normally did with the boys talking shit to other boys and flirting with girls. At the end of their lunch break the boys decided that they had enough school for one day and went to their skip spot. It was also only five minutes away from Delany, Tyrone's projects.

It was a graveyard five minutes away from the school. The usual routine was chatting, wrestling and then talking more shit. Today they played a game called Gangsta. They'd pick gangsters from the mob movies and pretended to be them. The boys ran around the grave yard for about thirty minutes fake shooting at one another. Then they'd get into wrestling matches. Don and Kay were in the middle getting down. Tyrone and two older boys they'd never seen before walked up sipping on 40 ounces of Colt 45 and passing a swisher around.

"What do we have here?" Tyrone said passing the blunt to one of his boys. "I told y'all little bitches this wasn't over."

He dropped his 40 ounce and charged Don. Don swung as Tyrone rushed him but he missed and Tyrone scooped him up and slammed him hard on his back. Within seconds Tyrone was on top of him pounding away connecting forceful blows to his face.

"This what you wanted, right? This what yo lil' ass wanted?" Tyrone repeated.

"Get off my brother!"

Immediately after the words left Jon's mouth, he let loose three hollow point bullets from his .32 handgun. All three shots caught Tyrone in his back. He slumped forward onto Don who quickly pushed him off. The two other boys dropped their 40's and ran. Kay walked up to Tyrone and put his gun to the back of Tyrone's head and fired twice.

"Hey, better safe than sorry," Kay said kicking Tyrone's lifeless body. "Let's get outta here."

The boys went straight to the Dungeon and just sat in Don's room saying nothing. Thirty minutes passed before Kay finally spoke.

"Look y'all, what's done is done. Ain't no need worrying about it now. Dude came looking for trouble and got what he had coming. We can't change what happened, but we definitely sent a message. Now we just have to stick together, keep our mouths shut and watch each other's back. Y'all know them niggas from Delaney gone be out for blood. But as long as we stick together and watch out for one another they ain't gone be able to touch us.

Now shake that shit off and let's play some Madden."

Kay and Zoe were playing the football game while Twon had his own thoughts of the repercussions that were sure to follow. Don and Jon were carrying on their own conversation.

"I ain't never heard Kay talk so much at one time." Don said trying to lighten the mood.

"He has a point. Them cats from Delany are going to be at us and we're gonna have to be ready for whatever." Don said and pumped Scarface's *Diary* CD. "You my brother and I love you more than I love myself. I can't speak for the rest of the crew but I know that we got each other's back. Our lives changed today and only time will tell if it was for the best or the worst. The only thing I do know is that today we graduated from boys to men," Don said.

"I heard everything that you just said and I promise you that you can always count on me to be there for you," Jon said.

Delany housing project was notorious for killing. The place was also filled with Vice Lords. While the boys were playing video games in the Dungeon, the two boys who were with Tyrone were in the projects at Cash's house telling him what had happened at the grave yard.

"You telling me that ya'll two let some little kids stank Tyrone?" Cash asked while lighting a Newport. "What the fuck good is ya'll?"

One of them, Pee-wee spoke up not wanting to let Cash get too agitated.

"Cash man, we didn't have no heat on us and all five of

them little muthafucka's had they shit out and ready."

The other, Doug, followed up.

"Yeah Cash, they came out of nowhere with all these guns and shit. Man, we barely got away ourselves. We could be lying next to Tyrone right now."

Delany projects produced a lot of killers, but the man out there was Cash. At sixteen he shot and killed two Gary police officers. The court had very little evidence and the case was dropped. After that incident no one messed with Cash. Now twenty-four, he stood six-feet even and weighed two hundred pounds. He was more of a force.

Cash sat at the kitchen table blowing smoke rings and contemplated what to do about the boys who had just killed his cousin. Finally he spoke.

"These lil' boys wanna play in the big leagues, huh? They killed my cousin, so now I'm gonna kill them. First thing, I'm gonna have a little fun. I want ya'll to find out who they are? Where they from? What school they go to? And who they affiliated with? That shouldn't be too hard for ya'll to do?"

Cash was putting his cigarette out when Pee-Wee said, "They play for Beckman. I saw a couple of the games. They hot shit."

"I don't give a damn if they hot shit or not because they dead." After cooling down he finished saying, "Well now all ya'll got to do is find out where they from and who they with. I don't want no surprises because if them lil' niggas got heat like that, no doubt that they plugged. I just hope they ain't from 11th because if they is? We got a war on our hands, in the worse way." Cash was clearly pissed.

Weeks passed and nothing was heard about the murder. The boys felt relieved and started getting back to their routine. It was a Friday and Norton's gym was packed.

Even though the gym was located on 13th Avenue in the boy's hood, people from all over the city came to play ball. Pee-Wee stood talking to some chick when the boys rolled up in the gym. Since this was their hood people gave them their due respect.

"There go Don and Jon." The girl said.

"Do you know them?" Pee-Wee asked.

"Hell yeah I know them. They from 11th Avenue," the girl said.

Pee-Wee knew their names, what school they went to and where they were from. Cash would be pleased.

"What up old man?" Jon asked.

Bay Bro sitting in the bleachers talking to some young, sexy chocolate female looked up smiling.

"What's up lil' soldiers?" he greeted shaking their hands. "Ya'll all right?"

"We're now," Don said relieved that a big deal wasn't made about Tyrone's murder. Bay Bro shot him a curious look.

"Ya'll gone play some ball or what?" He asked knowing that the boys would put on a show for the crowd.

"Nah, we just hear to watch tonight," Twon said finding a seat.

While the boys watched the game and talked to Bay Bro, Pee-Wee was out in the hall telling Cash about the twins.

"Who…?" Cash asked.

"They up in here talking to Bay Bro and it seem like they

real close." Pee-Wee looked around to make sure that no one around was listening.

Cash already had a feeling that the boys were plugged and was just hoping that it wasn't with Bay Bro, anybody but him. No one close knew that five years ago when Bay Bro first moved to Gary, he and Cash had beef. Cash could remember the time.

It was a dreadful hot July night and everybody was at the beach flossing in their rides. Cash was there in a red 87 Chevy, a flock of females around him telling him how he got it going on. Two hours later Cash was about to leave when Bay Bro pulled up in his gold Cherokee with gold deep-dish Daytona's'. He had a sound system that put everyone else's to shame. Heads turned and Cash was in awe. As the night went on more and more females flocked to Bay Bro, even the women that were around Cash. Cash was hot and decided to step to Bay Bro and see what he was about.

"What's up Playboy?" Cash asked sizing up Bay Bro.

"Coolin," Bay Bro said watching every move of the fake ass nigga before him. The two stared at each other and Bay Bro could see the hate in Cash's eye. "Do you have a problem?" Bay Bro asked staring Cash straight in his eyes.

"Nah man, I was just trying to remember where I know you from." Cash responded feeling disrespected at how Bay Bro had just came at him. "What hood you from?"

Bay Bro could tell that Cash was fishing and really didn't know him. Cash was looking for trouble and Bay Bro was just the person to give him what he was looking for.

"I'm from the City." Bay Bro proclaimed with a smile on his face.

This frontn' ass nigga think he better than me, Cash thought taking it to another level.

"Oh yeah," Cash said looking around noticing that the cars were steadily leaving. "If you from the soft-ass Chi, then." The rest of his sentence never got out.

Bay Bro slapped him upside his head with a 9mm. Cash fell. Bay Bro was on top on him slapping Cash a couple of times with the pistol.

"Ain't this what ya bitch ass wanted?"

The females had backed up from the two. Bay Bro dragged Cash down to the freezing cold water of Lake Michigan, stripped him and threw Cash in. Too hysterical to realize he was only in three feet of water, Cash flopped around. Bay Bro laughed then stepped off with the girls.

"Cash, Cash." Pee-Wee shouted in the phone.

"Look man, we got to plan this shit out because there can be no mistakes. Just hold tight and let me put something together." Cash hung up the phone. Mixed feelings were brewing.

2

The spring of 93 brought everyone out. Girls were in tight dresses, mini skirts and Daisy Dukes. Boys flossed tank tops and jerseys. They wore caps tilted to one side depending on the organization.

The boys were on the basketball court at Norton Park, putting on a show like they were Globetrotters. Each team that stepped on the court left embarrassed and befuddled. The crowd loved it. No one noticed Cash, Pee-Wee and Doug blending in. They weren't there just for the show.

The next five came to the court and from the start the unknown players made it clear; there would be pain. On the opening possession Jon went strong to the rim only to be elbowed by one of the opposing players. Jon grabbed his jaw while trying to shake off the pain.

"What the fuck is your problem?" Don screamed running up to the big man.

"It was my mistake," the player said trying to sound as sincere as possible.

"Let's just play ball," Jon said taking the ball out. The crowd was on their feet ready to attack and Cash just stood in the crowd with a smile on his face as he watched the first part of his plan take effect.

The big men continued carrying out their dirty tactics tripping and throwing 'bows. Hard fouls aimed at intimidating the boys. Kay went for a lay-up and a player pulled him down from behind. He fell hard on his upper back. Jon hit the bigger player in his throat then kicked him in the groin. He screamed like a stuck pig. Jon stomped him in the face and head. Kay regained his composure and joined in kicking the player. Blood leaked from his eyes and nose. Another player ran up behind Jon blindsiding him.

The bleachers cleared with Bay Bro leading the way. The five henchmen Cash sent to deliver pain were soon swarmed by nearly everyone in the bleachers. Cash, Pee-Wee and Doug crept to the exit. Police sirens were heard and the mob stampeded the nearest exit.

Jon didn't hear the sirens. He continued supplying kicks to the player. Don ran over pulling him away.

"One-time!" Don shouted.

The gym cleared except for Cash's five soldiers who were on the floor and unconscious.

The boys made it inside the Dungeon. They were trying to figure out what had happened.

"Man, what the fuck was that?" Jon asked examining his left eye in a mirror.

"Think it had sump'n to do with what happened to Tyrone?"

Twon asked fidgeting with his hands.

"I don't care who the fuck they was," Don said turning up the volume on DOC's *No One Can Do It Better.* "We sent whoever a muthafucking message. Niggas just can't come to our hood, thinking they can get with us. We sent a message loud and clear that we not to be fucked with and if niggas want to try then let 'em bring it."

"A whole lot a shit gone down since we took our oath," Twon said. Jon started to pace back and forth.

"You alright, Jon?" Don asked staring at Jon still pacing.

Jon sometimes blacked out when upset. He once stabbed their father with a butcher knife. Don decided to keep a closer eye on Jon. Jon was compassionate and unforgiving.

"I'll be fine," Jon said rewinding *The Formula.* "I'm just thirsty."

The mood lightened and the boys played Sega, drank pops and made fun of Jon's black eye.

Back in Delany projects, Cash Pee-Wee and Doug puffed a Swisher while sipping E&J.

"You...you think this gonna be a war? It's gonna start a war right?" Doug asked sounding shook.

"What you think? We started sump'n big, big..." Pee-Wee was tripping, he knew that this was just the beginning of a war that would cost many lives.

"It was like the whole hood got behind 'em boys," Cash said shaking his head. He saw Bay Bro leading the pack. "We gotta go to Chi and get our arsenal right." Cash puffed and passed the blunt to Pee-Wee. "This gonna be a hot summer." He exhaled.

"I think we should get this shit over with as soon as possible." Pee-Wee smoked and continued. "If Bay Bro got wind of us being involved in this shit, y'all know, he gone come out on full blast."

Cash knew Pee-Wee was right. Pride might get him killed. Apprehension tightened like a noose around his neck.

A week later, the boys were hanging in the Dungeon playing Sega. They started talking about the Spring Fling dance and who would have the prettiest date. None of them had asked a girl or were seriously thinking of going. But money was involved.

"This little bet is tight. We need to start making real money." Don said watching Jon and Twon play NBA Showtime basketball. "We need to get a hustle going."

"We can learn how to steal cars and since Deuce got a chop shop right in the hood we ain't got to fuck with nobody we don't know." Kay said from the sideline.

The twins and Kay knew how to drive. Kay figured it wouldn't take but a couple of minutes to teach Twon and Zoe. Kay had been waiting on some type of come-up. Since his pop got laid off from the Steel Mill he went from Jordan's to regular Nikes.

Jon put a pause to the game and said, "We don't know nothing about stealing cars and niggas get shot to steal another muthafucka's shit."

"Man, Deuce can show us how to steal a car and we got burners. We talking come-up and that's the sure way. Man, I heard you can steal a car in a minute and make a G off it. Think about that, a thousand a minute...? Man, us five can put that work in and make ten G's a day." Kay said.

"I feel you and I'm with you but we've to put this one to a vote. We'll go around the room. It's yeah or nay." Don said.

"Yeah!" was echoed by all.

"Then it's on,'" Don said smiling and thinking about all the dough.

Later the boys went by Deuce's garage. They were familiar with him but Kay was the closest to him because every summer he worked at the garage running to get food, sweeping up the floors and look-out. The garage was only one block over from the twin's house and it was on the same block as Kay's house. It was connected to a fast food restaurant slash ice cream shop.

When the boys finally made it to the garage it was Kay who was suppose to do all the talking since he messed with Deuce like that.

"Deuce man, we trying to stack some paper," Kay said sitting in a chair in Deuce's office. "The problem is; you need to show us how to steal cars."

Deuce was thirty-seven years-old, dark complexion six-footer. He had a gut that kept getting bigger with each bite that he took. Rumors floated that he killed two men who tried to rob him one night at the garage. Most people took Deuce for soft because his wife had him in check. The chop-shop had been running smoothly going on two years. Deuce smiled at Kay. This was inevitable. He knew that Kay was hungry.

"I'm gone sho' y'all little asses what ya'll need to do, but Kay, do not make my spot hot."

"Nah, I'll keep this on the low," Kay said.

Deuce showed them some stolen cars. They saw how it should look after. He liked neat work. Sloppy work would get you pulled over. He took them to the junkyard to demonstrate every step of stealing cars. After the demonstration he took them one by one and watched them duplicate what they had just seen. They all succeeded, but it was Jon who stood out. Jon had done the whole process accurately and neatly in less than one minute and Deuce was impressed. He knew that this was a come-up for everybody, especially himself.

"Ya'll ready to get that paper," Deuce said smiling at them.

"It's on."

In the weeks that followed, the boys went on a car stealing rampage turning Merriville upside down. Twon and Zoe learned to drive. They stole ten cars a day and although they were pumping in money, it was not as much as Kay figured. They were making three to four hundred dollars a car and felt like they were getting cheated. Deuce was paying his other car thieves seven to eight hundred for the same cars the twins were bringing. Deuce exploited them since they didn't know the car game.

One day the boys delivered their cars to the shop and ran into an older car thief who had been with the Deuce since the beginning. They noticed that he was delivering the same type of Cadillac.

"What up Cheese?" Jon said looking at how dapper Cheese was dressed in a cream color Pelle Pelle outfit that ain't even made it down to Gary yet.

"Putting that work in," Cheese responded smiling.

"Let me talk to you fro a minute playboy," Jon said.

They walked off. Jon picked Cheese's brain about the dough he was getting for his work.

"You just got twelve hundred for that 'lac?"

Jon was unable to hide his surprise. Deuce had just paid

them four hundred and fifty dollars for the same car with better rims and in better condition. Jon returned with fury in his eyes and payback on his mind.

"Do ya'll know that bitch-ass nigga, Deuce been playing us this whole time?" Jon asked calmly.

"What's on your mind brother?" Don asked seeing his brother had something up his sleeve.

"I'll explain everything to ya'll back in the dungeon," Jon said as they made their way across the street. "Let's just say we about to come up, fo' real."

When the boys made it back to the Dungeon, nobody ran to the Sega game. Instead they waited to hear what Jon had to say. Jon had gone upstairs to the kitchen. He grabbed a Sunny Delight and bumped into his mom.

"What are you boys up to?" She asked looking at Jon with a worried expression on her face.

"Nothing ma, we playing video games and just chillin," Jon smiled.

"I don't want y'all getting into no trouble," she said rinsing a cup.

"Ma, you know we good fellas." He hugged her and kissed her on the cheek then went back downstairs.

"So what's the plan?" Zoe asked.

"All right, I need ya'll to hear me out on everything before ya'll start interrupting," Jon said. He put Scarface's CD before continuing. "We gone hem his ass up in the garage and demand some changes. He pay Cheese twelve hundred for some busted-ass 'Lac. I ain't no sucka. He ain't gone play us or 'em hollows will ring. I'm tired of niggas not taking us serious because we shorties. Fuck that! It's time muthafuckas know bout SCC."

Jon sat down sipping his orange juice and surveying the room. No one said anything. Zoe looked at Jon.

"When do we put it into action?"

"One week from tomorrow," Jon said looking at the four others. They moved in closer as Jon went over the details.

The Spring Fling dance was quickly approaching. With the exception of Jon, the other boys had their eyes set on Vanessa, the prettiest girl in the school. Twon was the first one to approach her and quickly got dismissed. Zoe was next and tried to win her over but got turned down. Kay approached her at lunch time in the cafeteria and things were going well for him until he looked at another cutie wearing a skin tight Guess dress. Vanessa was so upset she threw a carton of milk at him. Luckily the carton of milk wasn't open. His brand new Pelle Pelle outfit wasn't damage.

Jon witnessed the whole thing and had a good laugh. He was sure to bring it up later so all the boys could clown Kay. Jon saw the cutie sit at a table and made his move. Jon didn't think that she would go to the dance with him but figured it was worth a shot.

"How you doing Lynette?" he asked standing in front of her.

"What do you want?" Lynette looked up mean as ever and said.

Jon was prepared for the attitude. He was always soft on Lynette and went out of his way to give her special gifts. Jon had a huge crush on her since she moved to Gary.

"I'm not trying to start no trouble with you. I just have sump'n I wanna ask," Jon said. He lowered himself and sat.

"I don't have all day." Lynette was impatient.

"Will you go to the dance with me?"

Lynette screwed up her face but on the inside she was smiling. She knew he was sprung and wasn't about to let him off the hook without making him sweat.

"Why should I go to the dance with you?" She asked with her ghetto girl attitude.

"Lynette, you know how I've been feelin you for some time." He fidgeted with a napkin. "I just never approach you because you treat me so bad."

She saw that he was being sincere. Lynette knew the twins apart whenever they would speak. Jon was so sweet to her while Don was a plague.

"Yes I will go to the dance with you."

Jon was shocked and just stared for a moment then a wide smile stretched across his face. He was speechless.

"Call me," Lynette said getting up from the table.

She made it to the door and turned to see if Jon was wearing that same big-ass smile. It didn't take much for Don to get Vanessa to agree to go with him to the dance. He couldn't wait to tell everybody to pay up and forget about competing because he was a lock.

Deuce's one week was up and the boys were at the shop to let him know how they were feeling. Waiting to get paid, they kept looking around to see who was coming and going. They had to execute the plan while only Shady and Tony were in the shop. Shady and Tony were the two workers who did all the work on the cars and had been with Deuce from jump. They were no killers. This was the boys' lucky day. Only Tony was in the shop. Deuce paid the boys. Then Jon and the rest of the boys pulled out 32's catching Deuce by surprise.

"What up Deuce?" Jon asked. Anger filled eyes.

"Man, what the fuck y'all doing...?" Deuce asked looking confused.

"We here to get our right due," Jon said pointing his gun at Deuce's head.

"I don't' know what y'all talking bout. Things was all good just a week ago." There was panic in Deuce's voice.

"Let's step into your office and talk about it," Jon said pointing.

Tony saw what was happening and decided to make his exit. Deuce and the boys entered the office. Jon sat in behind Deuce's desk.

"Keep your hands on the desk at all times," Jon said. The boys lowered their guns and Deuce felt a little relieved. "The reason it got to be like this is because you been playing us." Jon was looking straight in Deuce's eyes. "You been paying the older cats way more money than you been paying us and we here to collect what's owed us." Jon had a serious look on.

"I'm begging you, don't hurt me. I was the one who hooked y'all up. I'd never play y'all. I..."

"Shut the fuck up!" Jon shouted. "Look, this is a one time non-negotiable offer. You owe each of us a Mustang, hooked up of course. Then you'll pay us what you pay the others. The alternative

is to just pay us what you owe us and we'll go holla at dude on the 25th."

Deuce knew that he would lose out on a whole lot of money if he let the boys go. Deuce weighed his options before speaking.

"Deal," he said knowing no money was subtracted. "Next time ya'll have a problem just come and talk to me. Ain't no need for no guns. Ya'll know me and ya'll know we can work out whatever. Give me a couple days to get the paperwork right on the Mustangs." Deuce's smile didn't reveal the plot taking shape.

"All right," The boys said. They left laughing and joking.

3

Back up in the Dungeon, Don and Jon were playing Sega. Kay searched the music collection. They drank from a couple of 40 ounces of Colt 45, an old-timer copped for them earlier.

"Oh yeah," Don said pausing the game. "Y'all owe me five hundred a piece."

"For what?" Zoe asked.

"I know ya'll didn't forget about the little bet we got. I got the baddest chick in school for a date and unless ya'll can pull a rabbit out ya'll ass and get Janet Jackson, I suggest ya'll pay up now and save ya'll selves some dignity." Don said.

"I wouldn't count my chickens before they hatched if I was you." Jon said.

"Who's your date, Jon?" Don asked wanting to know who was better than Vanessa.

"It's a surprise. Everyone will see when I arrive at the dance with the finest girl in Gary." Jon said smiling.

Don looked at his brother and started laughing.

"What's so funny?" Jon asked.

"Man everybody knows that Lynette hates your guts. If you not bringing Janet Jackson forget about it," Don said.

The rest of the night went with the boys having a ball talking shit, raiding the fridge and playing Sega. Jon managed to get away for awhile and had a long conversation with Lynette. Then fell asleep happy, dreaming of Lynette.

Three days later, Deuce had the paperwork on all five 1992 Mustangs in order. When the boys delivered their next shipment of cars Deuce only paid all of them two hundred and fifty dollars.

"What the fuck is this." Don said reaching for the .32.

"Hold up, Don." Deuce said.

He walked to the back of the garage where the finished cars were kept. "It cost me way more than I expected. My man said it would draw a bust getting all five of them done at once." Deuce was lying through his teeth. The boys still was not getting their full pay but they didn't complain. Their mouths dropped when they walked into the area. Sitting in front of their eyes were five Mustangs with the wettest paint and all sitting on Dayton's.

The boys was about to run to their car of choice but Deuce stepped in front of them.

"Twon you get the candy apple red, Kay, the black one with gold flakes in it. Zoe you get the deep plum purple color red one. Don, you get the money green one with gold flakes. And Jon the cocaine white one is yours."

They went straight to get personalized license plates that read SCC. Gary and Chicago would hear more from them.

Doug, Pee-Wee, Darnell and Cash were sitting at Cash's kitchen table going over the plan.

"I done got all the heat we need. If we fuck this up, then we'll need everything." Cash sipped Hennessy as he spoke. "We can't afford mistakes."

"I want one of the little muthafucka's for that bullshit at the gym." Darnell said passing the blunt to his left. "We got to make sure that all of them little punks end up dead."

It was a week since Darnell was out the hospital. There were stitches on his chin and his lower lip. They shaved his head and put seventeen stitches to the back of his head. He had two painful ribs that were fractured. The crowd had really worked him over and the team. The other four members were out of the hospital. They quit messing with Cash and also warned Darnell to do the same. Darnell wanted revenge. Cash received a lot of criticism for leaving his guys hanging. He brushed it off.

"Man, we got to get this plan done up right because I ain't trying to fuck up and then have to see all of the 11th. Specially, Bay Bro stupid ass," Doug said and passed the blunt to Pee-Wee.

"Man shut the fuck up." Pee-Wee said. He snatched the blunt from Doug. "You too soft, complaining and acting all scared like a little bitch. You better hope a nigga do you a favor and kill you because you'll be somebody's bitch in the joint." Pee Wee laughed.

"Cool out Pee-Wee. Doug was telling it how he sees it that's all." Cash said.

They went over the plan changing what to do, finally demonstrating how it was going down. Cash felt satisfied.

The day of the dance the boys were running around trying to find Twon who had been missing since the night before. He had told his moms that he was spending the night with the twins but never showed up. The boys spent the morning driving around their hood and the adjoining hoods, trying to spot Twon's car. It was damn near two o'clock and they still hadn't heard a peep from him.

"You don't think it was them dudes from the gym, do you?" Zoe asked leaning on a tree in front of the twin's house.

"I don't know," Don said sipping a Hawaiian Punch. "But this shit ain't adding up."

The boys were about to go back into the house when they heard *Deep Cover* by Dr Dre and Snoop blaring from a car system. They stared at each other realizing it was Twon's favorite. A few seconds later they saw the candy apple red 5.0 bend the corner. Twon pulled in front of the twin's house.

"Get the fuck round the corner!" Jon yelled over the music.

Tina was in the house. Twon quickly pulled off and the boys walked to the next block.

"Man what the fuck is your problem?" Twon shot back.

All the boys knew that when Tina was home they had to park on the next block. There were no excuses. Jon grabbed Twon by the throat and forced him to bend over backwards falling onto the hood of Twon's car.

"I'm not my brother! I will choke yo ass to death out here. If you ever disrespect me again, I will punish yo bitch ass. Do you understand me?" Jon spat everywhere and looked as if he was foaming at the mouth. Twon nodded.

"Jon! Jon! Man you gone kill him. Come on brother let up. It's going to be all right."

Jon slowly released his grip on Twon's neck.

"You're... you're fucking crazy, man," Twon said rubbing his neck.

Zoe watched, his mouth hanging open. He knew Jon had a bad temper, now he saw it.

"It's ahight brother," Kay said. He grabbed Jon around the shoulders leading him back to the Dungeon. The others followed.

"Man Don, that brother of yours is nuts. How he gone disrespect me like that?" Twon said walking next to Don.

"Man, you had everyone worried. He was going crazy trying to find you. You know how he takes shit personal. You're lucky he didn't kill yo ass for not telling us where you were going to be last night." Don said.

They sat in silence. Jon and Kay were at the foot of Don's bed. Don and Twon sat at the head of the bed. Zoe decided to sit on the couch. Jon had calmed down and finally spoke.

"Where the fuck was you at?"

"I've been meaning to tell ya'll. I met this chick. She got a spot deep on the West side and from time to time, I fill in for some of her workers." Twon answered evenly.

Don stared in wide-eye surprise.

"So let me get this straight," he started, "You gotta plug and ain't turned us on to it. What the fuck is up with that?" Don

sounded pissed off after finding out that his friend was hustling on the side.

"It ain't even like that y'all. I already told her about y'all and she said that she didn't do business with people that she didn't know. So I figured that I would work for her for awhile and let her see that she could trust me and then introduce her to y'all." Twon knew he had fucked up and was looking for a way.

They had known each other for a long time and all felt Twon was lying through his teeth.

"So how did you meet this woman?" Jon asked.

"She's cool with my cousin Mike from the East side."

"How we gone shake y'all moms?" Zoe asked wanting to floss ride and not get dropped off at the dance.

"I already took care of everything." Jon said.

"What do you mean you took care of it? When? How come I ain't know anything?" Don asked looking at his brother.

"I hollered at Bay Bro and he got us covered. Just be ready at six o'clock."

5:45PM

The boys stood in Don's room. They were dressed in black Hugo Boss suits with gold Versace silk shirts and black gators on their feet.

5:50PM

Bay Bro rang the twin's doorbell to pick them up. The boys rushed upstairs and found Tina and Bay Bro carrying on like childhood friends.

"Ready to go, old man?" Don asked itching to get in his ride.

"Yeah, little men, I'm ready if y'all are." Bay Bro said with a smile.

"Don't forget, I want pictures," Tina said hugging all the boys.

"Don't worry Tina," Bay Bro said then passed out five black canes and five black Dobbs hats to the boys. "We'll be right back. You jut have that camera of yours ready." Jon kissed his mother as they went out.

"I see ya'll done came up in the world." Bay Bro said as they got into the van he rented for the evening.

"We doing ahight, but we could always be doing a lot better?" Zoe winked as he spoke.

"Y'all not ready yet," Bay Bro said choosing his words carefully. "Y'all got y'all hustle going for y'all. It might seem like slow money right now, but it's money. Y'all still a little young and right now school is important. When I think the time is right, I got y'all. Don't worry. So where we headed?" Bay Bro asked Jon since he had not spoke up to tell him where to go.

"Back to my moms," Jon said and all eyes went on him. "I need to talk to you about something important first." Bay Bro nodded and headed back to Tina's after picking up the dates.

Tina snapped pictures of the boys and their dates. She just kept going on and on about how handsome the boys were and how pretty the girls were. While Tina was enjoying the moment, Jon tapped Bay Bro on the shoulder and nodded his head towards the porch.

"What's on your mind?" Bay Bro asked.

"Well," Jon seemed to be trying to build up strength and choose the right words. "I didn't tell you where to pick up my date

up because I don't even know if I have one."

"I don't understand lil brother."

"It's like this. Now you have to hear me all the way out before you start telling me how crazy it sounds."

Bay Bro nodded with a serious expression on his face and Jon continued.

"My date is a girl that I have a huge crush on. I don't really know too much about love but I can say that I do love her. The problem is I have a lot of respect for her family and don't want to burn any bridges. She's the girl for me and I don't know if I should take the chance of going to pick her up and ruining my relationship with her family. What do you think I should do?"

"If you really like this girl then you should go for it." Bay Bro lit a cigarette and continued. "The family should either embrace you or warn her, but never have ill feelings towards you. Now you do have people that will kill to protect their loved ones." Bay Bro was looking straight in Jon's eyes. "If one of y'all tried to talk to my baby girl, we'd definitely have problems. I wouldn't say that I would kill y'all, but it would definitely be some repercussion."

"Bay Bro, I love you like a father and I mean no disrespect, but my date is Lynette. I'm willing to get punished for my feeling but please let it be after the dance. I don't want to take no pictures with bumps and bruises. Plus I…"

"Boy, who did you think you getting over on? I saw Tina Jenkins name at least fifty times on the caller ID this past week. I also knew for about two years now that you and Lynette liked each other. It was just a matter of time. I do like that you didn't let my little speech deter you from your goal. Out of all y'all, it's you that I don't have to worry about. Because you're smart, but at the same time you don't take no shit. Let's go get Lynette."

"I got love for you, old man and oh, don't tell the others." Jon whistled in relief.

"That's ahight with me."

Tina was still taking snap shots while the boys mugged.

"That's enough Tina," Bay Bro said reaching for the camera. "Save some for Jon and his date."

"Oh no, I don't," Tina said switching the camera from her right hand to her left one. Don walked over to Jon.

"What's up? Everything all right, Jon?"

Jon smiled and hugged his brother. "I'll tell you everything later," he said.

Tina finally let the boys on their way but was sure to tell Jon to hurry back. Bay Bro dropped the boys off around the corner where their Mustangs were parked. He and Jon chat as they headed to his house.

"You know that I tell everybody that I got three kids, a girl and two boys-twins. I love Lynette with all my heart. She's my baby girl and I would do anything to protect her. If I thought that you wasn't good enough for her we wouldn't even be having this conversation. Just remember that ya'll two are the same, hard on the outside and soft on the inside."

Jon listened and realized that this was forever. Bay Bro stopped the van in front of his house and stayed inside. Jon got out the van and went to the front door. Lynette was pissed about them taking so long. She didn't wait for Jon to make it all the way to the door. As soon as Jon put one foot on the top step, Lynette snatched the door open.

"What the fuck took ya'll so long!"

Jon stood frozen, not by her anger but her beauty. He had never seen a more beautiful girl than Lynette in his whole life. She stood in the doorway with her hands on her hips wearing a from-fitting gold Versace dress to her ankles. Her long hair hung down her back. A bang covered her left eye. She wore a matching gold silk shawl.

"Well Jon," she said.

"You're beautiful," Jon muttered nervously.

"Boy, quit playing and let's go."

Lynette grabbed her black clutch-purse, locked the door and headed to the van. Bay Bro smiled all the way back to Jon's house.

"Oh my God!" Tina screamed when she saw Lynette. "You're so beautiful." She continued. "I can see why my Jon be up late nights on the phone. You are really beautiful."

"Thank you," Bay Bro said proudly.

"I'm not complimenting you," Tina said looking at Bay Bro. "I'm talking to this beautiful young lady."

"Well, she's shy right now. I guess a cat got her tongue." Bay Bro said still smiling.

"Daddy stop," Lynette said softly.

"Daddy...?" Tina blurted out surprised.

"Yeah, this beautiful young lady is my daughter." Bay Bro said looking at Lynette.

Tina nodded her head and smiled. She grabbed her camera and started clicking away. Tina and Bay Bro took turns snapping pictures.

"All right mom," Jon said grabbing Lynette's hand and leading her towards the door. Tina hugged Jon and Lynette.

"Have a great time," she said.

They got into the van and Bay Bro went directly to Jon's car and stopped.

"What are you doing daddy?" Lynette asked confused.

"I'll be driving us to the dance," Jon said as he slid out the door and hit the remote to his car.

"What the…"

Lynette stared in surprise at the Mustang, her mouth wide open.

"Have fun," Bay Bro said as Jon helped Lynette out of the van and then opened the passenger door to his car for her.

"We will," Jon said smiling at Bay Bro.

4

Saturday night and Beckman Middle School was off the hook. The Spring Fling dance was in full effect. All the girls were looking pretty. Hairstyles were the latest designs and make-up was sharp. The fellows broke out dressed in two and three-piece suits. The festivities attracted students from other schools. Everyone was having fun up in the place.

Zoe, Twon and Kay were already at the dance. Their dates were stars. Ten minutes later, Don arrived with beautiful Vanessa. All eyes were on them as they headed to the dance floor and grooved to *Let's Chill* by Guy. Don wore a smile, he knew once the dance was over and they saw what he had in the parking lot, the hollering and gawking would begin. Don was too busy daydreaming to realize that he and Vanessa were the only couple still dancing. Jon and Lynette entered the gymnasium and one by one everybody froze.

"They staring cause you're the most beautiful girl at this

dance." Jon smiled.

"Oh, so it's only at this dance," Lynette said pinching his arm.

Jon led her to the dance floor. Don looked up to see what the distraction was about. At first he saw Jon walking in his direction. Then out of nowhere a gorgeous girl came into his view. Don did the double take when he recognized Lynette with Jon holding her hand. He thought she couldn't stand them. Jon and Lynette walked over to Don and Vanessa. Don smiled, hugged his brother and whispered.

"You won."

An hour had passed since Jon, Bay Bro, and Lynette had left. Tina heard her door bell ring. She was stretched out in her bed watching *The Bodyguard*. She hesitantly slid her feet into her slippers and made her way to the front door. Looking out the window on her front door, she was stunned to see Bay Bro standing on her porch. Tina opened the door.

"May I help you? You must be lost," she greeted.

"I'm not lost and actually you can help me. May I come in?"

Tina let him in then closed the door.

"So, what can I do for you?" she asked waving him to sit.

"Your boys are gone and my little girl is gone. So I thought that you'd be lonely, because I am, and I'm also hungry. I stopped by to check on you and also to see if you want to grab a quick bite to eat."

"No thank you. I already ate and I was trying to relax a little bit."

Bay Bro's smile vanished.

"I'll tell you what I can do," Tina said getting up from the couch. "I'll warm you up some of what I had and we can talk."

"Deal," Bay Bro said admiring Tina as she walked away.

A couple minutes later she returned with a plate filled with roast beef, mashed potatoes, green beans and corn bread.

"I forgot to tell you, I don't eat pork," Bay Bro said looking at the plate.

"Boy, you gone eat my cooking," Tina said placing the plate in Bay Bro hands. "Besides, I don't eat pork either. Now what would you like to drink?"

"Orange juice," he said walking to the dining room.

"You know what, you just like Jon," Tina said smiling. "All he drinks is orange juice."

Moments later she sat in the chair next to Bay Bro. They talked, laughed and joked for three hours. Bay Bro left and they both promised to stay in touch.

At the dance, two girls wearing the same dress but different colors got into a fight over who looked better. The fight started and ended with them pulling at each other's dress trying to rip it off of the other. A boy vomitted all over his date's dress. Another was caught jacking off. A girl was letting several popular boys finger her. The crew enjoyed themselves throughout. It was an hour till the dance was over. Don started to push-up hard on Vanessa.

"It'll stay between us," Don begged as they slow-drag.

Vanessa liked Don and knew that if they were a couple

she wouldn't have to worry about money, since he was rolling in a tricked out 5.0.

"I don't know Don. Can we wait for another day?"

The whole school knew that she wasn't a virgin. Her ex-best friend had dished the dirt on the whole incident.

"I can wait. But that doesn't mean that I'll wait. Just let me know because I can easily find somebody else."

"Tomorrow baby," she whispered in his ear. Don's smile widened.

All the boys were still virgins but tonight Kay was prepared and his date was willing. Twon wasn't prepared but his date didn't care. Zoe was prepared but his date was still playing hard to get. He wasn't worried because he had all the confidence in the world that he could break her. Jon and Lynette had heard all the talk about people getting it on this night. Jon eased Lynette's fear.

"The time's not right," he said kissing her on the cheek. The DJ announced last dance and the couples fled back to the floor.

"They should be coming out any minute. Get in position and don't fuck this up!" Cash said.

Pee-Wee, Doug and Darnell got out of his Chevy Blazer. The four men ran to the positions and waited. The kids started to file out the school.

"This is it."

The crew and their dates finally made it out of the school and into the parking lot, where they went straight to their cars and hit the alarms. They opened their doors and cranked their system drawing all attention to them. They then posted up by their own shit. After a minute had passed Don, Jon, Kay and Zoe turned their radios off and all of them went to Twon's car. Thirty seconds later gunfire broke out. The students, teachers and parents hit the ground or ran for cover.

Kay saw gunfire coming from three different directions. "Man, we surrounded." He said reaching for his 32 and a 9mm.

"We got to come up with something."

Jon peeked up above the car. "Let's get our shit and bust back. Don't waste y'all shells. Cover us, Kay."

Kay fired a couple times. The others made their way to get their burners.

Jon had Lynette by the arm making sure that she stayed safe. Kay couldn't believe what Twon was doing.

"This nigga done bitched up," Kay said watching Twon sitting on his knees praying. It appeared as if he was crying.

"Nigga snap out of it. If you don't pull yourself together you gone die. Get you shit and get ready." Twon got his gun out of the car and started inhaling and exhaling very quickly.

"I'm sorry I got you in this mess," Jon said to Lynette as he pulled out two baby 9mms.

"Apologize after you get us out of here," Lynette said calmly.

"Lay down in the back on the floor. I'll be back."

"You better," Lynette said crawling in the backseat.

"I love you," he said making his way back to Twon's car.

Jon was the last one back. Kay had his 9mm and 32, Twon had his 32, Jon had two 9mm's, Zoe had two 38's and Don had a 45 Desert Eagle and a Tech 22 with extended clips. Cash, Darnell and Pee-Wee kept shooting in the area the boys were at as they slowly advanced. Doug was no where to be seen or heard from because he had the AK.

"What the fuck is they shooting?" Zoe wondered aloud.

"Man we got to get the fuck up out of here," Twon said still sounding shook.

"We'll never make it. Just let them get a little closer," Don said.

Pee-Wee and Darnell kept shooting their carbines while every time one of the boys would stick their heads up, Cash would fire his twin Glock 45s.

"We got to spread out. We like sitting ducks," Jon said.

They split into two groups and made their way.

"I got one coming into my view," Zoe said ready to bust his gun.

"Let 'em get a little bit closer and when I give the signal we'll shoot," Kay said.

"Ready," Don said.

"Let 'em get a little closer," Jon said.

Pee-Wee and Darnell kept letting off shots as they approached.

"Now!" Kay said letting loose his 9mm.

"Fuck it!" Twon screamed letting off his two .38's.

Don and Jon heard the shots they looked at each other and jumped up letting their guns go. Darnell caught five from the Tec 22. Bullets ripped his chest open. The twins heard shots and started seeing leaves and branches fall around them.

Don turned in the direction of the shots and emptied the rest of his clip.

"I'm out!" He shouted to Jon who started letting his baby

9's go until Don put in his other clip.

Pee-Wee ran out of bullets and was busy changing the magazine to his carbine when Kay, Zoe and Twon popped out from behind the car and busted off in his direction. He was stunned and ended up dropping the magazine. On his knees, he was feeling for it. A bullet ripped through his right shoulder before he could reload.

"Ah-h shit!" He cried in pain.

Another bullet hit him in the left shoulder and he dropped the carbine and clumsily tried to put the magazine into the gun. He finally gave up and pulled out the Glock 9 that he had in his back. He looked up and saw three figures running at him. He slowly raised his gun and just as he was about to shoot, a bullet caught him straight in the middle of his head, killing him instantly.

Meanwhile, the boys had made their way to Darnell and was now standing over him kicking Darnell as he lay unconscious.

"What the fuck...?"Darnell said as he opened his eyes.. "Please don't kill me." He pleaded looking up at the barrels of the guns in the hands of the twins.

"Who the fuck are you?" Don asked.

"Where the fuck you from?" Jon asked.

"I'm from Delany," Darnell answered his hands covering his face. "They call me Dee. Cash told me he only wanted to scare y'all. We wasn't gone kill y'all. I'll swear."

Don looked at his brother and pulled out his Desert Eagle.

"That's too bad," He said pulling the trigger and emptying the gun. The bulletproof vest that Darnell was wearing couldn't save him from the onslaught that came down on his head.

"Now we know," Don said to his brother as he turned to leave.

On the way back to Twon's car, Jon stopped at his car and opened the door to see if Lynette was alright.

"What the hell took you so long?" She smiled. Jon helped her out of the car and they made it to where the rest of the crew were standing. All their dates were shaking and crying.

"I'm telling y'all that was the dude from the gym." Don said as Jon and Lynette joined the rest.

"We got to get out of here. Everybody meet in front of the Dungeon in an hour." Jon said looking around.

The boys and their dates hurried to the cars.

"What the fuck! Look at my shit." Twon shouted. The driver's side was riddled with bullets. Both Don's and Kay's Mustangs had bullet holes in them. Jon's was untouched.

"Don't worry about that right now. Let's get the fuck out of here," Jon said.

"That's easy for his ass to say." Twon mumbled under his breath. The boys got into their cars and left in different directions to drop their dates off.

"I don't think that you should tell my daddy," Lynette said turning down Shai on the CD player.

"It'll be alright Boo. We together now and I'm going to always keep you safe." Jon said smiling at her while they waited for the red light at Van Buren Street.

Cash had seen it with his own eyes but still couldn't believe it. The boys that he thought would be easy to eliminate ended up smashing his men and the plan. The whole scene replayed in his head like a comedy of errors. Cash struggled to the kitchen table. He sat recalling how Pee-Wee stupidly fumbled with the magazine to the carbine instead of reaching for this Glock. He tried to justify his own cowardice by telling himself he did shoot at the twins. Doug abandoned them without even firing one shot.

"If I ever see Doug again, I'll kill him." He swore as the ringing phone brought him away from his thoughts. "Hello," he said.

"I know it was you." The voice on the other end said. Then the phone went dead.

Cash hung the phone up and wondered who it could have been.

"Gots to be Bay Bro," he said running to his bedroom.

In the bedroom Cash packed one gym bag full of clothes and grabbed all of the money that he had stashed. He ran out of his house and jumped in his truck heading to the highway.

On the expressway, Cash headed straight to Chicago. He didn't want to go far away from Gary. Cash had several four corner hustlers he could have stayed with but chose Erica. She was average looking and wore long extensions. Most importantly, Erica stayed out of his business and didn't sweat him. Now lying in her bed, he watched the news. Cash's pride had him on the run.

5

"So how was the dance?" Bay Bro said looking up from the Chicago Bulls game recorded earlier.

"I'll let Jon tell you," Lynette said kissing her father on the cheek. "I'm going to go change clothes." Lynette left the living room walking in the direction of her bedroom.

Bay Bro turned off the big screen TV and Jon took a seat in the chair.

"What did Lynette mean by that?"

"We had a problem after the dance. See, right after we took our oath all of us were skipping at the graveyard-no, it started at the Boys Club...." Jon continued to tell what all happened.

"You did what?" Bay Bro asked.

Jon didn't know how upset Bay Bro was but he repeated it anyway.

"I shot Tyrone three times in the back and then Kay shot him twice in the head to make sure he was dead."

"Please, tell me y'all got rid of those guns," Bay Bro said reaching for a Newport.

"Nah, we still got em."

Lynette walked in wearing a T-shirt and jogging pants. She sat on the couch with Bay Bro.

"Do I even to want to hear the rest?" Bay Bro said shaking his head.

Jon nodded his head.

"All right then, go ahead."

Jon continued going into the incident at the gym, how they bought guns from crack-heads and found several in the cars they stole. He told Bay Bro every detail he could remember.

"Is that it?" Bay Bro said lighting another Newport.

"Yeah, that's it. I just want to say that I'd never let anything happen to Lynette, Bay Bro. I would take a bullet for her. I'd…"

"Hold up, Jon." Bay Bro said sucking on the cigarette. "I'm mad for two reasons. One, y'all should have told me about the graveyard and it probably wouldn't have gotten this far. Two, by you not telling me you put my baby girl in danger. I'm not y'all mentor, I'm y'all friend and sometimes y'all father. You should know that y'all can tell me anything. It won't change nothing." Bay Bro put the cigarette out and took a deep breath. "I don't know who saw what, but I dropped y'all off and picked y'all up. Get rid of them cars tonight and if somebody ask, y'all don't know who was in them cars. Get rid of all the guns y'all used tonight and just be cool. As for you and Lynette…"

Bay Bro paused with the kids looking at him hanging on his next sentence. He looked at Jon first and then Lynette before he continued. "I could say that it's too dangerous for y'all to be together, but I'm not. Jon, I know that you'll keep her safe. You have my permission to date Lynette, just don't involve me in y'all mess."

Lynette smiled and threw her arms around Bay Bro kissing him all over his face.

"I love you! I love you!"

"Thanks, I'll talk to you tomorrow about everything I'm going to get on top of that right now." Jon said and got up. Bay Bro hugged him and walked back to the kitchen.

Lynette walked Jon to the door.

"I got a lot to do tonight so I'll call you tomorrow." Jon said with his arms wrapped around Lynette's waist. "I love you."

"I love you too," Lynette said. Their lips locked as they kissed each other goodnight.

Lynette watched Jon drive away then she returned to the living room.

Bay Bro hugged and kissed Lynette goodnight.

"Goodnight, my baby girl," he said heading for his bedroom.

"Goodnight, dad, I love you."

Bay Bro laid on his bed thinking about everything Jon had told him. Even though he was impressed, he was also very concerned. Bay Bro reached for the phone and dialed.

"Yo what's up?" A husky voice answered.

"Not good Goldie," Bay Bro said lighting a cigarette.

"If it's that important I can be there in a half." Goldie said.

"I'll see you then," Bay Bro said.

Jon parked his car and walked over to his block. Don, Kay and Zoe were standing out front waiting while Twon hadn't arrived yet.

"Where's Twon?" Jon asked walking up to the group.

"I don't know," Don said chugging a bottle of Dom Perignon.

"Fuck it!" Jon said sounding annoyed. "I talked to Bay Bro and…"

"What you mean you talked to Bay Bro?" Zoe asked.

"Just listen, Bay Bro ain't mad about what happened. He is mad at us because we didn't tell him about it from jump."

"My fault fellas." Twon said as he came running from in between the next door house. "I had to calm baby girl down before I let her outta the car. It's straight though," he continued trying to catch his breath.

"Like I was saying," Jon said shaking his head at Twon. "Bay Bro said in the future to bring him all problems. He said to get rid of the cars and all the guns we used. He also said the he dropped us off and picked us up and that we don't know who was in the Mustangs. It's time to be smart. I got a plan for the cars but we got to come up with matching stories to feed them broads."

They had been out there for twenty minutes going over what to say before Tina stepped onto the porch.

"How long ya'll been out here?" She asked.

"Not long Ma." Jon said motioning for everybody to go into the house. "We were just on our way in." All of the boys hugged Tina and kissed her on the cheek as they went in. Tina could smell the alcohol on a couple of the boys, including Don.

Later when they knew Tina was asleep, the boys left out the back door. Don and Kay had complained about having to get rid of their guns. Kay didn't need a lot of persuasion. Once Jon said how stupid it was to be walking around with guns that had murders on them, Kay wanted to let them go.

The boys doubled up heavy duty garbage bags and put all of the guns that they had a used inside, along with some heavy bricks to keep the bags grounded. They drove down to First and threw the bag in Lake Michigan. Next they took their cars to a stash spot on the 25th Avenue and parked them. Back in the Dungeon, they chatted about all the girls at the dance, jiving on Jon about finally getting Lynette.

When Goldie arrived at Bay Bro's house they spoke about what had gone down. Goldie was Lynette's godfather and was pissed that she wound up in the middle of a gunfight. He knew the boys and was surprised how the boys handled their business.

The next day Bay Bro found out where Cash lived. Goldie and Bay Bro rode in Goldie's girlfriend's red, ninety-eight Oldsmobile. They wore grim masks on their faces headed for Delany projects.

"I'm telling you Goldie," Bay Bro said sipping Hennessy. "I'm going to do this dude real bad."

"I'm with you brother," Goldie said pulling up on Cash's block.

"That's the house right here." Bay Bro said pointing to

Cash's house on 21st and Polk.

"It's time to give this stunt what he wants," Goldie said parking the car.

The two men got out of the car and looked around. Some crack-heads were out late searching for a high. When they made it to the front door, Bay Bro noticed that the door was opened. He paused. Cautiously they entered the house. Guns ready, they were prepared for whatever surprises they could encounter. They searched the whole house. No sign of Cash made them angrier than they had been.

"Get the gas." Bay Bro said spreading clothes all over the house. Seconds later, Goldie returned with two gas cans and gave one to Bay Bro. The two men spread the gasoline all around the house and then stood at front door where Bay Bro lit some newspapers and threw them in the house.

"Good riddance." Goldie said.

The next day Don, Jon, and Kay went to see Deuce. They found him in the back.

"What's up Deuce?" Jon said looking around at the Chevys and Oldsmobiles that lined the walls.

"What's going on fellas?" Deuce said sounding stressed.

"We got a problem," Don said.

"Like I said, if there's a problem, I'm sure we can work it out." Deuce's eyes widened and he started sweating.

"This is the problem," Jon said eyeing a big-body two door,

cream colored Impala. "We need to get rid of the Mustangs fast. We trying to get you to do a trade with us, say a couple of these Chevys."

Deuce couldn't believe his ears. They were trying to trade-in the Mustangs, cars that easily sold for $10,000. "What's the problem?" Deuce smiled in relief.

"Three of the cars got a whole lot of bullet holes in them and the other two still in mint condition. Five Mustangs for five Chevys and I want the Impala over there," Jon said pointing to the car he had been eye-balling.

"I'll tell you what." Deuce said looking around the garage at the cars. "I'll give you two Chevys, including the Impala and three Oldsmobiles."

"Deal," Jon said without a second thought.

"Just bring the Mustangs back and they're yours."

The boys left to go get Twon and Zoe who were still sleeping then they'd get the Mustangs. They took alleys and back-ways back to the garage.

"I didn't know that they were this fucked up. We-we got to come up with something different." Deuce stuttered when he saw the three Mustangs with bullet holes in them.

"Look Deuce, we got a deal. I told you that the cars had a lot of holes in them and you shook on it. Now you can honor our agreement or we can take matters to the next level."

"I'm going to do this time, but no more trade-ins," Deuce said reluctantly.

The boys were happy with the deal as they drove off in the cars.

Later, Jon went by Bay Bro's to fill him in on what they had done and most importantly, see Lynette. Jon was disappointed to find that she wasn't there. Bay Bro filled him on the plan. The visit was brief. Bay Bro had business to attend to. On the way out he gave Jon a duffel bag filled with guns.

"Take it easy, don't kill everything," Bay Bro said.

Jon took the duffel bag back to the dungeon and went through it. There were Glocks, Macs, a couple AR's and two Tec 9s.

When Don and Twon walked in they were mesmerized by the guns spread across the bed.

"Where did you get these from?" Don asked picking up a Mac 11.

"Bay Bro gave them to me today," Jon said passing his brother a Tec 9. "I made him a promise we wouldn't go on any killing spree."

"I love you boy," Don said with a smile.

Monday morning came too early. Figuring the police to be all over the school asking questions, the boys decided keep things low-pro and walked. They told their dates the stories to tell. They were the hottest up and coming crew in Gary and the cars they were in Saturday proved it.

Don, Jon and Twon were put in three separate rooms where detectives questioned them. When they were called Kay and Zoe offered no information. They all played dumb. Lynette and the other four girls represented. No one volunteered information. They made it through the school with no mention of the incident. The teachers looked at them differently and other students gave them more respect. The police never came back. People talked about the incident and even added bits. The boys put it in their rearview mirrors and acted like it never happened. Their names continued to grow in infamy.

6

School was out. It was summer and the boys had no plans for a real vacation. They began playing video games regularly and were able to do ten cars a day. Things had changed since the incident. The news of what they did to Darnell and Pee-Wee had spread throughout the city. Everyone gave them much respect. No one wanted to tangle with the crew and it was widely known they had backing from Bay Bro.

The detectives came back with bullying tactics, it didn't work. The boys stuck to their stories. They were no longer referred to by their names, they were known as SCC. Don, Kay, Twon and Zoe lost their virginity. Jon was still taking things slow with Lynette. The two had decided to wait and not rush into doing it.

The boys were sitting on the twin's front porch when Calvin, Joe and Lee pulled up in front of the house. Calvin was a sloppy five-ten, dark skin, two hundred and twelve pound, sixteen year-old who called the shots for the youngsters on 21st Avenue. He looked much older and was able to go in liquor stores. Joe and Lee were his two most trusted flunkies.

"What's up, SCC?" Calvin greeted walking up the stairs leading to the front porch.

"What's going on, Calvin?" Don said warily.

"Trying to get down with y'all," Calvin said talking with his hands. "You know we'll take this city over. Gary be ours."

"Are you serious? What do y'all have to offer?" Jon tried but couldn't stop chuckling.

Calvin knew better than to piss the boys off.

"It's only five of y'all and pretty soon a lot of up and coming dudes gone test y'all. I know y'all done held y'all own so far, but with my boys peeps would think twice."

"We don't draw off numbers and we can hold our own," Jon said.

Calvin was undeterred and kept going.

"I'm not saying that y'all can't hold your own. All I'm saying is that y'all will have strength in numbers. Plus, I know y'all do the car thing and we get paid like that too. We also get paid off this." Calvin pulled out a bag with crack cocaine. "I'm telling ya'll, we can get paid. I got a plug that can't be beat," he said.

Jon looked at the others and shrugged his shoulders.

"I'll tell you what. Y'all come with us tonight on our run and if y'all all that, we'll see" Don said sitting in his chair and pointing at Calvin.

"Bet," Calvin said confidently. Calvin, Joe and Lee sat down with the boys.

The sun was going down. It was time. The crew got ready for work. They locked up the house and got into two cars. Jon, Kay,

Zoe and Lee rode in Jon's Impala. Don, Twon, Calvin and Joe rode in Calvin's Cutlass.

Riding around Chicago for an hour and half they stole six cars. The boys along with Calvin's gang headed back to Gary. Calvin wanted to stop in Calumet, Illinois. On the way back they drove around the apartment complex. There were Caddys, Jeeps, Mustangs, Benzs and BM's parked in a lot unattended.

They took the cars to Deuce and told him that they'd be back and rolled to the apartment complex. Jon stole a '92 black Benz. Kay stole a '93 Deville, Lee a '91 BM, Zoe had a Jeep Cherokee. Don took off in a '91 ZR1 Corvette. Calvin spotted a black Mercedes-Benz 300e that he just had to have. There was no one in the parking lot so the group didn't have any standing security. Calvin disabled the car's alarm, unlocked the door and was in. He was having a difficult time with the ignition.

A man came walking in Calvin's direction. Jon blew his horn but Calvin kept trying to start the car. The man got closer to Calvin.

"Hey, what in God's name you think you're doing?"

Calvin reached for his gun. The others hurried over.

"Get the fuck on!" Calvin shouted at the man raising his gun.

The man reached for his waistband. Calvin let out two shots from his .380 hitting the man in his leg. The man aimed and fired. The bullet found its mark in the middle of Calvin's chest. His upper body dropped back into the car while his legs rested on the parking lot pavement. The man on the pavement was trying to get up.

"This nigga killed him!" Lee screamed and started shooting. The man caught one in the stomach. He turned to shoot at Lee when bullets from Jon's 45 tore through his back. Silently they stared at Calvin's life-less body. The man was gone. They ran back to the cars and headed for the expressway to Gary.

The cars were taken to Deuce's and the boys were paid well. They went to the Dungeon.

"Hold up," Jon sounded pissed about a comment Joe made. "What the fuck you mean, it's our fault? I blew the horn and his ass stayed in the car. Plus, we took care of dude."

"I'm not saying that y'all the reason he dead, I'm just saying, Calvin was trying to impress y'all and that's the reason he got killed. What we do now?" He asked.

"Look, I know Calvin was a soldier and y'all fucked up about his death. We were never in Calumet and don't know nothing. Now, earlier when Calvin was talking, he made a point. We know how y'all get down and y'all know how we get down. If y'all want to be part of SCC y'all more than welcome. Think about it and let us know."

Joe and Lee left. The boys decided to put the incident in Calumet to bed.

A week later, Joe and Lee never contacted them. The boys had an alibi with Bay Bro just in case. Jon had told him about the Calvin incident the day after it happened. Bay Bro wasn't pleased to hear about another murder but he couldn't say much because they were getting money the only way that they knew. All he could do was to caution Jon about the things they were doing and assured him that he had their backs.

Don, Jon, Kay and Zoe were sitting in the Dungeon playing Sega. There was a knock on the door. Zoe answered the door. It was Twon and another person.

"What's up brothers?" Twon said sounding happier than he had been in a long time. "This is my cousin Ron from Milwaukee."

The boys greeted Ron. Jon and Kay continued to play Madden football.

"So what part of Milwaukee you from?" Don asked.

"The North side," Ron said trying to seem hard.

"Oh yeah" Don answered smiling. "My peoples from the North side, do you know Chris and Bo?"

"Yeah, them my peoples, we were getting a lot of money together," Ron said.

His body language spoke differently. Ron was high yellow with brown eyes. He had a medium frame and corn rolls. He dressed a little country.

"How long you staying?" Zoe asked.

"I'm here for the whole summer but I'm thinking 'bout moving down permanently."

Zoe shook his head up and down like it was cool but was thinking that Ron would be trouble.

Don and Jon walked into Jon's room.

"What do you think?" Don asked his brother.

"I don't know. I'll call up Chris and Bo."

"Yeah, I got a bad vibe."

In two days, Ron had gotten on everybody's nerves. He talked all the time and a lot of slick shit came out his mouth. If it wasn't for Twon, Don would have been shut Ron's mouth up. Jon wasn't around to get the full effect of Ron's mouth because he would be at Bay Bro's talking and kicking it with Lynette. Jon would leave the room. Now on this day Lynette was with him and they were in his room away from the others. Jon was lying on the bed with Lynette resting beside him with her head on his chest.

"Wanna play spades?"

"I'm chilling right now, maybe later," Jon said.

Lynette picking her head off his chest looked Jon in the face and said, "Come on Smooch, I want to see you kick they ass. Nobody talks shit to my man."

"All right, this one's for you," Jon said getting up from his bed.

Kay, Jon and Lynette joined the others in the downstairs kitchen. Twon and Ron were slaying Don and Zoe. Ron looked up from the table and saw Lynette, he smiled flirtingly at her. Kay and Jon sat down. The boys started to play cards and Jon thought he saw a signal. After a couple of hands the game was tied up and the deal was in Ron's hands. He dealt the first four cards then Twon shot Ron a look and Ron skipped himself.

"You missed yourself," Jon said putting his arm on the table.

"No I didn't," Ron said staring at Jon.

"All I'm saying is count your cards," Jon said keeping cool.

"Count my cards, for what?" Ron asked raising his voice.

"Wait a minute. It's only a card game. No need to cheat," Twon said.

"Exactly," Jon and Ron said at the same time.

"Look Jon," Ron said with sarcasm leaking. "I ain't no muthafuckin' liar and I don't cheat. I ain't my cousin either. Shit, I put in work too."

Zoe backed away from the table as did Kay. Twon stood

up and so did Ron. Don told Lynette to go into Jon's room. She didn't budge.

"Look, y'all my family, my brothers, but Ron my family too. For me, give him a pass."

"It's cool," Jon said maintaining a calm composure.

"I know it's cool. Y'all need to calm y'all young asses down," Ron said trying not to look intimidated.

"Nigga, shut the fuck up!" Lynette screamed pissed off because Ron kept running his mouth. "You ain't built like that and the only reason you still breathing is because of Twon."

"Bitch…! Mind your-"

Ron didn't get the last word out. Jon jumped over the table and was choking him.

"Do something, Don!" Twon screamed.

Don looked down at Ron's eyes rolling to the back of his head. He kicked him twice in the side of the head before pulling Jon off of him.

Jon pushed his brother to the side and kicked Ron in the face. Twon pushed Jon in the chest. Kay punched Twon right in the eye and was now throwing combinations to the face and body of Twon. Jon got back on Ron throwing rights and lefts to his face.

"Zoe! Grab Kay and I'm a get Jon," Don said.

Zoe wrestled Kay off Twon. Jon was fed up with Ron's mouth.

"He talk too much shit," Jon said still pushing his way past Don.

Lynette wanted Jon to finish the job, slowly walked over and hugged Jon.

"It's all right baby."

"Let's go Kay," Jon said spitting on Ron. Jon, Kay and Lynette left. Lynette drove.

"I think you made a bad move. You never go against family," Zoe said pulling Don to the bathroom.

"I didn't go against Jon. I was just trying to keep him from killing that boy."

"Hey, it's not me you got to convince," Zoe said.

"He'll be alright," Don said.

Jon, Kay and Lynette drove to the beach. Lynette figured that water, fresh air and kids would be good for Jon. She parked the car. He refused to get out.

"Come on, baby," Lynette said rubbing Jon's shoulder.

"In a minute, let me talk to Kay for a minute and I promise you that I'll get out."

Lynette kissed Jon on the forehead and got out of the car leaving Jon to talk with Kay.

"I can't believe Don went against me like that," Jon said turning around to face Kay sitting in the backseat. "He's my blood brother. Shit, we twins!"

"I know what you saying. But you was fucking that boy up. I wasn't gone jump in it because dude mouth is off the chain. I think Don did what he thought was best."

"If you didn't jump in, then why should he? It's like Twon his brother and not me." Jon shot back.

"Come on Jon, it ain't ever like that. You knew that Don

would kill Twon in a minute if it came down to you or Twon, y'all brothers man, it be like that."

"You know what, you right. I call you my cousin but you my brother and I mean that. We go back to kindergarten and you've always been there for me. I thank you."

"Thank me for what? Man we'll get through this. Shit, we done been through too much. Go have fun with Lyn."

Jon got out of the car and joined Lynette sitting on the hood. He wrapped his arm around her.

Jon dropped Lynette off around eleven o'clock that night. He and Kay drove around talking. One in the morning they made it back to the Dungeon. Twon and Ron were still there sitting on Don's bed watching *The King of New York*. Zoe was on the couch. Ron had two black eyes and some red marks around his neck while Twon had a swollen lip and his left eye was black.

"What's up?" Don said.

"I'm gone lay down," Jon said.

"Hold up, we gone work this shit tonight," Don said.

"I said I'm going to bed," Jon said walking to his room.

Don ran to his doorway not letting Jon leave the room.

"What's up brother? I know you ain't still mad." Jon ignored him. Don was determined to reach his brother. "We boys and shit happens. You know that."

Jon just kept looking at Don not saying a word. "All right, it's like that," Don said getting upset. "Well what you want to do, hit me?"

Jon stepped back and looked at this brother with a frown on his face.

"I'm just trying to go to bed. It's been a long day and I'm tired," Jon said. "If you want to fight take your best shot. I don't give a fuck if you're pissed about Twon and his cousin. Hey, that's your brother and I can respect you taking up for him. No hard feelings. Now, if you'd move so me and my brother can go to my room, I'd appreciate it."

"So it's like that?" Don asked not believing what he'd just heard.

"Exactly like that. You chose your side," Jon said turning to go back the way he came. "No love lost." Jon walked back out the door, got in his car and left.

After Jon left Don got really upset. "What the fuck y'all do all day?" Don asked Kay.

"I ain't Twon, so check your attitude and tone," Kay said. He never backed down.

"I don't give a fuck who you is," Don said walking towards Kay.

"Hold up Don," Zoe said jumping up and putting his arms out to stop Don. Kay was strapped and wasn't afraid to use it. "Haven't we been through enough bullshit today? Let's chill."

Don stopped and stared at Kay standing five feet away. He walked away and sat on his bed. Kay went into Jon's room and sat on the bed turning the radio to WGCI.

Jon needed space. It took everything to restrain himself from hitting Don straight in the mouth. He wouldn't give Twon the pleasure of seeing them fight. Instead he walked out of his house.

Jon thought about going to Bay Bro's house but chose to drive back out to the beach instead.

Morning came and no one in the house had slept the night before except Ron. Don was awake all night thinking about the events that had led up to his brother making the statements that hurt. He wondered if Jon really felt that way, or was Jon just upset? Don called Bay Bro at four in the morning. Bay Bro hadn't seen Jon since last night. Bay Bro wanted to talk to all of them, including Ron.

Twon stayed up hoping that Jon didn't come back and kill him and Ron. He knew that Jon had a temper and anything was possible. Twon hoped that Ron would leave. They were never really that close. If another incident happens between Ron and any of his boys Ron was on his own, he thought.

Kay kept tripping on how Don approached him. Don knew that he wouldn't back down. He couldn't believe that an outsider had them going from being a tight knit family to a dysfunctional one, in a day. If something happened to Jon, something surely would happen to Twon and his punk-ass cousin.

Zoe wondered what he could've done to prevent everything from happening. He knew that things will probably never be the same. He kept blaming himself for not speaking up when they were playing cards. He had seen Ron cheating twice but decided not to say anything because it was petty. He was going to have to choose a side, something he never wanted to do.

Tina came downstairs in the morning to check on the boys and was panicking when she didn't see her Jon. Don told her that he went fishing with Bay Bro and that he didn't want to wake her. It was midday and Jon hadn't turned up. Don was becoming extremely worried.

"Do any of y'all know where my brother can be?" Don asked as they sat on the front porch. Everybody looked around at each other. "Man, if something…

"Jon is fine," Kay said cutting Don off. "He just needed to cool off."

"Cool off…?" Don asked.

"For starters, Jon thinks that you went against him. He thinks that you sided with Twon over him. He also thinks that you see Twon as your brother instead of him. And worst that stunt that you pulled last night with him in front of everybody was straight disrespect."

The boys spent the rest of the afternoon just sitting on the porch. They didn't even go out to steal no cars. Around nine o'clock that night Jon came walking up. The boys were still sitting on the porch lost in thoughts and hadn't paid attention to him until Jon was on the first step.

"Are you all right?" Don asked calmly.

"Yeah, I'm cool." Jon said.

"I told ma that you went fishing with Bay Bro. He said for us to come by his house when you showed up."

"What you mean when I showed up?"

"He just want to make sure we ain't killed nobody lately."

Don laughed hoping that his brother would see that he wasn't mad. Jon let his guard down and relaxed.

"Ahight," Jon said rubbing the top of Zoe's head as he walked by him. "Let me jump in the shower first." All of them were relieved that Jon had calmed down.

Jon took his shower and went to his bedroom. He walked in and found Don sitting on his bed flipping through some CD's.

"What's up?" Jon asked.

"After you left last night I did a lot of thinking. I heard what you said last night and I also heard Kay earlier."

"Kay...?" Jon asked.

"Yeah, Kay, that's your man, right? The same way you feel about me and Twon's friendship. I feel the same way about you and Kay's. Look Jon." Don said standing. "You my brother and I'm always gone worry bout you. Please, don't stay away again without anyone knowing where you are."

Jon looked at his brother and smiled. "All right, now can I get dressed?"

The brothers laughed and hugged.

7

The boys arrived at Bay Bro's house and found him and Lynette sitting in the living room watching her favorite movie, *Ghost*.

"What's up old man?" Don said shaking Bay Bro's hand. Don pointed at Ron. "This is who I told you about."

Bay Bro looked at the teenager and wanted to laugh at the sight of Ron's black and blue eyes compliments of Jon. Instead he extended his hand.

"What's up, young brother?"

Ron shook his hand and said nothing. He was busy gazing at Bay Bro's toned upper body under the wife-beater.

Jon went straight to Lynette.

"What's wrong baby?" she asked caressing Jon's face.

"I'll tell you 'bout it later." He responded.

Bay Bro looked over at Jon and Lynette and shook his head laughing.

"Y'all two better not make me a grandfather no time soon. I think we should go out front and talk. I'll be back in fifteen minutes baby girl."

Outside no one said anything for a minute.

"What's going on?" Bay Bro asked.

"With what?" Ron responded with intense curiosity. Bay Bro glanced at him and lit a Newport.

"What's up with you and Twon's eyes...?"

"I got a little out of line yesterday and we fell out. But it's cool though, we done squashed all that." Ron said.

"I don't get y'all." Bay Bro said inhaling. "Y'all egos so bad... y'all go to war with anybody, even y'all selves." Bay Bro exhaled the smoke then continued. "I've never been ashamed or threatened by y'all. My ego is in check. I don't have to beef with my boys about who's the man, because you know what?" Bay Bro paused. "At different times we all play the man. Y'all have different qualities and at different times you'll have to step up and put those qualities to use. No one should be mad or jealous because it's for all y'all. Each of you'll benefit from each other." Bay Bro flicked his cigarette in the air. "Y'all brothers and brothers will fight. Now if y'all can't resolve y'all differences on y'all own then I'm a get involved then we all be fighting. Now just put this behind y'all."

The boys looked at each other as if they didn't know what to do. Jon walked over to Ron and shook his hand. He did the same with Twon. Everyone followed Jon.

Later they sat watching Ghost. Jon didn't care what movie it was, he and his boo were cuddled together on the love seat. Bay Bro went to his bedroom after his speech glad that they showed up because he didn't want to watch *Ghost* for the hundredth time. The boys sat around cracking jokes about the movie and about Jon and Lynette. In the past Lynette would have told them off but now that she was with Jon she let them slide. After about thirty minutes Lynette got up to go to the bathroom and when she left Don went and sat beside his brother.

"We need to start thinking about making some real money," Don whispered to Jon.

"What you got in mind?" Jon asked suspecting drugs would be involved.

"Jackin," Don smiled. Jon looked surprised. Don continued. "I figured it's too much risk in selling the stuff ourselves, so we let other niggas take the risks and then we come and get they riches. And we open up spots." Jon nodded his head.

Ron approached Lynette when she came out of the bathroom.

"What do you want?" She crossed her arms.

Ron was enchanted and was determined to try and take her.

"I'm not trying to start no trouble. I just wanted to talk to you. You know? One on one," Ron smiled.

"Whatever you got to say to me, you can say in front of my man," Lynette said peeping game.

"Look Lynette, I think that you're a very beautiful young lady and I'm not trying to disrespect you but I thought that you and Jon had an open relationship, especially the way he's out there."

"An open relationship...?" Lynette laughed. "Nah, we got a closed relationship and if it were open," she paused and took a step back looking Ron up and down, "Honey, you wouldn't have a

chance."

"I'm just a stubborn kinda fella and I got my mind made up on you…" Ron smiled. Without answering Lynette walked away.

"Stupid little bitch," Ron said under his breath. Smiling thinking that all he wanted to do was zoom-zoom in her poom-poom. He watched her backside sashaying back and forth as she walked away. It was best not to tell Jon, she thought. Lynette snuggled up under Jon's arm and continued to watch the movie.

The boys functioned as a unit for the next two weeks. Ron continued hanging with them and even made money with them. The fourth of July was hot. The boys were in the Dungeon debating stealing cars.

"I'm telling you man, we should roll out to Gleason," Zoe said on the phone to a girl.

"I'm not trying to go to Taste," Jon said wanting to spend time with Lynette.

"All the girls gone be out there," Zoe said covering the phone with his hand.

"I don't care what we do," Jon said.

"All right," Zoe said jumping up from the couch. "The Taste is it."

The Taste of Gary was a knock-off from the Chicago's Taste of Chicago. Only unlike Chicago, there is food from all over to taste. The Taste of Gary is a huge carnival with singers, usually old school singers like the Gap Band, the O'Jays and other soul groups from the seventy's. This year TLC was scheduled. Zoe loved Left Eye. It was the determining factor he wanted to go.

Around seven that night they arrived at Taste. Kay, Jon and

Zoe rode in Jon's Impala while Twon, Don and Ron rode in Twon's Delta 88. It'd be less hassle to find parking. It still took twenty minutes to find a spot. Zoe kept carrying on that the Taste was packed with honeys.

They made it inside the concert. TLC were already on stage performing. The stadium was packed to the rafters with people from all over Gary. The boys got as close to the stage as possible. Zoe was really enjoying the concert, loving every song the group sung. They started singing What About Your Friends. Zoe spotted a golden complexion, five-foot one with long black hair, hazel eyed beauty standing a couple feet away. He thought she winked at him. He decided to kick it to her.

"Do I know you?" the girl shouted over the music.

"You probably seen me play ball," Zoe said smiling before he continued. "We got this squad that the city be talking about."

"No," she said with a blank expression.

"You're joking right?"

"I don't watch sports." The girl said moving her hair away from her eyes. "I might catch a game a year." Zoe knew she was lying, he could see right through her flirty moves. He had seen her in the stands before. She was a true basketball fan and had seen most of Zoe's games. The girl had done her homework and found out that Zoe and his crew were up-and-coming gold-getters.

"My name's Zoe," He extended his hand.

"Shawn," she said smiling and holding his hand. A six-foot three, dark skinned, slender man grabbed Shawn by the waist from behind.

"Get your young ass on somewhere!"

Zoe looked up and the first thing he saw was a gold six

point star with diamonds on each point hanging from a gold Rolex link chain.

"Do I know you playboy?" Zoe asked.

"Who the fuck is this lil' boy…?" The man said frowning.

"Baby," Shawn started as she turned and kissed the man on the side of his face. "He play on the Double One's summer team."

"Oh yeah," the man said covering his mouth with his fist trying to look cool as he now realized who Zoe was. "Y'all from Beckman, right? I'm Shine." He said reaching out his hand.

"Zoe," he said faking a smile while shaking Shine's hand. Jon went to get a drink.

"Kay," he said pointing over at Zoe. "Who that frontin'-ass nigga Zoe talking to?"

Kay looked over to see who Jon was talking about and couldn't believe it.

"That's the nigga Shine from Miller projects," Kay said. "Shine got the whole eastside and Miller on lock. He's only eighteen and damn near a millionaire."

"Miller projects is all Gangster Disciples, why is he talking to Zoe?" Jon asked.

"He probably caught Zoe hollering at his woman. Might as well go over and say hi," Kay said.

Jon saw Shine's gigantic six point star confirming what he thought. Shine was a G.D.

"What's up Zoe?" Jon asked.

"You know me," Zoe said cutting his eyes at Shawn. "Just trying to get in where I fit in."

Shine looked at Kay and Jon. He had the stories now he stood looking at them and wondering if they were true.

"My name's Shine," he said extending his hand.

Kay looked at Jon and then shook Shine's hand.

"Kay…"

Jon didn't really want to shake his hand but did anyway.

"Call me Jay, what you and my guy talking 'bout?" Jon asked.

"Oh, we were just talking about basketball, you know?" Shine paused motioning for someone to come over. "We hold pick-up games at the Hudson Campbell, a thousand dollars a man every Saturday and Sunday."

"That's good to know, we definitely gone fall through," Kay said cutting his eyes at Shawn.

"Excuse me," Shine said and then walked over to talk to the gentleman he motioned to.

"My name's Shawn," his girl said looking at Kay.

Kay looked at her and wondered if she was testing him.

"Kay," he said looking in Shine's direction.

She turned to Jon and said, "Ain't y'all from 11th?"

Jon turned his nose up at her and said with an attitude, "If you already know the answer you shouldn't ask the question, it makes you look stupid."

Shawn took a step back and said, "Excuse me for being polite to your sorry ass." She rolled her eyes at Jon and turned her head.

"Whatever," Jon said laughing at her hood rat attitude.

"You know what," Jon said looking at Kay talking loud enough for Shawn to hear him. "Bitch must be spoiled."

"Nigga please, I ain't spoiled."

She started laughing. Jon joined her. Zoe and Kay stood there watching the two.

"Are you sure it was these little niggas that did it?" Shine asked. He already knew the answer.

"My man ain't never been wrong."

"All right," Shine looked over and saw Shawn pointing her finger at Jon. "Get everybody ready and don't lose them. We hit 'em up when they leaving."

"Man, what's your problem?"

"What G...?" Shine asked. His man wondered how Shine had managed to stay on top for three years.

"Look Shine," G said with concerned in his tone. "You got to quit slipping. I already told you that they don't separate. The other two around here somewhere, don't worry bout it folks, I'm a take care of everything." The two threw up Gangster Disciples sign and went their ways. Shine walked over to Shawn.

"Everything alright baby?" He asked.

"Oh yeah, we just tripping," Shawn replied still smiling.

Shine shrugged at her response. She'd gotten a little too friendly. He decided to let it go.

"Yo Zoe," he said trying to sound even. "Where's the rest of your team?"

"What team?" The boys answered dumbfounded.

"I was just trying to make sure that y'all straight. I hope y'all didn't come up here three deep, especially with all the bullshit that be happening at functions like this."

"Nah, we got some peeps up in here. Matter fact, it's time

for us to go find them." Jon said.

They walked away looking for Don, Twon and Ron.

Jon, Kay and Zoe found the others at the free throw shooting booth betting.

"It's time to go," Jon said to Don.

"What's up?" Don said and sank a free throw.

"This G.D. thing, I'll tell you bout it later."

The boys headed to the cars without paying attention to the person following behind them. It was time for payback and for him to prove to the others, he had heart. The boys kept walking and was now outside in the parking area. The man came running behind the boys with two Smith and Wesson .45 pointing at them.

From behind a parked car across the street some people started shooting in their direction.

"What the fuck!" Kay shouted as he ducked down behind a van and pulled out his Glock .45. The others also got low and pulled out weapons. Bullets hit the cars and van that the boys were hiding behind. Don recognized one of them.

"Yo Jon," Don said pointing his Glock. "It's Delany," and started shooting. There were other people entering and leaving the park. Confusion reigned as four others started shooting in both directions. The boys kept shooting while moving to Jon's and Twon's cars.

One of the four teenagers that were drawn into this gunfight stuck his head up a little too far and caught a blast to his face from a 12 gauge shotgun. One of the boys that was with him saw what had happened and jumped up from behind the car that was shielding him and proceeded to run across the street firing shots at the group that had just shot his man. The two other boys that were with this soldier followed him. They were running into the street shooting at the group hiding behind parked cars. Jon fired shots at both groups on both sides of the street.

"What the fuck you doing?" Twon said.

"Shut the fuck up and shoot across the street!"

With the three boys in the middle of the road letting off shots and the barrage of bullets coming from SCC, the group that was behind the cars started running into the woods that were behind them.

Bullets whizzed by as the boys made it to their cars. Don joined Jon, Kay and Zoe in Jon's car.

"I'm telling ya'll," Don said catching his breath. "It was them Delany niggas."

"Are you sure it was Delany? Cause Cash left town," Jon said.

"It was Delany. The same dude from the grave yard that was with Tyrone, I'm telling y'all. I know what I saw."

"I'm tired of bothering the old man with this bullshit," Jon said turning on the street where Bay Bro lived.

"We ain't gotta tell him. I can't stand another lecture." Zoe said.

"We could take care of it ourselves," Kay said reloading a full clip in his Glock.

"No," Don said. He turned the radio off. "We might need some assistance taking on a whole project."

"Man, they ain't got no structure," Kay said.

"It's a right way to do everything," Jon said and pulled up in front of Bay Bro's house. "We gone end this once and for all."

The news of the shoot-out spread like wildfire. Within minutes it had burnt through the whole city and even reached Chicago. Cash's cousin called to tell him that she saw Doug at the Taste. He started wiping down his Tec 9 as soon as he hung up the phone. He checked his AK, SK, and his twin .45 Glocks. Cash couldn't believe that Doug would show his face at a public event like he was Mr. Clean. He thought about how Doug was out and about without a care while he was in the next state laying low trying to blend in. Cash still associated with the same people in Chicago that he partied and hung out with when he used to come and visit, but it felt different for him now that he actually lived there. He missed Gary and wanted to go home to bed. Cash polished the shells to all of his guns.

"Revenge is mine," he repeated.

Bay Bro was sitting on his front porch smoking a cigarette when the boys pulled up.

"What's up old man?" Kay said as they exited the cars.

"What's going on little soldiers?" Bay Bro responded tossing the cigarette.

"Bad news," Jon said as he sat on the porch across from Bay Bro.

"Give it to me," Bay Bro shouted.

"It wasn't our fault," Zoe said.

"Yeah, we was minding our business," Ron said nervously.

"Old man, Don saw dude from Delany trying to sneak behind us but before he got close enough his boys started shooting from the opposite side of the street. It wasn't our fault."

"Are ya'll sure it was Delany?" Bay Bro asked wondering if Cash was back in town and his source hadn't told him.

"We sure," Kay said getting hyper. "We need to go out

there and let them feel us. I'm tired of them niggas, old man. I say it's time to dig some ditches."

"Hold up, hold up, let me check around and see what's really going on. If they're responsible," he said looking at a car driving slowly down the street. "We'll bless 'em."

They watched the car going by. An elderly woman was behind the wheel. Jon went in the house to see Lynette.

The others focused on getting Shine. Jon and Kay had told the rest of the group that if they were going to come up it would have to be off of Shine. They told them about the millionaire stories. He was soft and slipping. Jon didn't want to rob small time drug dealers. He wanted it to be a one-time thing because to him anything could go wrong. If he had the millions that everyone said he did, it was worth the risk. They were going to try and get as close as possible to Shine. The plan was to befriend him and watch his moves to see where he was vulnerable. They'd find out who was dearest to him. They wanted to exploit any weaknesses. The boys wanted to start right away.

Hudson Campbell on a Saturday morning was the place to be. The gym wasn't as packed like the boys had hoped. Only four teams were there to play ball. Shine wasn't playing ball. He and Shawn sat in the bleachers watching the teams. When Shine saw Zoe and the rest of the boys walked in, they stood.

"What's up fellas?" Shine greeted.

"What's up Shine?"

Don turned to his brother and whispered, "So this Shine. Seems like we hit the jackpot," Don said looking at the six-point star medallion hanging from Shine's neck.

Jon was walking with Lynette under his arm while he

whispered, "Be cool. We got this."

Shine shook the boy's hand and introduced Shawn. Jon introduced Lynette as Lyn trying to disguise identities.

"I didn't expect to see ya'll here," Shine said and sat back down.

"Why you ain't playing?" Jon asked sitting next to Shawn. Lynette sat on his other side.

"I'm retired," Shine said smiling. He was a star at Wirt High School. Shine averaged thirty-one points and thirteen rebounds as a senior.

"You too young," Twon said.

Shine traded in scholarships, college and a shot at the NBA for fast money and drugs. "I used to be all right but I had other obligations," he said reminiscing.

"I hear you on that one," Jon said knowingly.

"Enough talking, y'all up."

They easily won all the games they played. The oppositions had only one or two players that could really ball. The boys did some trash-talking while punishing the other teams. Shine paid no attention to the talk. Then Ron spoke.

"My man, is this the best ya'll hood got to offer? They gotta be some loyal soldiers for you to just watch this kinda slaughter and be cool with it."

Shine became furious and decided to come out of retirement.

"They are killers. Now let's see who gets slaughtered," Shine said getting off the bench.

"Let's up the stakes to say five thousand a man," Shine

said.

The boys thought that it would be easy money.

"Let's make it ten," Kay said.

"Ten it is. I know ya'll good for it."

The game began and on the first play Shine shook Don and went high in the air tomahawking over Kay. The boys all looked at each other while Shine back paddled down the court with a smile on his face.

"I told ya'll that I was all right," he yelled.

The boys decided to run some set plays that had won them all of their championships. If they played street ball with Shine, they'd lose. Shine tried to keep the game fast paced while the boys slowed it down. Both teams went back and forth exchanging baskets while Shawn cheered for her man's team, especially Shine.

The boys pulled it together and buckled down on Shine thinking that the four other players couldn't beat them. They were right. The boys went on to win by ten points and Shine decided to run it back because he enjoyed the competition. The boys also won the second game. They played a little loose doing playground tricks and even let Shine do his thing.

"That's twenty G's a piece." Jon said walking back to the bleachers.

Shine's boys were looking at him to settle their debts.

"I don't have all the money here," Shine said toweling his face off. "But ya'll know I'm good. I'll bring the whole thing next Saturday."

"Um baby, I betted on y'all too," Shawn said in a baby's voice.

Shine looked at her and smiled. He kissed her on the

forehead

"How much?"

"Ten thousand," Shawn cooed.

"I got that now."

Shine went into his pocket and pulled out two rolls of hundred dollar bills wrapped in rubber bands. "That should cover it."

He handed the money to Jon.

"I'm sure it's all there." Jon said taking the rolls from Shine. They all walked out of the fitness center and went their separate ways.

Cash crept back into Gary. He had been sneaking around for two days but had no luck finding Doug. Cash visited his mom, aunt and cousin. He was staying with his son's mother, Victoria, who loved him but couldn't stand him. Victoria was the color of peanut butter with black hair and a curvaceous body. She was a nineteen year old who ran Cash's life.

Cash was relishing being back in Gary. It didn't bother him too much that he had to be creeping. He couldn't find Doug and that bothered him. Cash checked with all of the women Doug messed with, his family members and even Doug's mom. No luck. It had been a week and Cash became impatient. He knew it was only a matter of time before Doug would come out of hiding. Cash had put the word out on Doug, along with a fifty thousand reward.

All week long the boys worked on a plan to persuade Shine to sell them five bricks and front them another five. He knew they had money and would be good for the dough. It made no difference. The boys didn't plan on paying.

Saturday rolled around. The boys were at Hudson Campbell ready to win more money and to bait Shine. Shawn was in the bleachers watching as Shine practiced sets.

The boys walked in at nine confident that Shine would agree to do business with them. Shawn waved and smiled. Zoe and Kay returned the greetings.

"What's up fellas? Y'all ready to get it on?"

Shine made a cut then crossover between his legs. He probably traveled on the play Jon thought but hollered back at him.

"What's the price?" Jon asked lacing his sneaks.

"I figure we play a series, best of five. If I win I keep my hundred thousand and if y'all win, well..." Shine paused smiling, picked up his gym bag and tossed it to Zoe. "Y'all get this."

Zoe opened the bag and his mouth dropped open. "Two hundred G's in there." Shine said. The rest of the boys looked in the bag.

"Bet," Jon said.

This time Shine and his team played with more enthusiasm. They executed plays Shine had worked out with them. The boys had seen the Benjamin's' in the gym bag and stepped up their game. They pulled away and easily won the first game. Shawn and Ron were in the bleachers cheering. Even though Shawn was supposed to be cheering only for Shine's team, she couldn't help clapping for the boys. The second game was a repeat performance. The boys huddled and Jon spoke.

"Let them win the next two. Keep it close. But let 'em win, build their confidence up. We got some suckers here and we can do this every weekend. It's an easy come up until we come off. The last game we'll win coming back." The boys agreed with Jon. If they could do this every weekend there wouldn't be a need to rob anybody.

The next two games went according to plan with the boys taking bad shots and missing easy lay-ups. Shine's teammates started talking trash. Halfway through the final game the boys were down to two shots and didn't have the ball. It was time to turn it up Zoe and Twon were worn down by the bigger opposing players and couldn't deliver. Jon scored the next seven baskets, putting them up by two points. Kay provided a needed basket on a reverse lay-up.

"Y'all earned that," Shine said in between breaths.

"Y'all played a hell of a lot better today," Jon said sipping orange juice.

"You real nice with it don't fuck up and throw it away like I did," Shine said.

"Thanks," Jon picking up the gym bag filled with dough.

"I really need to talk to you about something," Shine said.

Jon already knew what he wanted to talk about. They walked to an area of the gym where they could be alone.

"So what's up, Jay?"

"Yeah, we trying to lock the west down but we need a real

plug. I heard that you was doing big thangs and maybe you can show us some love."

Shine didn't like doing business with kids. He decided to entertain Jon.

"What y'all trying to cop?"

Jon didn't know what number to throw out there since Shine knew that they had at least two hundred to spend.

"Make me an offer," Jon said smiling.

"I'll tell you what," Shine said looking at his Rolex. "I'll fuck with y'all. I think y'all some cool lil dudes. Bring the two hundred thousand with y'all tomorrow and I'll bring fifteen bricks. You know you can't beat that price around here."

Jon nodded in agreement even though he really didn't know if he could've done better.

"Tomorrow," Jon said shaking Shine's hand.

Jon walked back over to his crew smiling. "It's a go. I'll tell y'all the happenings back in the Dungeon."

The boys walked towards the exit with Shine, Shawn and the rest of Shine's entourage right behind them. In the parking lot all were going separate ways.

"See ya'll later," Shine called out raising his fist. Gunfire erupted as soon as his fist came down. Shine grabbed Shawn and led her to safety. The boys paired up and scattered trying to see where the shots were coming from. Jon and Kay ducked behind a car and pulled out their Glocks. Don and Zoe were hiding behind a Chevy Blazer while Ron and Twon were five cars up hiding behind a blue Nova.

"Ya'll strap?" Jon called out to Don and Zoe.

"I am but Zoe not," Don yelled back.

"Where the fuck is it coming from?" Kay asked still unable to pinpoint the location of the shooters.

"They straight ahead," Jon said looking to see how far away their rides were parked. We just gone have to let off a couple and ease forward. Kay, don't get trigger happy. Save some bullets."

He readied himself to dash across to where Don and Zoe were. Shine had made it to his two-door '63 sky blue Impala, sitting on deep-dish Dayton's and equipped with sixteen switches.

"Aren't you going too help them?" Shawn asked concerned for the boy's safety.

"Hell no!" Shine turned the key in the ignition. "Let them deal with their own shit."

"I can't believe big bad Shine, gone leave some little kids he likes get killed. I thought I knew you. I guess I was wrong."

"I got you with me. I have to think about your safety."

Shawn didn't even blink. Shine became angry and said, "Fuck it! Get in the backseat and lay down." He reached for his Tec 9 as Shawn crawled to the back of the car. Seeing where the boys were pinned down, he made his move to be the hero Shawn wanted.

The boys saw the '63 Chevy racing towards them with the driver holding a gun out of the window. Thinking that the driver was part of the group shooting at them, the boys turned and were about to fire when the driver started busting in the direction of the shooters. Shine unload seventy-five shots, then came to a stop in front of the boys. "Get in."

The boys jumped in the car with Kay letting off a couple more shots.

"Thanks man, that was on time," Jon said from the backseat.

"No big deal." Shine said stopping to pick up Ron and Twon.

"Man, who the fuck was that?" Ron asked getting in the car and looking around to see if all the shooters were gone.

"We'll discuss it later." Jon said glancing back.

"We right here," Don said pointing to their cars.

"What do the SCC stand for?" Shine asked. The boys looked at each other. A minute later Jon spoke.

"It stands for Straight Conservative Clique."

Shine looked at Don, smiled and said, "I knew y'all were Vice Lords the first time I met Jay. He kinda turned his nose up at my chain. Its cool though. Y'all good little dudes. We straight." He nodded.

The boys exited Shine's car and Jon lost his balance landing with his left hand on Shawn's lap and his head on her breast. "My fault," he said smiling awkwardly.

"It's all right," Shawn said smiling at him. Shine saw nothing.

"Be cool," Jon said as he got out of the car.

"Tomorrow," Shine said as he pulled out a CD case.

Jon held the door open as Shawn got out the backseat. He waited for her to sit before closing the door. "Take care," he said.

"You too," Shawn said.

Cash had a huge fight with his son's mom after refusing to

fuck her. Victoria loved to fuck. Victoria held on to her feelings for Cash but he didn't have any for her. Victoria smacked him in the head with a coffee mug.

"Get the fuck out," she ordered. Cash did but not before busting her nose, splitting her lip and blackening both her eyes. It all started when Cash's cousin called him telling him that Doug was living with a girl who worked at McDonald's. Cash planned to follow her home and enter the house, catching Doug by surprise.

He entered the Mickey-D's looking around for any female he had seen Doug with. Having no success, he went on line hoping someone would call out her name. A pretty, light skinned woman was at the counter. She asked for his order. Cash was ordering and noticed how cute the woman was and his eyes started roaming over parts of her body not covered by the counter.

"Jossie..." Cash said aloud when his eyes came across her name tag.

"Yes," the woman responded with a beautiful smile.

"I've never met anyone with the name Jossie before. I have a God-daughter named Josephine and we call her Jossie."

"That's my real name." Jossie said pointing at herself before she added, "And I have a niece named Josephine, we also call her Jossie."

Now Cash knew exactly why Doug was staying with her. Cash started to have doubts. He now remembered Jossie from when she was a little girl. Although Cash was six years older than Jossie he had a crush on her. When he was younger, he called her his Angel. Cash placed his order and went and sat in a booth.

"Fuck that nigga, he ain't shit no way," Victoria said into her phone.

"Why are you now telling me all this now?" A man's voice on the other end asked.

"I don't know. I guess I call myself trying to save a nigga that didn't want to be saved," Victoria said visibly upset about the ass kicking she took.

"I been told you that he didn't love you the way I do. Don't worry bout it. I'm about to call my peoples and we gone take care of him sump'n good."

"Thanks, I love you daddy," Victoria purred.

"Yeah, I love you too, baby."

"Excuse me sir, but do I know you?" Cash looked up from his table with a smile that spread from ear-to ear.

"No, I don't think so," Cash said staring in her light green eyes. "But I would love to get to know you."

Jossie smiled and politely said, "I would love to because it's something familiar about you. It's just that right now is not a good time."

"That's my cell number and my pager number. If you need anything at all, please, don't hesitate to give me a call."

"Goodbye," she said and put the number in her pocketbook.

The boys really didn't want to check in with Bay Bro. They all felt like they were bothering him too much with their petty wars. They weren't little boys anymore who needed to check in with a keeper whenever they ran into problems. They were hyped to let Bay Bro know how they were feeling. The boys had a change of heart when they pulled in front of his house.

"What's up old man?" Don said as he sat down on the couch.

"I'm glad ya'll here because I need ya'll to make a run with me," Bay Bro said.

The boys looked at each other smiling. It was their time to shine.

"What we waiting on," Kay said jumping up from his chair.

"Calm down," Bay Bro smiled. "Let me grab something and then we can be out."

Lynette was asleep on the sofa. Jon went over to Lynette and started rubbing her forehead when Bay Bro left.

"Man, it's about time that Bay Bro took notice," Twon said.

"Yeah man, it's long overdue," Kay agreed.

"I wonder what's up," Don pondered.

"It's probably nothing," Jon said and continued to lightly rub Lynette's head.

Bay Bro came back out and saw Jon sitting on the armrest of the sofa rubbing Lynette's head.

"You can stay here with Lynette," he said.

"After we done I'll just come back and spend some time with her," Jon said.

"Jon." Bay Bro said putting his hand on Jon's shoulder. "Trust me. This nothing, I need you to stay here with Lynette because she's sick. When she wakes up, I want someone be here."

Jon looked down at Lynette sleeping peacefully and then he looked at Don.

"Old man, I love Lynette and I also love my brother. I don't know what you got planned but please watch out for Don and the rest."

Bay Bro looked at Jon and smiled. "I got you, son."

Jossie lived twenty minutes away from McDonalds. She occupied one of the beach houses spread along Lake Michigan. She liked the quietness of being out there and loved the sound of the water at night. There was something familiar about the guy she had met earlier. Jossie couldn't quite figure it out. She stared at him for five minutes before approaching him. She pulled the piece of paper out of her pocket that he had given her and there was no name, just two numbers. If not for Doug she thought, then surely she would've given him a call. Doug knew how she felt about him being out there in the streets and now he had done something where he can't even leave the house. That was so stupid, Jossie thought. She paid attention to the beige wagon following her. She turned into her driveway, parked and exited.

The butt of the .45 caliber handgun caught her hard in the back of her head and left her sprawled in the doorway. The intruder jumped over her unconscious body and went about his business searching the house, turning things over as he made his way to the bedroom. He opened one of the bedrooms. Doug was sleeping on his stomach in a king size waterbed.

"Get the fuck up!"

Doug reached under his pillow for his Glock but knew that his time was up.

"Cash man," Doug said on his stomach. He didn't have to see Cash's face to know that it was him. "Let me explain, man."

"Shut the fuck up!" Cash placed the gun to the back of Doug's head.

"Wait! Please wait," Doug shouted trying to reach for his gun. It wasn't under that pillow but was under the next one. "Don't let Jossie find me like this, please, Cash man. Remember how you used to adore her, please man, this would really fuck her up. Please don't…"

"Didn't I say shut the fuck up!" Cash shouted as his conscience came into play. "Get the fuck up and be real easy." Cash didn't know what to expect from Doug but he wasn't taking any chances keeping the gun close to Doug's head.

Doug got to his feet and Cash placed the .45 in the center of Doug's chest while patting him down.

"Your bitch-ass gone take a ride with me," Cash said after making sure he had no weapon on him. Cash took the gun from Doug's chest and placed it in his lower back pushing him forward.

"It ain't even gotta be like this," Doug said as they moved to the front of the house. "I'm saying, we boys. I know I fucked up but," Doug stopped in his tracks and stared at Jossie lying unconscious in the doorway. He became furious. "Why the fuck you had to hit her? Huh? Why?"

Cash bitch-slapped Doug with the .45 cutting Doug's right ear.

"Don't piss me off. Now get the fuck to the car."

Doug held his ear and stepped over his sister. He grimaced as he thought he should've listened to her warnings. Cash threw Doug the keys.

"Drive and don't try any slick shit," Cash said looking around. "First, I'll kill you then I'll come back and kill Jossie."

"What the fuck is your problem?" G asked into the phone.

"Cool out," Shine said looking around to make sure Shawn wasn't listening.

"What you mean, cool out? We had them little niggas boxed in and then you come to they rescue. You're making my job harder." G sounded real upset.

"Shawn was talking all this shit about me and I didn't want to look like a punk. Look G, tomorrow will be different, I promise. I'm gonna leave Shawn at the house and we can take care of them little niggas."

"Ahight," G said smiling. "Catch you later, seven-four."

"G.D."

Shine hung up the phone. Shawn placed the receiver down and couldn't believe what she had just heard. She couldn't believe that Shine had played her like a fool and was planning to kill the boys.

Cash had Doug drive to a wooded area. There was no traffic. The two men got out of the station wagon and started walking into the woods.

"Cash, it ain't even got to be like this," Doug pleaded with his old friend.

"Oh, it's going to be exactly like this."

"We go way back and you know that I would never leave you hanging like that."

"Shit, I can't tell."

"I been by your side since I was eleven. Eleven years old and I always been there for you, man." Tears were rolling down his face. "I was the one who killed dude when he tried to creep you on the ball court. I was the one made those witnesses disappear when you had that double murder. I was the one..."

"Shut the fuck up!" Cash shouted.

Doug was right. He'd been there when no one else cared. Doug never betrayed him or really left him out. But the incident with the boys was a small issue that they could have handled if Doug hadn't run.

"That was then, you deserted us, Pee-Wee and Darnell paid the price. True soldiers got bodied because you didn't hold down your post. You got scared and ran like a bitch. I could be dead right now."

Cash shot Doug in the right leg. He fell on his side holding his leg and screaming like a stuck pig.

"Cash man, I didn't want to leave you. The plan..."

"The plan what...?" Cash asked then fired into Doug's other leg. "Now, you want to run, don't you?"

Doug's lower body was on fire.

"Cash man, I'm sorry man. If you let me live, I'll leave."

Cash looked down at his friend and shook his head. He placed the nozzle inches from Doug's face and opened fire, still shaking his head. Cash pulled off the dark blue Golden State Warriors warm-up suit that he had put on to prevent any blood from staining the tan Pelle Pelle outfit he was wearing.

Cash went back to Jossie's house and saw that she was no longer lying in the front doorway. He parked his car, walked up to the door and rung the doorbell. Jossie was sitting on her living room couch holding a towel filled with ice to the back of her head. She was having a hard time trying to figure out what happened. The doorbell startled her. She thought it was Doug or her mom. Jossie opened the door. Jossie dropped her towel with the ice.

"Are you all right?" Cash asked bending down to pick the ice up.

"What are you doing here?" Jossie asked recovering from the shock.

Cash was prepared for that question. "Doug called me and..."

"Doug called you. Who are you? I mean, you give me your numbers and you didn't even put your name down. What is going on?" Jossie began to cry.

Cash pulled her close to his chest and rubbed her back. "Now I see why I'm so familiar to you, I used to spoil you when you was little. My name is Cash."

Jossie pulled her head away from Cash's chest and looked in his face.

"I remembered you from somewhere. I'm still confused. Why are you here?"

Cash took a deep breath.

"Brace yourself. Doug was involved in the Beckman shooting. The police and some other people are looking for him. I tried to warn him about the life that he was leading. Doug been doing some heavy drugs. You know where he is?" Cash asked.

Jossie's head now hurt from what she had just heard. She still hadn't figured what had happened.

"I don't know where Doug at. I was coming in the house and someone mugged me." Jossie continued to rub the back of her head.

Cash pager went off twice with 911 behind the number. Before he could call the number back, his cell phone started ringing.

"Hello," he said and listened. Cash received news that made him back away from Jossie wearing a look of confusion. "I'll be there in ten minutes," Cash said and hung up. "Something important just came up and I've to go. Tell Doug to call me and if I don't hear anything from him or you, I'll be back. Don't worry. Everything will be alright, I promise," he said and left.

The boys were confused. They had misread Bay Bro's intentions. They had planned on showing Bay Bro that they could handle whatever needed to be handled. Bay Bro had told the boys that he wanted to make a run with him and nothing else. Bay Bro hadn't planned on his business taking as long as it was. He thought that they would be done in no more than fifteen minutes. It had been over an hour and they still sat around waiting.

"Be patient Don, we'll be out of here real soon," Bay Bro said.

He walked to the back bedroom. "What's up? I thought that we'd be gone by now, I ain't with the waiting." He said to the woman sitting in there.

"It shouldn't be too much longer baby," she said looking out the window.

"When lil' Dee coming back?" Bay Bro asked peeking out the window.

"Hurry up! Here he comes." She said as the car rolled to a stop.

Bay Bro ran in the living room.

"It's that time," he said pulling out his .44 Desert Eagle. "Blast only if you have to."

The boys jumped and pulled out their guns.

"Oh shit!" Cash's mouth dropped open. He looked around and couldn't believe his eyes, the bitch set him up.

"You want to fuck with the little C's," Bay Bro said aiming the Desert Eagle at Cash's chest. The boys had no idea of what was going on because they never seen Cash before, they had only heard stories about him.

"Who is this?" Twon asked.

"This is Cash."

The name came out of Bay Bro's mouth, Don slapped Cash

in the mouth with his Glock.   Blood squirted out along with two teeth.

"Fuck you…" Cash screamed and grabbed his mouth.

"Bitch ass nigga, why you keep fucking with us?"

Don raised his Glock to smack Cash again.

"Tyrone was my cousin. I had a lot of pressure on me. It was nothing personal."

"Nothing personal my ass," Kay said pointing his Glock at Cash's head.

"Wait Kay, hold on a minute," Bay Bro said.

"Don't do it here, take his sorry ass to the alley where the trash at," Victoria said before looking Cash in his eye.

"Let's do it then," Ron jumped in ready to prove loyalty.

"Daddy, daddy," Lil' Dee screamed out as he ran into the living room just as Bay Bro was about to speak. Cash grabbed his son and held him close covering his chest. Suddenly he pulled out his .45.

All the weapons in the room was cocked and aimed in Cash's direction.

"Wait! Everybody just wait a minute." Bay Bro said.

Victoria standing behind Bay Bro screamed at Cash. The boys kept their guns trained on him.

"Ain't no kids getting killed today or any other day." Bay Bro said and put down his Desert Eagle. "You got this one. Take it as a gift from the almighty Himself. Keep on running and don't ever come back."

Cash pulled Lil' Dee close to his chest and eased out of the living room.

"You had the nerve to lie about my son's health, just to set me up? Bitch, I got you," he said gazing on Victoria.

Cash made it outside to the station wagon and let Lil' Dee go. The boy ran back inside the house screaming.

"Daddy…! Daddy…!" He ran up to Bay Bro. "Why you mad at my other daddy?" Three year-old Lil' Dee asked.

"Cash isn't your other daddy, Dee. I'm your one and only daddy and I'll always be your daddy. I love you." Bay Bro hugged his son and gave him kiss. "Pack some of y'all things." He said looking at Victoria. "Cash might try and come back and I want both of y'all safe."

"Where are we going to stay? I ain't trying to go back to Delany." Victoria said wrinkling her brow.

"Y'all gone stay with me. It's bout time I give the family thing a try anyway." Victoria rushed off to pack leaving.

Cash drove with thoughts racing through his head. Questions were going through his head. That bitch Victoria was dead. Cash pulled in front of Jossies's place. He'd tell her whatever he had to in order to stay with her.

Jossie answered the door wearing a long Chicago Cub T-shirt with baggy jogging pants. She smiled and let Cash in.

"What happened to you?" She asked seeing his mouth.

Cash looked in her light green eyes and said, "I have some bad news. Doug is dead."

"No-o-o…!" Jossie screamed and fell to the floor.

"I did everything I could to save him."

Cash joined her on the floor, wrapping his arms around her. "The call I got was from one of my boys and by the time I got to them, they already had Doug. I lied for him, I tried everything. I got hit in the mouth with a gun then they shot him. I pulled my gun and started shooting but it was too late. I'm sorry."

Jossie kept crying as Cash consoled her.

Bay Bro, Victoria and the rest of the boys entered his house. Jon and Lynette were watching *Ghost*. Don walked over to Jon and Lynette.

"You ain't gone believe this," he said just as Bay Bro started speaking.

"I know that this is going to be a lot to deal with, especially for you," he said eyeing Lynette. He lit a Newport then continued. "This your little brother Devon and his mother Victoria. I've been seeing Victoria for four years. I cheated on your mother with her. She found out and that's the reason she left."

"What? I don't understand…"

"Baby, I know that I messed up. I'm sorry. I love Lil' Dee just as much as I love you. Something came up today and they have to stay with us. I want y'all to grow up like brother and sister. I want y'all to know each other and I want you to be all right with this move."

Lynette looked at her handsome little brother and called him over holding her arms out. Lil' Dee went to her. Later as Bay Bro continued to answer questions, Lil' Dee fell asleep in Lynette's arms. She was cool with it.

The boys went to the Dungeon and watched a bootleg copy of *Menace II Society*. The phone rang. Zoe answered it and passed it to Jon.

"What up?"

"How you doing?" the voice at the other end said.

"Who this?" Jon said not recognizing the voice.

Ten seconds went by before the voice on the other end said, "You know who this is. I'm a very concerned friend."

The caller had Jon's attention.

"Y'all being set-up… Shine gone kill ya'll tomorrow…"

"Shawn…?" Jon said into the phone.

"Just listen… I'm sure you'll thank me properly later…"

Jon listened intently then hung up the phone.

"Man, ya'll not gone believe this."

"Who was that?" Zoe asked.

"It was Shawn."

"Shawn!" They all screamed at once.

"She said Shine setting us up."

"I wouldn't believe no bitch. She probably mad at her man," Ron said.

"What do you think Jon?" Kay asked.

"I believe her," Jon replied solemnly.

"Bullshit!" Ron sounded disgusted. "I can't believe you gone let her play you like this. We came into some money, real money. I ain't trying to fuck it up."

"Sit yo ass down and listen. Remember the first time we met Shine? He walked off to meet his man and came back different. They went they way and we went ours and got shot at."

"But Don saw dude from Delany," Twon sounded confused.

"You right," Jon said pointing at Twon. "Maybe it was dude or maybe it was coincidence. Dude didn't know that we were going to be at the Hudson Campbell. Shine did and Shawn said that she had to beg him to help us." Jon looked around the room and said, "It's better to be safe than sorry."

They all agreed and started to discuss a counter-plan.

Cash managed to get Jossie to stop crying. He told her that he would stay with her just in case the people who killed Doug were the ones who had knocked her out and trashed her house. He told her that he would die protecting her. Jossie composed herself and tended to Cash's mouth. Jossie led Cash to the back porch. They fell asleep in each other's arms.

Shawn didn't like being Shine's girlfriend and really wanted out of the relationship. She had been stashing away money, close to quarter of million dollars. Shawn was waiting for the right time to make her exit. She cared for Jon and even convinced herself that she might be in love with him. She pictured Jon making big bucks in the NBA. She'd be by his side with their children at all the home games cheering him on. Shawn was determined not to let anyone get in the way of her dream.

Jon couldn't sleep. Shawn was on his mind. Did she really like him? What about Lynette? Was Shawn setting them up? The thoughts went on and on.

The boys wanted to get an early jump on Shine and his crew so they were at the Hudson Campbell at seven in the morning. They planned on being the aggressors. The minutes ticked away as the boys sat back and waited for Shine to arrive.

Five minutes after eight, four vans and two trucks pulled into the parking lot. Shine was driving a 1993 dark blue Jeep Grand Cherokee fully equipped with rims, switches and a sound system that could be heard for blocks. His main man G wasn't half-stepping with a 1992 money-green Ford Explorer. The men piled out of vans and their total count was twenty-four, including G and Shine. The boys watched as G barked out orders to the crew. Shawn was telling the truth, she put them on point.

Shine's men ran to their positions the boys kept watching from where they were parked.

"We should've got 'em niggas when they were huddled up." Kay sounded frustrated.

"Be patient Kay," Jon said pointing to Shine carrying a back pack. "We not gone come out of this empty handed. That bag belongs to SCC."

Jon and Kay walked into the Hudson Campbell while Don, Twon and Zoe made their way to where Shine's men were. Ron went to his post and started assembling the Mini 14 Jon had given him.

"Lights out, baby," Ron kept saying to himself. They had counted five groups of three leaving nine inside the Hudson Campbell.

Jon and Kay were in the gym area ready to hear Shine bullshit.

"What's up, fellas?" Shine greeted walking up to the two. "Where the rest of the team at?"

"Oh, we didn't think you wanted to play today so they stayed in bed."

"Fuck it," Shine said looking at G and gave a half smile. Then he turned to Jon and Kay. "We might as well get this over with. I see you didn't bring the money."

"We left it in the car. I didn't think that you'd bring all of it in the gym so I figured after we test it we'd do exchange at the same time."

"Let's do this," Shine said handing Jon the knapsack.

"This is too light." Jon said.

"You're right," Shine said and glanced at G. "That's three. The rest is in my truck."

They walked through the parking lot and made it to Shine's car. Jon gave Kay the bag.

"Test it and bring the dough," Jon said to Kay.

Kay walked off with Don, Twon and Zoe watching from the side street. It didn't take the three a long time to locate and took care of Shine's crew using silencers. The boys snuck up on each catching them slipping. Now it was up to Ron to finish the job.

Shine saw Kay walking back with a different color book bag and he started stretching his arms above his head like he was tired. When Kay reached them Shine stretched again looking at G. He appeared dumbfounded.

"You tired?" Jon asked Shine taking the book bag from

Kay.

"I'm cool," Shine said.

"I guess all you have to do is give us the rest of the dope," Jon said.

Shine looked nervous and once again he raised his arms above his head.

"Is there a problem?" Jon asked smiling.

"Nah Jay," Shine said looking at G. Shine hit the remote car alarm to his Cherokee and went to open the back door.

"What the fuck?" G screamed as two of his folks dropped to the ground. Shine spun around just in time to see his man drop.

"Just give us the rest of the shit and we gone," Jon said pulling two 9mm's from the gym bag and tossing one to Kay. The fourth man dropped and G ducked behind the front of his Explorer puling out his Desert Eagle.

Jon and Kay took their eyes off of Shine to see where G was. It was enough time for Shine to run to the front of his Cherokee and duck down. He pulled out two 9mm Berettas. Ron dropped two more of Shine's men with the Mini 14 and he was enjoying it.

"All we want is the dope." Jon said looking at the last soldier. Jon put up a finger. Ron stopped shooting.

"Shine, you got one man left. If you don't tell me where the dope is? He fittin' to get it."

"Fuck you!" Shine screamed.

Jon put two fingers in the air and Ron shot the last member of Shine's hit team leaving only Shine and G. Jon shot three times into Shine's truck. "All you got to do is tell me where it's at and we out."

"Fuck you!" Shine screamed.

G stuck his head around the front fender of his truck to see where Jon and Kay were and Ron fired a shot barely missing G but hitting the Explorer's headlight. Kay turned his focus on G and shot six times at the front end of the Explorer causing G to run to the rear of the truck.

The boys watched everything from Don's car. This was taking too long for Don, especially with Jon and Kay having to shoot Glocks. Those were the only guns they didn't have silencers for. The police would be on the scene soon. Don started the 98 and headed straight to where the action was.

"What the fuck is taking so long?" Don asked getting out the car.

"He won't tell us where the shit at," Jon said.

"Shine, if y'all try any bullshit we gone kill y'all." Don called out.

He walked to the back door of Shine's truck and searched for the cocaine. Don didn't find anything and was more pissed.

"The nigga played us."

"What?" Jon asked.

"Ain't shit here! Kill 'em muthafuckas 'fore the cops come." Don said signaling.

The boys opened fire on the two trucks. Shine and G hit the ground. The sound of police sirens were getting closer. Shine let off three shots catching Zoe in the calf. He fell to the ground. Ron sprayed shots from the Mini 14 at the two trucks. Jon and Kay grabbed Zoe pulling him to Jon's car while the others jumped in Don's car.

Shine was still on the ground and saw the boys leave the

parking lot. Hearing the police siren, he jumped to his feet and ran to the closest van.

"G bring yo ass on!"

When they got into the van Shine discovered that there were no keys. Shine grabbed the seat belt and went to work on the steering column with the metal piece. By the time the police were pulling in, Shine and G were exiting.

"Them little niggas are gangstas." Shine said as he drove home.

"Zoe, you all right?" Jon asked as he saw two police cars racing by.

"I'm cool," Zoe said holding his leg. "I think it only skinned me."

Jon parked in front of Bay Bro's house and turned to Zoe.

"Bay Bro will know how he we should play it. Give us an alibi and see if we should take you to the hospital."

Jon, Kay and Zoe got out of the car. Zoe leaned on Kay for support.

Don turned with his tires screeching. Jon, Kay and Zoe pulled out their Glocks.

"What the fuck is his problem?" A jumpy Kay said.

"I don't know," Zoe said limping off.

Don, Ron and Twon jumped from Don's 98 and ran to Zoe.

"You alright…?" They kept asking.

"I'll be even better when I get in the house and sit down."

"What happened to Zoe?" Bay Bro asked when he saw the blood.

"Zoe got shot," Jon said sitting next Lynette.

"Victoria!" Bay Bro screamed.

"What...?" Victoria said running into the living room, a walking cane raised above her head. She lowered the cane after seeing it was the boys. "Don't be scaring me like that."

"I think she's a soldier." Jon laughed and said.

"What's the problem?" she asked.

"It's Zoe. Look at his leg," Bay Bro said pointing to Zoe.

"What happened to you?" She asked blotting some blood.

"I was shot."

Victoria nodded to Bay Bro. He was satisfied that Victoria could take care of Zoe's wound. It was time for him to talk with the boys.

"Y'all know the drill. We need to talk outside," he said waving his hand.

"Alright, alright," Jon said clearing his throat. "We made a mistake at the Taste. Don saw dude from Delany and I guess we just assumed that it was them. We met Shine, he's a GD. He acted like he was cool with us, shot ball with us and everything. We got word that he was setting us up. Today we took it to him before he brought it."

"Shine from Miller," Bay Bro lit a Newport and asked.

"Yeah," Don answered. Don also went on to tell Bay Bro about the three bricks of cocaine.

Bay Bro couldn't believe his ears. "How many?" he asked puffing on the cigarette.

"Three and we don't know anything about coke. We need your help."

"I'll teach ya'll the game," Bay Bro said tossing the butt.

They went back to the house. Victoria was busy taping Zoe's calf.

"He'll be alright. It was only a skin wound."

"I'm worried about you and you come up in here and Zoe got shot. What if it was you?" Lynette asked. Bay Bro walked away and came back carrying a knapsack on his shoulder.

"I know that you worry but I'll be ahight. I wasn't in the streets wildin' out," Jon said smiling and caressing Lynette's cheek. "Everything will be alright."

They headed to the kitchen where Bay Bro took over the stove. The boys paid close attention to Bay Bro cooking the cocaine with the baking soda. They broke all three kilos down into twenty dollar rocks and baked cake.

"Old man," Jon said counting the bagged up product. "We really want to sell weed but we ain't got no connect."

"I got the best hydro connect in the Midwest," Bay Bro said smiling.

"How soon?" Twon asked. He was ready to see major paper.

"As soon as we finished here," Bay Bro said.

They learned to cut, cook and bag the coke.

"I'm glad it was seven of us," Bay Bro said and lit a cigarette. "Let's go see the medicine man."

Shine and G had spent the whole day riding around talking about what happened and what went wrong.

"Man, we done been over this shit a hundred times," Shine said as he pulled in front of his house. "I still can't figure out how them little niggas knew what was going down."

"Somebody had to tell them in order for them to take out our guys." G pulled on the blunt and exhaled.

"Them little niggas are serious," Shine said with a smile.

"Fuck them little niggas. All we got to do is put a contract out on they asses."

"Nah," Shine said pulling on the blunt.

"Shine, I'll take care of it. Don't even stress it."

Shine looked at G and smiled. They shook hands and he got out of the van.

"Where the hell you been?" Shawn said with her hands on her hips. Shine knew she was pissed.

"I'm not in the mood Shawn," Shine said plopping onto a leather sofa.

"Did you at least win your money back?"

"Them little niggas robbed me. Can you believe that shit?" Shine lit a blunt.

"What you mean they robbed you?" Shawn asked sounding concerned.

Shine was high but not that high. He never discussed his

business with Shawn and he had no plans on starting that night.

"I don't talk about my business," Shine said stretching out on the sofa. "Can I get something to eat please?"

BLOODY SUNDAY-12 KILLED... It was reported that there was no witness or leads.

The story was all over the front page of the morning paper. Ron read the article and the other boys listened. The boys planned on using two abandoned houses next to theirs for setting up shop. Weed would be sold from one and crack the other. Don, Twon and Zoe were in charge of selling crack. Jon, Kay and Ron sold weed. The boys opened shop and relied on satisfied customers to spread the word.

"God...!" Jossie screamed and dropped the newspaper. Cash ran into the living room and found Jossie staring. The front page caught his attention. He read the story and not only recognized the names, but also the crews.

"You knew some of these people?" Cash asked.

"No, the bottom of the page," she said pointing.

Cash looked at the article on the bottom of the front and read it. It was about Doug.

"I have to go down to the morgue..."

"I don't think that you're ready to see Doug like that," Cash said.

"I have to claim the body and make arrangements."

"I'll take care of it," Cash said hugging Jossie.

"I have to, you can come with me."

One week passed. The boys had stopped stealing cars. They directed their energy to success in the dope game. All profits from their transactions were stored in a safe. Business was booming. They structured another deal with the weed connect and was copping crack also.

The boys started treating Ron like one of the clique. Jon and Kay bought him a new 5.0 Mustang from the Ford lot. Don, Twon and Zoe paid for some new rims and an expensive sound system. They presented the car to Ron with a personalized SCC license plate. Ron loved the treatment.

"What's up Cash?" Shine said watching Doug's casket being lowered into the cold ground. Cash looked at his friend. "It looks like you can't take care of your people."

Cash couldn't believe Shine's arrogance. "Don't look like you can take care of yours either. Twelve dead, right?" Cash shot back. Shine frowned.

"I don't know what you talking bout," Shine said looking away.

"Yeah, I know," Cash said with a chuckle.

"What's up cuz? Are you alright?" Shawn greeted.

"Yeah, I'm alright. How you doing cousin?"

"I'm cool," Lynette answered.

Jossie came over and Cash introduced her to Shawn. They talked a little while and then they all left the cemetery.

Ron needed insurance on the Mustang. He drove downtown to Miller. After getting the insurance, Ron decided to front. He pulled up on every group of females that were out. He was standing outside his car talking to the girls and didn't know G was in the house watching.

"I'm telling you Shine, one of them little niggas is in front of my house talking to Bianca and her little friends right now," G said on the phone.

"Follow his ass and call me on my cellie."

Shine headed out the door leaving Shawn on the living room couch. She heard enough and called Jon as soon as Shine left. Ron pulled off and G jumped into his '78 Cadi.

Five blocks from G's house, a car coming in the opposite direction, started shooting at Ron. He ducked down and tried to reverse but the Cadillac right behind him opened up fire on him. Ron didn't know what to do and he panicked. Bullets were coming at him, hitting the car. One caught Ron in his left hand. He hit the gas. Ron stuck his head up and saw Shine with a Tec .22 hanging out. Shine passed Ron and opened fire hitting Ron twice. The car swerved and crashed into a parked car. Shine turned the Bronco around. Finishing Ron off was the fury burning his mind. He saw Jon's car speeding in his direction. Shine and G both sped off. Jon pulled up to Ron's car and all of the boys jumped out. Jon ran to the car and saw blood coming from Ron's face.

"Call an ambulance," he shouted. Zoe took off running across the street to a flower shop.

Jon and Kay jumped in the Impala then sped off.

"Where we going?" Kay asked.

Kay saw the rage on Jon's face as he continued to weave through traffic.

"Miller project," Jon finally said.

On the street watching the Impala, Don threw up his hands. Twon stayed at the Mustang with his cousin, tears coming down.

"Where the fuck Jon and Kay go?" Zoe shouted as he ran across the street. Twon didn't even bother answering and kept staring at Ron.

"I don't know," Don saying as he walked away from Ron's car. "Jon left before I could ask him."

Zoe shook his head. He knew where Jon was headed. "I called Bay Bro. He's on his way."

"That's cool," Don said rubbing his forehead.

Jon fingered the Mac 11 and two 9mm Beretas sitting in his lap. He pulled up in front of the Miller project basketball court.

The Mac and the 9mms were in his waist. Kay had two Glocks. Strapped and ready, they jumped from the Impala and headed in the direction of the courts. Children, mothers and fathers were there enjoying the sunshine and sitting in the bleachers. A pick-up game was in progress.

"It's a good day to die!" Jon suddenly screamed.

Everyone froze. Shells rained from the Mac11. Two players were felled by the barrage of shots. It was then that the crowd panicked and started a stampede.

Jon kept his finger on the trigger waving the gun from right to left till the extended clip was empty. He dropped the Mac 11 and out came the Beretas firing. The two kept firing and Kay dropped four dudes and a woman. They emptied couple more clips.

"Let's get the fuck outta here!" Kay shouted and grabbed Jon by the arm. They ran back to Jon's Impala. Kay hopped into the driver's seat and peeled off.

Bay Bro arrived two minutes before the police arrived. The boys were quickly briefed. The police interviewed Bay Bro for a minute then the ambulance came. The paramedics pulled Ron from his Mustang and administered CPR. They ran the gurney to the ambulance and pulled off. Bay Bro was still answering the police questions when Kay pulled next to the Explorer.

"What's up?" Kay asked Don.

"I don't know, Bay Bro said he'll handle things." Don said. He looked at Jon leaning against the truck crying. "Where ya'll go?"

"Shit's fucked up, man. We went out there to the projects and left niggas and bitches stankin." He paused shaking his head. "Maybe some kids too."

"That's fucked up!" Zoe screamed from the backseat.

"What's fucked up is Ron. He got shot the fuck up. What's fucked up is that we didn't have his back. What's fucked up is you sitting here crying like a little bitch. Man, you disgust me. I'm going to the hospital," Jon said getting back in his car with Kay riding shotgun.

10

It was all over the news. Eight dead, including two little girls, nine others injured. A sixteen year-old basketball phenom named Jason was one of the injured. Shine heard but couldn't believe.

"These little niggas done took this to another level." Shine shouted in his phone. "They sprayed my hood, my territory, my brother..."

G knew that a war had just started. He knew how Shine was about his friends and family, especially his only brother, Jason.

"He alright man..."

"We need to talk..." Shine said walking into his bedroom. "Meet me at old girl crib. I'm a go check on Jason."

"Alright I'm with you, man," G said.

Jon and Kay had been in the waiting area. Bay Bro and the rest of the crew joined them.

"How you feel, Jon?" Bay Bro asked.

"I'm all right," Jon said staring straight ahead.

"I know what you mean," Bay Bro said putting an arm around Jon's shoulders. "Don told me what you and Kay done did. I don't object. Shit, I'd have done the same thing. I'm pretty sure that your car is going to be hot, you gone have to get rid of it." The doctor came out and spoke to Bay Bro.

"He's going to be all right," Bay Bro said. A morose expression was written on his face.

"If Ron's going to be alright, then why aren't you happy?" Jon asked feeling Bay Bro's unhappiness.

"Let's go outside. I'll tell ya'll what's up," Bay Bro said as he started to walk towards the sliding doors.

Once outside, Bay Bro explained to the anxious boys. "Ron's going to need another surgery in a couple of months for his hand. That's not the worst part. Ron lost one of his eyes."

"What you mean he lost one of his eyes?" Twon said agitated by the news.

"One of the bullets somehow caught Ron right here," Bay Bro said pointing to his temple. "It exited through his eye socket."

The boys couldn't believe. Twon plopped down on a bench dazed as everyone rushed over trying to console him.

Cash sat in Jossie's bedroom waiting on her to get out of the shower. He heard about the shooting at the basketball court. It was time for him to go. Cash had deep feelings for Jossie and didn't want harm coming to her. The beef with Bay Bro and the twins had just begun. They were winning the battle by taking the fight to Shine's hood. Jossie was not safe. Cash no longer had the resources or soldiers it would take to win. The best thing for him to do was leave.

"What's up boo?" Jossie asked walking in the bedroom.

Cash watched her gliding seductive in the bedroom. The erection caused a lump in his throat. Jossie wore a pink see-through black, silk negligee. His eyes scanned her 36C breasts plunging out with dime sized nipples poking at her negligee. Cash's lump extended as Jossies's neatly trimmed pubic hair peeked at him. He was aroused but patted a spot on the mattress next to him.

"We need to talk. I've things that I need to tell you, right now."

She knew that it had to be something serious. Cash could not hide his depression. Jossie sat next to him and started massaging his neck.

"Talk to me. Please, you can tell me," Jossie said moving her fingers gently up and down Cash's neck. Jossie's touch sent thoughts racing through Cash's spine. He was about to leave and quickly dismissed them.

"I've been here too long. I think it's time for me to leave."

Jossie stopped and stared wide-eyed.

Cash smiled uncomfortably as he continued. "We both knew that this was only temporary. I like you a lot, shit, since this my last night with you. I might as well tell you my true feelings, I love you. I guess I always been."

Cash glanced at her and lowered his head. Jossie stared saying nothing. Cash continued. "There was a shooting out here today and some people got killed. It was the same people that killed Doug. They the same ones that killed the people at the Hudson Campbell, and they're looking for me."

"Who…?" Jossie asked with frustration written all over her face.

"Dude name Bay Bro from 11th. He been hating from way back. That's not the point. I don't care about me, I ain't shit. I've done a lot of things that I ain't proud of. You're smart, beautiful, funny, caring I can go on and on but I love you too much to bring danger to you. You have everything to live for. That's why I think its best I leave."

Jossie never once looked away. She felt that Cash was sincere.

"Wait, I'm not going to let you off that easy. You can protect me better from here." She pointed at the bed. "How you gone tell me that you love me and then try to leave me? Now I got something to tell you too. I love you."

"You love me?" He asked incredulously. "You can't be serious. I'm not going to make it Jossie. It's a miracle I'm alive today."

"You're my miracle. I love you and I'm not going to let you go." Jossie whispered and pulled Cash's head to her breast.

He was intoxicated by the scent of her perfume. Cash rested his head on Jossie's soft breast. Suddenly he started sucking and nibbling. He jerked his head away from her embrace.

"I…I really should go. I'm not thinking clearly and I might do something that…" Cash got up.

Jossie sat on the edge of the bed befuddled and breathing hard. She was overwhelmed by emotions and tears rolled down her face. Cash bent down to kiss Jossie and she pulled him down on top of her. They kissed passionately. Her tongue darted in Cash's mouth. Jossie's hands on Cash's ass squeezing his cheeks causing him to forget about leaving and focusing on the moment.

Cash's fingernails moved teasingly up and down the side of Jossie's body. He continued kissing her and slipped his right hand under her night gown. He massaged her breast.

"Oh-h…" Jossie moaned tugging Cash's shirt.

She went low for his shorts, pulling them down just barely pass Cash's butt. Cash still snaked his tongue in and out of Jossie's mouth he continued to massage her breast with one hand and pulled his shorts and boxers off with the other.

Cash eased the negligee down and softly kissed Jossie's exposed flesh. Jossie was naked and Cash kissed and licked her inner thighs. She stopped him.

"I think that I should tell you that this is my first time."

Cash's jaw dropped in disbelief. He normally dealt with hood rats who would say that they were virgins, but had fucked the whole town.

"Don't worry. I'm going to make your first time memorable," Cash said moving Jossie's hair from her face.

Cash kissed her forehead softly. Next he kissed both her eyelids, then nose. Cash ran his tongue in and around both of Jossie's ears. He softly bit the top and bottom of both ears. He returned to her lips, before moving down to her chin, neck and right breast. Cash licked Jossie's right tit while gently massaging her left. He rotated sucking, licking and kissing her left tit. Cash carefully squeezed both her breasts together. He opened his mouth as wide as possible, sucking, licking, kissing and softly biting her nipples.

Cash's tongue slid up and down Jossie's belly, skipping her sweet spot and focusing on her inner thighs. The tongue licking continued to her lower body and thighs. Jossie wiggled. He made his way down to her toes taking each one into his mouth one at a time and repeated the process on her other thigh till he was at Jossie's moistness.

She was soaking wet. Cash parted Jossie's swollen outer lips tasting the juices seeping.

"You taste just like honey," he said.

His head went downtown licking Jossie's pussy while softly biting her clit. Jossie's legs shook as she experienced continuous orgasms. Cash kissed his way back up her stomach replacing his tongue with a finger in her pussy.

"Oh yeah...ah..." Jossie moaned in pleasure. Jossie humped Cash's finger.

"Please stick it in. Ooh...yeah do me..."

Cash smiled and stuck his tongue deep inside Jossie's mouth.

"We almost ready baby," he said prying a second finger inside her.

"Oh shit!" she screamed from the pain and pleasure of Cash working his fingers in and out of her.

"It's time," he announced removing his fingers.

Cash put his dick close to Jossie's pussy lips. He eased

three inches inside her and moved in and out of Jossie's pussy. Cash added a half inch every time he went inside her.

"Oh...yes-s-s..." Jossie moaned.

Cash worked six inches inside of her. Jossie wrapped her arms around Cash.

"I love you," she whispered.

Cash finally managed to get his entire dick inside her. He stroked her long and slow.

"You gone make me bust early," Cash said after couple minutes of fucking.

Jossie climaxed once and was on the verge of another.

"Don't stop! It feels soo good. Keep going, please, keep going. Ah-ah-ah! Yes-s-s...!" She exploded.

"Ooh, ah...I'm coming!" Cash grunted.

Cash skeeted deep inside Jossie. He later regained his strength and fucked the dog-shit out of Jossie for the rest of the night. Cash showed her different positions and ate the pussy time and time again.

It was the brother's fourteenth birthday. Tina took the day off to throw a surprise celebration. She was convinced that Ron's so-called accident was no one's fault. Tina was worried about the boys, especially her two. She could no longer live in denial. Tina saw the change in their clothing, the new jewelry and was finding hundreds, sometimes thousands of dollars left in pants pockets.

She heard rumors about the killings they were supposed to have been involved in and about them selling drugs. She failed them, Tina thought. She broke her promise and lost her sons to the streets. Her little babies were grown men.

Ron didn't want any visitors. His mind relived the journey that led to him losing an eye. Money, fame, girls, none of what the streets offered was worth his sight. Decisions about his future had to be made. He wanted to make them before he spoke to anyone. Moving back to Milwaukee was not the answer. He would stay in Gary. It was a matter of whether he'd stay in the clique.

The boys spent the day in their hood getting drunk the whole day. Business was up and their product was by far the best around. Customers came and left, they'd talk about Ron. The day seemed to drag. Jon took a couple sips of Hennessy. Lynette came around eight in the evening. Lil' Dee was hanging on to her Guess shorts. She hung out for twenty minutes and then went in to talk to Tina.

The boys were getting ready to close shop for the night when gunfire erupted on the av.

"Get Dee in the house!" Jon yelled running to 11th.

Twon grabbed Lil' Dee rushing into Tina's basement. The rest of the boys headed up the street after Jon. They saw the same three vans from the Hudson Campbell followed by two Chevys flying by the block.

"Shine." Jon said and stopped.

The gunfire now seemed like it was coming from the next block causing the boys to turn around and run back up the block where they ran into Twon carrying a pump in one hand and a carbine in the other hand. Don grabbed the carbine and the boys headed back up the block. They were two houses from the twin's house when the first van turned on the block.

Jon posted Kay, Don and Twon on one side of the street. He and Zoe took the other side. Don walked into the middle of street, raised the carbine and opened fire. The driver caught it twice in the chest. The van sped up, swerved left off the road and hit a tree. People stumbled out of the van Jon and Zoe gunned them down. Shots were fired from the second van at Don.

He took aim and let a barrage loose on the second van. It stopped at the entrance of an alley. Twon joined Don in the middle of the street squeezing off. The two vans and cars turned into the alley and sped off with a couple of people letting off shots. The boys chased them, emptying their clips.

Tina and Lynette came running from the house. The boys dropped their guns and kept walking around looking at the dead bodies.

"Stupid-fake asses!" Jon said.

"What happened?" What's going on?" Tina screamed.

"We don't know, ma," Don said as Tina checked him for injuries. "We were around the corner at Zoe's house."

"I want y'all to get in the house now," Tina said.

The boys along with Lynette went in the house. The setting sun reminded everyone that the eyes of war had blinked. Blood had been shed on the block.

There were forty-eight more murders that summer. The boys killed seventeen members of Shine's crew and fifteen innocent bystanders. Bay Bro kicked in Shine's door behind the drive-by incident. Jon alerted Shawn who was in the house and she left two minutes before Bay Bro and Goldie arrived.

Shine's crew killed sixteen innocent people during raids on 11th. Nothing was resolved from this high body count.

11

At the end of the school year, the boys' basketball team was undefeated. Jon and Lynette were crowned Mr. and Miss Beckman. Even though altercations between the boys and Shine were minimal, Don and Jon thought they needed more soldiers to back them. They formed cliques with two other neighborhoods. The move allowed them to lock down a significant portion of Midtown. They hooked up with a crew from 2nd avenue called pimp, macks, playas, PMP was headed by Pretty Ricky. They were seventy-five strong and had members from all over Gary. With the free coke they kept getting from Shine, the boys became major players in the drug game.

The events from the summer gave Don a big head. At school, he talked slick to everyone, even teachers weren't safe. All the girls were trying to be his next. Everyday Don was running-up in a different girl. Sometimes he'd double-up. He dropped out of school in April. His excuse was boredom and that he couldn't learn what he really needed to at school. Don met twenty-two year old Renee at a liquor store and made her his woman against his brother's wishes.

Jon was the opposite. He stayed mellow and treated everyone with respect. He made straight A's all school year. He could've skipped the ninth grade but declined. Jon crept several times with Shawn. They'd go to Griffin's to watch a movie or eat at Red Lobster. Jon was developing feelings for Shawn, but Lynette was the girl he planned to be with. He started investing the profits and learned stocks and bonds. He perused different legal money making schemes. Jon started boxing.

Lynette enjoyed her school year making a lot of new friends. She wasn't condescending anymore. She spent all of her free time with Lil' Dee. Lynette stayed in Jon's ear about getting out of the game. Even though she knew he couldn't, she stayed on him anyway.

Kay stayed the same. He was always close to Jon, especially after Don dropped out of school. Kay knew that the slightest thing could set Jon off. The girls also started swarming Kay. He knew that they were only trying to hook up with him because of his status.

"In order to be my woman you've gotta give good brains," Kay joked with Jon about perquisite drill girls endured. "Several have." He laughed. Kay was the main actor in a school play. It was clear that Kay was coming out of his shell.

Zoe always considered himself the playboy of the crew. It was no surprise that girls flocked to him. His flesh wound had healed nicely. He told all the girls crazy stories about how he received it. Mad girls were giving it up to Zoe and he was loving it. The sensitive side was leaving him slowly as each day passed. If you weren't down with the crew, Zoe was disrespecting you. Jon tried to talk to him but Zoe wouldn't change.

Twon wasn't the same. He withdrew from the crew and the girls trying to holler at him. Ron's incident did a number on him. Twon was having nightmares of being killed. He started hanging at Jackie's spot. The crew gave him space. At first Don tried talking to Twon, but Don started kicking it to Renee and backed off.

Ron accepted the loss of his eye. He and Jon talked about Ron's position. Jon agreed to let Ron operate the weed and crack houses. Ron had surgery on his hand then went through rehab and was able to regain full use of his left hand. Ron put in work with the boys from time to time just to get an adrenaline rush. He even took his GED and passed it. The girls found the patch that he wore over his eye sexy. This helped build his self-esteem up. Ron was doing well.

After Tina saw the four dead men on her block that night she realized that the stories about her sons were true. She tried talking to the boys but they denied everything. Although heartbroken she continued to work. The months went by and Tina accepted the boys' lifestyle. She kept her concerns to herself.

Bay Bro bonded with Lil' Dee and Victoria while Lynette was at school. At least once a week he'd speak with the boys. He helped them to expand business. Bay Bro had a hundred G's on Cash's head. He was thinking of marrying Victoria.

Victoria was high on life. All her dreams were coming true. She made the Dean's list both semesters and built a good relationship with Lynette. Victoria was pregnant.

Cash made changes. He and Jossie bonded and Cash

began to care about life again. He didn't want to lose her. He'd stay in the house all day and only come out at night. Cash wore a baldy and grew a full beard. Jossie became pregnant and Cash proposed to her. In April, they had a boy. Cash got out of the drug game completely. Cash invested in a clothing designer and opened a clothing store.

Jossie broke out of her good girl shell and had Cash teach her basic survival things that she was supposed to have known. She quit her job and enrolled at Indiana University Northwest. She majored in business management following Cash's request. She got a gun permit and purchased a .380 without Cash knowing. She loved Cash and equally loved being a mother. Jossie wanted to name their son after Doug. Cash insisted on their son being a junior.

Shine was having major problems. His luck went down since the boys came into his life. After finding his house ransacked he moved his family including Shawn, his brother, Jason and his sister Michelle, to Hobart. His spots kept getting robbed. He couldn't figure out who or how they knew where all of his spots were. Shawn changed up on him. She wouldn't listen to the advice he'd give. Sex with Shawn was almost nonexistent. Shine acquired a connect in the Gary police department. Not even officer Johnson could help Shine keep his dope houses from getting hit-up.

Shawn was tired of Shine. She was fed up with his lies and couldn't stand his ugly sister. His paper was why she was with him. Shawn got an abortion and never told Shine. She wanted Jon's seeds. Shawn put full-court press on Jon, trying to get him to see her and not Lynette. She fed him information on Shine's spots, to prove her loyalty. She warned him on times Shine was going to strike. She put herself out there in a bad way all in the name of love.

G was paranoid. All the spots were getting robbed and only three people knew where all of the spots were, Shine, G and Shawn. G knew Shine wouldn't let information about the business slip. He wasn't sure of Shawn. Since the Hudson Campbell incident, G lost trust for everyone, even Shine. Shawn pulled too many disappearing acts. He casually mentioned it to Shine.

"I think you ought to check your woman. She's always going out alone."

"Leave my woman and I biz alone," Shine angrily said.

G never spoke on the subject again. He began stacking dough planning not to be around for the finale.

The boys went undefeated and even had a couple scouts at some of the games. They found a heroin connect which allowed them to start their take over of the drug game in Gary. The only problem was the competition had moved into their neighborhood. After Ron's incident, Jon got everybody a cell phone.

Bay Bro had presented all of the boys with their brand new 1994 GMC Jimmy trucks on graduation day.

12

The summer was filled with promise. The boys were doing all they could to avoid their enemies and stay out of trouble. It was hard since Will lived only three blocks over from the twins. They saw him on the daily. Ron, Zoe, Kay and Don occupied their days by taking care of dope houses while Twon spent his days at Jackie's spot on Burr Street. Jon spent his days at the police gym. Jon fell in love with boxing and was in the ring at least five days a week. Sometimes Lynette and Lil' Dee watched him sparring.

The police didn't know how to take Jon. They heard stories about his involvement in numerous murders. Although some officers did talk to Jon they thought he was fishing for information.

The boys purchased an old club on the corner of 11th and Fillmore, one street over from the Dungeon. They turned the club into a game room for them and their affiliates. They named it SCC. Jon had a wall up. One section was an arcade for the kids to come and have fun. It didn't matter if they had money or not. Whoever

was behind the counter would give quarters to any kid that came in.

No Soliciting! No Drugs! Violators Will Be Dealt With!

The signs were posted on two walls outside. Jon wanted the arcade to be a safe haven for children. Even though it was a place to have fun, security personnel were at the corners surrounding the game room. The game room became the central place where the boys plotted and planned their moves.

Will wouldn't be around too much longer. The boys couldn't tolerate him. He was an only child who had it rough coming up. His father went to the state penitentiary when he was nine. At ten his mother was strung out on heroin. He had to fight for everything he got especially respect. Will was six-one and had jet black hair with waves all around.

He was born and grew up in New Brunswick, a place also called the Bronx. He moved on 11th in March of this year and was instantly not welcome. No one liked the electric blue Chevy Blazer that he drove and the six point star medallion didn't help his popularity. Will had a habit of calling everyone folks. He was an outsider who the boys didn't like trying to set up shop on the block.

Will had a run in with Don, Jon and Kay at Tolleston Park on Memorial Day. The courts were crowded and the bleachers were filled with kids and women from all over the city. Will's crew was forty-five members deep and rolled everywhere together. Kay bumped Will's man on purpose and ordered him to apologize. Dude looked at Kay like he was retarded and laughed. Infuriated Kay pulled out his Glock and smacked dude upside his head.

Will's crew ran over to help their man. Don and Twon pulled out Glocks stopping them in their tracks. Jon dialed a number while watching from the sidelines. Three minutes later, forty members of PMP led by Pretty Ricky were on the scene. Two minutes later twenty members from 17th arrived led by Smoke. Will and his crew were out numbered and would be out gunned. They had no choice but to watch their man get the shit beat out of him.

Will sat in his beaten up '83 Monte Carlo counting his money and waiting to re-up. Here it comes. The sight of the car pulling up next to him brought a smile to Will's face.

"What's up, Will?" Shine said slamming the door.

"Not too much, folks. Trying to get mines," Will smiled.

"I hear that," Shine replied.

The two went in a small restaurant and ordered. They talked about any and everything they could think of. Both had been busy and haven't hung in a while.

"You said having problems with them cats from your neighborhood?" Shine asked.

"First of all folks, it's not my hood," Will said with agitation. "And second, I can handle that."

"Ahight…" Shine said laughing. "So where did you move to?"

"13th and Buchanan."

"Oh yeah," Shine said pausing for the waitress to put their food down. After she left he continued. "This little beef you having, it wouldn't be with some lil' kids, would it?"

"Folks, how you know?"

Shine shook his head and told Will about his own feud with the boys. The two men talked a little while longer. They exchanged

car keys, paid the bill and left.

"Don't be a stranger," Will said.

"If you need some assistance, you call me." Shine started up the Monte Carlo.

"I got this, folks." Will lit a cigarette.

"Ahight gangsta, I'm out."

Will was moving keys and the boys decided the next time he made a big purchase they would stick him up for it. Steve called Jon. Will had a big duffel bag. Jon called Pretty Ricky and told him to bring Sam and Man. He also called Smoke and told him to bring Ty. Once all five of them arrived Jon went over the plan one last time before they left to meet Steve. It was going down.

Will's house had three entrances, the front door, the backdoor and a basement entrance. Jon, Zoe, Ron and Man were at the front door. Don, Twon, Steve and Sam were posted up at the back door while Kay, Pretty Ricky, Smoke and Ty were positioned at the basement door. Jon had Don on his cell phone and Twon had Kay on his cell phone line.

"One, two, three..." Jon counted. The doors were kicked-in and came crashing down.

At the time, Will was using the scales in a room at the back of his house. He was weighing the cocaine just purchased. On the floor next him, was his SK. After grabbing the gun Will turned the light off and backed into the closet. The boys were searching the house very slowly. The basement was empty. Kay and his crew joined the others upstairs.

They searched half the house. Steve turned on the light to the bedroom where Will was hiding. Will let off ten shots catching

Steve with seven of them killing him instantly. Three shots hit Ty leaving him on the hallway floor gasping.

"Get him outta here!" Jon shouted at Man.

Man bent down to pull Ty out of the hallway. It was too late. Ty had took his final breath.

Jon emptied the whole clip to his Tec 9 where Will hid.

"Give us the shit and we outta here," Jon shouted.

"Fuck you! The only way y'all getting my shit is over my dead body." Will said before firing five more times.

Jon saw the duffel bag on the floor and three keys on top of the table with the scales and other utensils. He huddled everybody up in the living room and began talking.

"We gotta get this over with early before the police get here. Zoe, Twon, Smoke and Man bust off till y'all empty. Kay, Don, Ron and Pretty Ricky to come behind them. I'm gone crawl on the floor and get the bag. Fuck what's on the table. I want two up and two down and don't shoot me." Jon looked at each one of them and said. "Let's get this money."

The boys set up on both sides of the hallway as planned.

"What the fuck y'all waiting on," Will shouted. "Y'all think I'm gonna let this shit slide? Shit! Y'all better kill me now because y'all fucking with the wrong one."

Will stuck the SK out letting off seven shots. Jon gave the signal and the first group started shooting. Jon got on his stomach and low-crawled as fast as he could. Four feet from the prize, the boys switched. Jon hurried as Will was preoccupied.

Jon secured the duffel and backtracked. The shooting stopped.

"Fuck!" Jon hissed jumping to his feet. Will peeked saw

Jon with the duffel bag and swung the SK at Jon.

"Get down, Jon!" Kay yelled fumbling to reload the Mac 11. Sam came around the corner pointing his Glock. Will saw Sam but focused on the duffel bag. With his finger on the trigger Will squeezed. Sam fired his Glock, hitting Will in the shoulder and sending him back into the closet. Jon was laid out on the floor not moving.

"Jon! Jon!" Don screamed out as he proceeded to run and get his brother. Kay finally reloaded and provided Don with cover. The others changed clips. Don threw the duffel bag into the hallway and dragged Jon by his shirt to safety.

Jon wasn't bleeding anywhere but he had a big-ass bump on his forehead.

"Let's get him to the car." Kay said grabbing the duffel bag. The boys ran out to the get-away cars. Don and Ron carried Jon while Pretty Ricky and Smoke emptied their clips as they backed out. Sirens were only a couple blocks away. The boys peeled off.

"That nigga gone come see us," Kay said steering Jon's truck.

"We got what we came for. Fuck' em!" Pretty Ricky said sparking a blunt.

"Pretty Ricky is what they call him..." Jon mumbled.

"You alright?" Don asked.

"My head is killing me. What happened?" Jon asked rubbing his forehead.

"Your goofy ass knocked yourself out," Kay answered chuckling.

"Fuck you," Jon said. Everybody laughed. The rest of the

ride was filled with jokes and laughs.

Back at Will's house, the police couldn't believe their eyes. Bullet holes were everywhere. At least two hundred empty shell casings were left behind. Will cleaned up and secured the caine left behind. He told the police the intruders broke in and he ran to get his gun and defended himself. Will had a permit and was protecting his property the police didn't give him a hard time. Will took the trip to the hospital vowing revenge.

The boys sat at a back room table in the game room planning their next move.

"I got a plan," Jon said sipping orange juice. "New Jack City."

"What!" Everyone shouted at once.

Jon slowly rose to his feet and cleared his throat. "I know we ain't gone take over no big ass housing complex, but we can get us an apartment building like the Carter. Three floors, the top floor we can sell heroin. Crack on the middle floor and in the basement we got weed."

"I don't know if we should put everything in one spot like that," Smoke said.

"Yeah Jon," Pretty Ricky said looking around. "It'll make it too easy for a nigga to rob us or for the police to bust us."

Jon took another swallow and spoke. "First off, who gone

rob us in our own hood? Second, our security is going to be airtight and third, it's riskier having our spots spread everywhere we can't keep a close eye on them. All I'm saying is we give it a try and see how it works. If it doesn't work then we'll go back to the old way."

13

Five days passed since the boys robbed and shot Will. They were starting to relax a little bit and felt like Will had gotten the message loud and clear. Jon didn't want to be looking over his shoulders anymore than he had to. He sat in the game room with Don, Kay, Zoe, Pretty Ricky and Smoke planning the move to the three-story apartment building. One of the kids from the neighborhood came running in.

"It's a man out there asking all kids if we want to sell drugs."

Jon was immediately pissed and jumped up. He ran to the door with the others in hot pursuit.

"What the fuck is your problem?" Jon asked walking towards the man. "Can you read? The sign says violators will be dealt with."

The man obviously was not from around the way because he had no idea of who Jon was.

"You better get yo little ass back up in there and play some video games before I treat you like my child."

Jon looked back at his crew and he could see in their eyes that they were waiting for him to make his move. Jon dropped him to one knee.

The man reached behind his back to retrieve his gun and Jon kicked him upside his head. Don and the rest of the crew came running over stomping him out. A crowd gathered.

"You can't read muthafucka? You can't read muthafucka?" Jon repeated with each kick.

"Throw his ass in the alley." Jon ordered.

They did and went back inside the game room.

"Who the hell was dude?" Smoke asked walking into the backroom.

"I don't know, but I bet he ain't coming back." Pretty Ricky laughed.

"Got that right," Zoe said laughing.

"I don't know why niggas keep trying us. It's like we still ain't got full respect," Don said and lit a blunt.

Jon was sitting at a back table. He seemed to have a lot of things on his mind. Respect wasn't one of them. He couldn't believe how reckless everybody had gotten. For the first time he wanted out.

Will needed to lay low for a couple days and went to the Bronx. He needed time to think about the huge loss. Not only did he lose twelve keys, he also lost the three keys that he stashed because somebody robbed him again. He knew who took the twelve keys and left him with a bullet. They would pay.

The boys had been at the game room all day working out details of opening the apartment building. They even placed a large order with the supplier confident that Jon's idea would work.

"Man, I'm about to be out," Smoke said yawning. "We been in here all day. I'm tired and hungry."

Everybody realized that they had not eaten and had been stuck in the back room making plans. Smoke left the game room headed back to 17th. Jon really wanted to stop by Lynette's but didn't want to bail on his boys.

Always wanting to party Zoe spoke up. "Let's go to the Savoy."

Pretty Ricky and Don were all for it. Jon and Kay reluctantly agreed.

The phone rang. Kay answered. Jumping to his feet he said. "We'll be right there." He hung up the phone and turned to the others. "Will got some people laid down on Fillmore Street."

"What!" Jon shouted in disbelief. "Let's take care of his ass once and for all."

The boys ran out the game room and headed for Fillmore. They arrived in time to see Will holding a gun and seven people lying in front of him. Jon directed Don, Zoe and Pretty Ricky through the alley. He and Kay attacked from the front. The three took off running. Jon turned to Kay.

"I can't believe this dude is this bold," Jon said pointing his gun up the street at Will. "This nigga in our hood by self, trying to put in work."

"Trying is right," Kay said staring at Will. "I'm a make sure I get his ass."

Smoke came running up startling the two boys. "What's up?" He asked holding the gun in his hand. Jon and Kay swung around pointing their gun.

"Chill, chill," Smoke said raising his arms above his head.

"Don't do that shit again," Jon said with clinched teeth.

"Where the others at?" Smoke asked lowering his arms.

"They went through the alley. We should make our way," Kay said.

Jon, Kay and Smoke made their way up the street keeping their eyes directly on the target. They were a couple houses away from him.

"Get the fuck on the ground." The three boys stopped in their tracks and Jon looked from side to side seeing no one. "I said get the fuck on the ground."

Will turned his attention behind him and saw Jon, Kay, and Smoke.

"Y'all thought it was going to be that easy," Will said then shot one of the dudes on the ground. "Where the rest of y'all?" he asked pointing his gun at another man lying on the ground.

"Fuck you!" Smoke shouted.

"Let me do them, Will." The voice called out.

"The dude is to our right," Jon said elbowing Kay.

Will shot a second person and then asked again. This time he got the answer he was looking for.

"Right here," Don said running up on Will's direction with the Glock blazing.

Jon turned to his right and started shooting wildly. Kay followed Jon's lead while Smoke's focus was on Will.

Will backed up in between two houses while Don kept running. When he passed the men lying on the ground three of them jumped up.

"Don!" Smoke shouted. "Watch your back!"

Don looked over his shoulder just in time to see the three men pulling out. Don dropped to the ground and shots rang. Pretty Ricky and Zoe shot the three men down from behind. Will took off for his car parked in the alley.

"It's a good thing we run slow," Pretty Ricky said pulling up Don up from the ground.

"Yeah...right on time," Don said smiling.

Zoe walked over to the bodies that were still on the ground. Holding his gun in front of him he saw couple of old-heads lying there, tape covering their mouths. Zoe took the tape off their mouths. He couldn't make out the other two. It didn't matter, they were dead. He joined Don and Pretty Ricky. They went after Will.

Jon, Kay and Smoke had emptied their clips and reloaded. They walked in the direction of where the voice was. They made it between the two houses and saw the man they stomped earlier, in a puddle of blood.

"I guess dude didn't know to leave shit alone," Jon said shaking his head.

"Damn," Kay said kicking the body. "This was Will's man?"

"You said that right," Smoke said turning to leave. "Was."

The boys all met up in the middle of Fillmore Street.

"Will got away," Don said disappointed.

"Don't even sweat it," Smoke said and lit a blunt. "Dude from earlier was one of his boys. We took care of that problem."

"Fuck it," Jon said hearing sirens. "Let's be out."

The boys went back to SCC. They talked about Will for a while.

"Fuck Will!" Jon said and took a swallow of orange juice. "We have to focus on where we setting up shop. The apartment building is on Pierce Street."

"We'll soon have them fiends leaning. Let's call it Pauline," Zoe said.

"Sounds good," Smoke agreed.

"There's nothing else to talk about." Don inhaled the blunt. "Everything's a go."

"Alright, I'll see y'all tomorrow. I'm out," Jon said thinking of Lynette.

"Me too," Zoe and Smoke said. Everybody left.

The day for the grand opening of Pauline's finally rolled around. Jon pulled twenty-two workers off the street to work in Pauline's. He put two men on each floor to work the apartments. They worked for twelve hours and were relieved by two more workers who finished the day off. Security worked the same way. Jon bought four junk cars and parked them at the four corners of Pierce Street. He put two men in each car equipped with walkie-talkie. They worked twelve hour shifts. Ron was in charge of running everything.

The apartments were half furnished. The kitchen had old stoves and refrigerators. In the living room were plush couches, stereos and big screen TV's. Jon ordered cable for the apartments and was debating video games. The doors had mail slots so customers were unable to see servers. Steel poles ran from the key hole to the floor fortifying the doors. Jon was taking no chances.

It was a hot Fourth of July day. The heat was too unbearable to play basketball so the boys stayed in the air conditioned game-room. The temperature rose to over a hundred degrees. In Gary, the high temperature had already claimed the lives of seventeen people. The only bright spot, no matter how hot, the fiends kept on coming back. Pauline had been open for six days and sales exceeded all expectations. The boys already made sixty-three thousand dollars. Word that Pauline having the best sacks was spreading like wildfire.

Pretty Ricky was introduced to an LSD connect although he didn't know much about acid. He knew that fiends in Hammond, Chicago's eastside and the northern Chicago, were going crazy for it. He wanted to expand clientele to the white preppy kids with money. Jon and the others were in agreement. The new connect not only sold cocaine and heroin but also guaranteed the best price in the Midwest if the quantity was right.

Pretty Ricky arranged for Jon and him to meet with the connect that very evening at four. It was two. Pretty Ricky was eager to get it over with. He had someone's wife on hold and her husband would be gone. The boys sat around the game room playing spades and talking trash. Twon was there enjoying himself.

"Hello," Jon said picking up the phone. The person on the other end said nothing. "Hello," Jon repeated.

"Who is this?" A male voice said on the other end.

"How may I help you?" Jon asked becoming annoyed.

The man on the other end laughed. "The question is, how may I help you?" the caller paused before continuing. "I know y'all got a little deal going down today and if I was you, I wouldn't show up. That is, if you value your freedom."

Jon was at a disadvantage and didn't know the proper way to deal with the caller. He panicked.

"Who is this? Do I know you a…"

"Calm down son," the man said. "Everybody knows y'all doing big things and people saying that y'all gone own this city. If that's the case," the man paused again. "I want to roll with the winning team."

Jon had no idea who the man was. The man found out about their deal.

"How do you know this?"

The man started talking very slowly. "Let's just say that a man who ain't to be trusted sings very loud. I will collect on my debt in the future." The man hung up.

"Pretty Ricky," Jon called out as he placed the receiver down. "How did you meet this plug?"

Pretty Ricky was sitting at the table playing spades with Don, Kay and Twon.

"It's cool, my man hooked me up."

Jon didn't think that Pretty Ricky was setting them up but didn't want to leave anything to chance.

"I got a bad feeling about this. Suppose you put my mind at ease? How'd you meet this connect? Who introduced y'all?"

"What's up Jon?" Pretty Ricky asked throwing his cards on the table and pulling his six-three two hundred five pound frame from the chair. "You got something to say?"

The room became quiet. Everyone looked from Jon to Pretty Ricky and back.

"All I'm saying," Jon started in a calm voice. "Is tell me who introduced you to the connect."

Pretty Ricky's golden complexion had turned beet red and his dark brown eyes, now looked black.

"I told you, Man introduced me to him," Pretty Ricky said with eyes fixed on Jon.

"Man!" Jon yelled. He told them about the conversation he had on the phone with the mystery man. There would be no meeting the connect that day, or any other. Jon made it clear that they'd stick with the usual connect.

"I'm going to take care of Man," Pretty Ricky said lighting a blunt. "We've to do it now before he finds out we were tipped off." He exhaled the smoke and shook his head from side to side. "I can't believe Man turned. We go back to second grade, almost fifteen years."

"Yeah, you just never know," Zoe said.

Don grabbed the blunt from Pretty Ricky and said, "Don't trip. It's just one less bitch we ain't got to put up with. Rats have to be exterminated."

Man was working his shift at Pauline's with Sam. Jon didn't know how Man had told the police so he put their security team on

high alert before they entered the apartment. "What's up peoples?" Man asked watching *Scarface* on the big screen.

Pretty Ricky was high and it showed in his slurred speech.

"Why don't you tell me what's really up, friend of mine."

Man paused the movie and looked at the group. Don, Jon, Kay, Ron, Twon, Zoe and Pretty Ricky weren't smiling.

"What's going on?" Man asked fidgeting with the remote.

"How fitting." Zoe said pointing at the TV. "We got our very own Omar right here."

Man looked puzzled. He didn't understand Pretty Ricky's attitude or Zoe's comment.

"Y'all done had y'all laugh. Ha, ha, jokes on me," Man said hoping this was only a test. "Rick, I thought y'all had a meeting?"

Pretty Ricky answered with a loud band from his .44 revolver catching Man in the shoulder and causing everybody else's ears to ring.

"You bitch-ass nigga." Pretty Ricky said looking down at Man.

"What the fuck is going on?" Man screamed clutching his right arm.

"I can't hear!" Zoe shouted as he put his index fingers in his ears and began wiggling them.

"Oh, you know what's going on," Pretty Ricky said still aiming his gun.

"I don't know what you talking about." Man said weakly. "We boys."

Pretty Ricky smacked Man across his forehead with the gun. "We ain't shit! You a snitch and no friends of mines are snitches."

Sam didn't know what was going on. "Am I next?" He asked cutting his eyes at the SK about seven feet away.

"Nah Sam, you cool," Jon said keeping his focus on Man. Jon paused for a couple of seconds before adding. "For all of us."

Man was still looking at Pretty Ricky and more importantly at the .44.

"I don't know what y'all talking bout," Man pleaded. "I ain't no snitch. Y'all got to know that."

Don had heard all that he wanted. He walked over to Man and said. "You have one chance and one chance only to make it out of here alive. Tell how you got trapped up?"

Man took several deep breaths. "Fuck it!" He hissed and began. "I got jammed up with a half a brick and they offered me a deal."

"What kind of deal?" Jon asked.

"They wanted me to set Rick up."

Pretty Ricky couldn't believe his ears. "Why me?"

"I don't know. All I know is they wanted you. They knew we was boys and said we would only do couple years."

"What else?" Pretty Rick asked.

"They didn't know much. They was trying to get me to talk." Man winced

"And did you?" Jon asked. Everybody in the room was anxious for Man's response.

"I couldn't do life in no jail cell. But don't y'all worry, I didn't tell them nothing."

"That's all I need to know." Pretty Ricky said.

He aimed the .44 at Man's chest. Man took a deep breath and closed his eyes. Pretty Ricky squeezed the trigger catching Man in the heart.

"Let's get this place cleaned up and get rid of this body," Jon said looking down at Man's body.

14

It was a good year for Cash. He celebrated the birth of his son by giving the dope game up. Cash had over a million dollars and invested in a designer with hot ideas. Together they started Hustlers clothing. They purchased a store selling only their line. Northern Indiana and Chicago flocked to the store, buying clothes. On July 5 Cash and Jossie were married. They had a small wedding at their home with only family in attendance. Shawn was there for her cousin's celebration. Cash was happy and tears of joy flowed.

It had been two weeks since the boys killed Man. Pretty Ricky was a nervous wreck. He was being very cautious and hung out more at the game room. He trusted the boys only.

"What's up Pretty Ricky?" Zoe said throwing his hands up

in the air.

The boys were playing cards and watching *Menace II Society*. Pretty Ricky was Zoe's partner and they were playing Don and Jon.

"My fault," Pretty Ricky said playing a card. "I spaced out."

"It'll be alright, Pretty Ricky," Jon said scooping the book. "Stay low. We got you."

"Yeah, we family," Kay said turning his head from the movie.

The boys played cards, talked shit, got high and watched a couple more movies. Later they all went their separate ways.

Don was hungry, high and horny. There was only one person who could satisfy his needs; Renee. Driving to the apartment he rented for Renee, Don became aroused. His lust for Renee's 36D's bouncing up and down made him go faster. Don turned into the parking lot. He noticed the living room lights were out. Don hoped Renee hadn't gone to sleep.

He entered the apartment and smelled the strange odor. The apartment was dark. The only light coming from the bathroom in the back. Don heard music playing from Renee's bedroom. He walked to the bedroom trying to figure out the strange smell. Don turned the knob on the bedroom door hoping Renee was sprawled out on the bed wearing something sexy. He slowly pushed the door open. Renee was lying but naked on the bed with a glass dick hanging from her hand.

"What the fuck is your problem!" Don screamed as he charged Renee.

Renee dropped the crack pipe to the floor turning white as ghost. Renee was beautiful. She stood five-foot one, had long black wavy hair, honey color eyes. She was half black half white, very light skinned with a body like a goddess.

"What the fuck you tripping for?" She shot back as if she had done nothing wrong.

"I can't believe you, you a crack-head."

"Shi-i-i-t nigga! I ain't the only one in this room that fucks around." She jumping from the bed with her big titties bouncing up and down.

"What the fuck you talking bout? I don't fuck with that shit."

Don was inches away from her face.

Renee poked out her lips and folded her arms. "I already know you ain't Mr. Clean, Twon told me."

Don smacked Renee across the bed.

"Bitch, don't be lying on my brother like that," he said then jumping on the bed and smacking her twice. "Bitch, get your shit and git the fuck up."

Don's handprints were implanted on the sides of Renee's face. Tears flowed as she crawled out of the bed and started dressing.

"I'm sorry. I'm soo sorry." She kept saying.

Once she was fully clothed she grabbed Don's arm and said. "Please baby I'm sorry. I know I fucked up but..."

"Get the fuck out!" Don said snatching his arm out of her grasp.

Renee slowly walked out of the room and slammed the apartment door.

Don put the incident behind him and took out his phone book. He was a player again.

15

The morning came quickly. It was the dawn of a new day. Different because it was twin's birthday. They planned on doing it real big all day getting high, drunk and driving Tina crazy. The Player's Ball was at the Savoy starting at ten that evening. Everybody who was anybody was sure to be there, including Shine and Will.

The boys weren't worried because they would be at least seventy-five deep and planned on sneaking a couple of guns inside. They were in the middle of pestering Tina for some food when Twon ran up the stairs screaming.

"We gotta get to the hospital! We gotta get to the hospital!"

"The hospital..? For what Twon?" A confused Tina asked.

Twon was still trying to catch his breath but managed to speak.

"Victoria's in labor."

The twins looked at each other and smiled. Everybody left

for the hospital.

Bay Bro was at the hospital pacing back and forth smoking Newport after Newport. Lynette tried to calm him down but gave up. She played games with Lil' Dee. By the time everybody arrived Bay Bro was a nervous wreck and Lynette relieved.

"You look like you haven't been through this before," Tina said smiling.

"I haven't," Bay Bro said as he put out one cigarette and lit another. "I was in Cook County when Lynette was born and Lil' Dee was...it doesn't matter."

"It'll be over before you know it." Tina said and gave Bay Bro a hug.

"She kicked me out of the room. Can you believe that?" Bay Bro said shaking his head.

"Yes, I can," Tina smiled.

Forty-eight minutes later the doctor came out and told Bay Bro that he had a healthy baby girl. The visiting room erupted with cheers. Jon turning to Lynette and whispering.

"If she's half as beautiful as you are, Bay Bro really got his hands full."

Lynette smiled and bumped Jon's shoulder. "Shut up, boy."

"We're really gone celebrate now. This a triple birthday," Don said.

It was almost midnight when the boys arrived at the Savoy.

Jon, Don, Kay, Ron, Twon, Zoe, Pretty Ricky and Smoke were the last to get there. Everybody else from the crew was already inside the Player's Ball checking things out. Sam called and told them that Will was already in there and that he had a couple of people with him. He also told them that Shine wasn't there and the word was that he wasn't going to show. Jon still didn't want to take any chances. He had four females sneak eight Glocks inside the ball and now it was their turn to try and bribe the security guard to get the rest in.

Jon was prepared to do all of the talking. When they got to the entrance, security let them in without searching them.

"I hope y'all packing because it's a lot of guns up in here," he warned.

The boys looked at each other and walked in. Kay stopped and turned around. "I'll be back in fifteen minutes." He said with a smile on his face. "I have to go change."

Jon looked puzzled because they all had on the same kind of outfit. "You want me to come with you?"

"Nah, I'm straight." Kay said then ran to his truck.

"Now that's smart man," the security guard said.

"Do I know you?" Jon asked the security.

"I don't think so. As you can see, my big ass can't be easily forgotten. I know ya'll though. SCC right?"

The boys stared at each other.

"Damn, it's about time we getting our props." Don said looking at Jon. "Shit, all the shit we been through."

"Come on, let's go inside," Jon said interrupting his brother before he got going. "Good looking," Jon said and gave him a thousand dollars.

Inside the Savoy, the men came dressed in leathers, gators, lizards, crocodiles and ostrich skin suits. The boys blended right with their dark green gator suits with matching shoes and hats. Jon, Don, Zoe and Pretty Ricky were even sporting pimp canes. The women wore form fitting dresses, mini skirts or leopard print suits. People were taking pictures with other people's women.

Groups of player's huddled together talking money, women and the game. The boys stayed within their circle talking among themselves. It wasn't too long before Kay came walking up to them wearing the same outfit.

"I thought you went to change?" Twon asked looking confused.

Kay looked at the group and smiled. "I had to get us right. I got three of the Mini 14's under my jacket."

"Now that's what I'm talking bout," Pretty Ricky said holding his hand out smiling. "Lemme get one."

Kay looked at Jon to see if it was all right to give Pretty Ricky one and Jon nodded his head giving his approval. Don received the second one Kay kept the third. The boys also passed out the guns that they snuck in to key members of their crew.

Twenty minutes after Kay arrived the boys spotted Will, definitely dressed to impress. He was wearing a baby blue gator suit with matching Kangol. In his ears were diamond earrings, the size of a gram rock and a six-point star chain that put all others to shame. He was surrounded by eight dudes. It didn't take Will long to realize that the boys were eyeing him and motioned for two of his men to round up their posse. The boys didn't waste time gathering the crew. Will's man came back and whispered something in his ear. He approached the boys.

"Y'all in the wrong neck-of-the woods," he said with a scowl.

The Savoy was located in the Brunswick area which meant the boys were now in Will's hood.

"We don't set trap," Jon said staring in Will's eyes. Twon and Smoke laughed.

"I don't want to mess up anybody's night," Will said looking from one SCC member to the next. "But I'm going to get my revenge."

The members of his crew nodded their heads up and down with some even smiling.

"How's the shoulder?" Don asked sarcasm dripping.

"Fuck you! You little bitch!"

Will was still pissed about being robbed and having a bullet deposited in him. Will's men were ready.

"I got your bitch right here, soft-ass mark." Don shot back. Will swung on Don and a battle royal ensued.

Don stumbled and regrouped. Before Don could fight back, Jon hit Will with a left-right-left combination that sent Will falling into the arms of one of his men. Kay took off on the closest Bronx boy he could find.

"0-9! 0-9! 0-9!" Was heard. It was the call the Bronx boys used to alert each other of danger. Within seconds close to two hundred people were rushing the boys. The rest of the SCC ran to the boys' aid.

"Ain't that them little niggas from the Taste?" A short brown skinned teenager asked pointing in the direction of the commotion.

"Yep, sho is." A six-foot dark skinned chubby boy responded. The two teenagers gathered up their crew and ran to the middle of the brawl.

Things weren't looking good for SCC. They were getting over powered and man handled by the bigger, stronger Bronx boys. Jon was about to pull his Glock and start dropping people when he saw a familiar face coming through the crowd. Jon couldn't place where he knew the individual from but he was thankful that he was with them instead of against them. He was giving the Bronx boys the business. Jon watched the short stocky teenager and noticed the dark skinned heavy set boy knocking the Bronx out one by one.

Will had enough fighting and pulled out his chrome .40 caliber handgun and started shooting. He had just played into the boys' hand. Don grabbed the Mini 14 that was strapped to his shoulder and started dropping people. Kay and Pretty Ricky followed his lead making almost everyone drop to the ground for cover. Those that tried to run caught bullets in their backs. Jon looked around for Will. He quietly slithered his way out the door once he saw his posse outgunned.

"Come on," the short stocky boy said pulling Jon by the arm. "We gotta go. Y'all chill in our hood till the police are gone."

Jon gathered up the SCC members and followed the boy out to the parking lot to the vehicles and left in hurry. "What you think of dude?" Ron asked as he rode with Jon.

"I don't know yet," Jon said still trying to place the boys face. "I guess we just gone have to wait and see."

The boys were led to the notorious Concord projects.

Concord and the Bronx were at war. They both had high number of casualties because of beefs. Concord was not set up like other projects in Gary, it had three sides. The apartment buildings, duplex houses and the flat houses, where everything went down. Concord projects was known and feared.

"Your face looks familiar. Do I know you?" Jon asked the stocky boy.

"Can you believe this dude?" he said to his man next to him. They looked at Jon. "I'm the dude from the Taste. The one that was drawn into y'all shootout."

"You the one that ran in the middle of the street, right? How's your man doing?"

"My bother's face still fucked up and he can't see out one eye but he's alive."

Ron bumped Jon and then pointed at the boy. "I told you he go hard."

The boy stood up extending his hand. "My name's J-Roc."

They introduced themselves and kicked it for the rest of the night.

Shawn was tired of Shine's bullshit. She planned time and time again to leave and now possessed both things she had been lacking. Money and nerves. She was in the middle of getting ready for her movie date with Jon. Shawn planned to tell him her plans hoping that this would bring them closer. Shine walked in as she was putting on her shoes.

"Where you going?" he asked.

"Out," Shawn said with a nasty attitude.

"Out where? Since we moved here a lot has changed between us," Shine said sitting on the bed.

"Oh well," Shawn said checking herself in the full length mirror. "You should've thought about that before you moved your stuck-up ass sister in here. I need some air. I'll be at the beach for a little while getting my head right."

Shawn grabbed her purse and car keys.

"You do that. And while you at it, think about who takes care of your ass."

Shawn walked out the house. She was supposed to meet Jon at the movies in the mall. Shawn pulled into the parking lot and saw Jon's truck parked on the side of the building. She parked in the spot next to his truck and got out.

"Look at you, Ms. Thang." Jon smiled getting out his truck.

Shawn wore a Hustlers T-shirt, some daisy dukes and sneakers. Jon's eyes were riveted on the daisy dukes.

"These old things," Shawn said hugging and kissing Jon.

"We should go in," Jon said grabbing her by the hand.

They were talking and playing with each other while G sat in his car observing it all.

"Shine," G said into his cell phone. "Shawn up here at the mall with Jay."

Shine was pissed. "You stay on they ass. I'm on my way out the door."

Shine grabbed the carbine from the closet.

"They at the movies out here. You'll find me parked."

Shine grabbed two 9's and headed for the door. "I'm out, Gangsta, seven-four."

Jon and Shawn went to see *Above the Rim* and now they were headed to Red Lobster. They were walking to their cars. Shawn noticed G's car parked an aisle behind them. Shawn stopped and looked at Jon.

"That's G's car parked over there."

"Are you sure?" Jon asked looking around the parking lot. G's 1994 ninety-eight was unmistakable. He had the only purple one in the city.

"Of course I'm sure," Shawn said.

She saw Shine's truck parked in the back of the parking lot. She pointed at it." "And that's Shine's truck."

Jon had a Glock but they had the advantage. He didn't know how many of Shine's men were there.

"Let's go back inside," Jon said grabbing Shawn by the shoulders and turning her around. Shine saw the change in their direction and opened fire with the carbine.

"Get behind the car!"

Jon pushed Shawn behind an old Cutlass, pulled out his Glock and peeked to see where the shots were coming from. He saw fire coming from the side of a Caravan five aisles away.

"Follow me," Jon said moving to the Cutlass's door.

He was in luck because the door was unlocked. He pushed Shawn inside the car and jumped in. Jon frantically searched for the car's seatbelt.

"What are you doing?" Shawn asked hysterically.

"Be cool," Jon said. Finally he located the driver's side seatbelt. "I said that I'm a get us outta here. Trust me."

Jon adjusted the steering wheel all the way up then he went to work breaking the steering column. Jon started the car. Shine realized that the two were trying to get-away. Shine ran up on the Cutlass letting off shots. G approached from the passenger side busting shots from his .40 caliber handgun.

"Get down on the floor," Jon shouted breaking the steering wheel free. Mall security was quickly closing in and Jon let off two shots from his Glock through the passenger window at G. Shawn screamed. Jon finally got the Cutlass ready to go and took off for the highway. Shine and G were running behind the car shooting.

Jon took Shawn to the apartment that Don had been renting for Renee. The two sat in the living room eating pizza Jon ordered. Shawn told him about her plans of leaving Shine anyway. She put the R *12 Play* in the CD changer.

"I don't want you to worry about nothing, I'm gonna take care of you till you decide what you want to do," Jon said sipping Hawaiian Punch. Shawn smiled and sat next to Jon on the black leather sofa.

"I know you will," she said leaning over and kissing Jon on his lips.

Shawn pushed Jon back onto the sofa and hopped on top of him. She kissed Jon letting her fingers caress his face and chest. She pulled Jon's shirt over his head and rubbed her finger nails up and down his torso. Shawn bent down and started kissing him from his head down to his chest and stomach while at the same time undoing Jon's belt and pants. Shawn yanked Jon's boxers and pants from up under him exposing a full erection. Shawn was surprised. Jon was huge. She smiled and kissed Jon's stomach.

"I don't think we should do this," Jon said groggily.

Shawn grabbed his dick and ran her tongue up and down the shaft. Her tongue snaked until his dick was in her mouth. Jon was going crazy shaking his leg. He never experienced anything like this before. Shawn deep-throated him and played with his balls. After couple minutes, Jon shot a gallon of sperm down her throat. She swallowed every bit. Shawn kept sucking trying to resuscitate it.

Shawn got Jon's dick rock-hard, she rode him like she was in a rodeo. The rest of the night was spent with her giving him a bath, a massage, licking his ass and showing him all the positions she knew.

It had been two days since he slept with Shawn and he was feeling terrible. Jon told Don what happened and that Shawn was staying at his apartment until she got on her feet. Don was against it but realized that she had saved their lives and had been feeding them info. Jon denied sleeping with Shawn.

One week passed and Jon still had not been able to contact their supplier. They had a stash on reserve but that was in case of a drought. He didn't want to dabble with the stash and decided to see Bay Bro for a new connect. It was either that or jacking every baller. Jon was on his way out the door when Pretty Ricky came running into the house.

"Did you see today's paper?" He asked slamming it down on Jon's bed. "I got knocked and so did eighty other muthafuckas."

"What!" Jon shouted unable to hide his shock. "That's why I haven't been able to get in touch with his ass."

Jon picked up the newspaper and read the article about the eighty-eighty count indictment that his plug kicked off. It was the connect. He was arrested with two hundred kilos of cocaine and that others would be indicted. "Damn! This is fucked up," Jon said.

"Fucked up!" Pretty Ricky repeated.

"We straight. Everything's cool."

"It better be," Pretty Ricky said with a scowl. He snatched the paper from Jon's hand and stormed out.

Shine also saw the morning paper and he knew every person that was mentioned in the article. The one name that stood out from the rest was Gordon Anderson, his right hand man G. Shine didn't understand how G's name made the list and his didn't. G was not in custody. He was one of the seven still at large. Shine sent G out of town to take care of some business. G was unaware of the indictment.

Shine wasn't concerned with G telling on him. He placed a call to Officer Johnson and asked how to make the problem go away. Shine was trying to be safe and not worry.

Three days before school was to start, the second indictment came down. The name in the paper read, Ricky Jones. The boys knew him as Pretty Ricky. Don, Jon, Kay, Twon and Smoke were in the game room waiting on Pretty Ricky. Jon didn't want Zoe around just in case things didn't go as Jon hoped.

The boys acted like that night was any other night but they knew it wasn't.

"What's up brothers?" Pretty Ricky greeted as he entered the back room. Jon immediately noticed Pretty Ricky's mood.

"You sure is in a good mood," Jon said putting on a fake smile. "What done changed?"

Pretty Ricky smiled back at Jon and took a seat at one of the tables.

"I talked to my lawyer. He said that I wouldn't get more than five years. Shit, I'll be out at twenty-four. That's still young."

"So how do you plan to get this five years?" Jon asked staring at Ricky.

Pretty Ricky sat straight up in his chair and placed his arms on the table.

"Say what's on your mind, brother."

"Who the fuck you telling on?" Don bellowed standing. "That's what we want to know."

Pretty Ricky also stood to his feet. "I'm tired of you and your brother accusing me of being a snitch. I ain't no snitch. The lawyer said the case is weak against me."

"How does your lawyer know anything? You haven't even been arrested," Jon said standing to his feet.

"What the fuck you talking bout?"

"I was going to get the best fed lawyer around. I went to talk to him and he said that he wouldn't know anything about the case until after you was arrested. Way after."

Pretty Ricky looked confused. "I'm telling y'all," he said looking around the room. "My lawyer told me…"

Kay hit him on the side of the head with his gun. "You lying piece of shit," Kay said hitting Pretty Ricky again. He fell. Kay started stomping away at Pretty Ricky lying defenseless on the ground.

"Let's get this over with," Don said thinking about his rendezvous with Shawn. Jon took out a switchblade and stabbed the unconscious Pretty Ricky twice in the chest. They wrapped him

up in a rug and buried him in a ditch, dug earlier that day.

"Rest in peace," Don said walking.

Shawn sat around the apartment thinking about her next move. She was pregnant. There was no question. Jon was the father. She contemplated telling him but knew that it would only complicate things. Since Jon and Don were twins, Don had some of Jon's good qualities in him. It was up to her to find them and bring them out.

"What's up boo?" Shawn greeted in a soft voice.

"You," Don said giving Shawn a hug and a long, slow tongue kiss.

Shawn pulled away.

"We need to talk."

Don took a step back and looked at Shawn tilting his head to one side. Shawn grabbed Don by his hand and led him into the living room. She sat down on the couch and Don did the same.

"You know that I'm a woman and I have needs."

"Yeah, I..."

Shawn put a finger over Don's lips. "Let me talk," she said removing her finger. "I like you a lot but I'm not trying to be in a relationship like the one I was just in. I'm a loyal woman who has her man's back as long as he's out there taking care of business. I'm tired of being alone. I need compassion, affection and love. I want to open myself up to you but I'm afraid of getting hurt." Shawn put her hands over her face and began to cry. "Men always try to hurt me and I'm tired."

"I got you now Boo. You don't have to worry," Don said hugging Shawn.

She kissed him passionately. They made love the rest of the night. Don was satiated and fell asleep. Shawn kneeled over him still dripping wet. She smiled.

"You don't know this baby, but I gotcha…"

There was no response. Don's chest heaved up and down, his breathing loud. Shawn wore a sinister grin as she rested her head.

16

School started off slow the following year. Jon, Kay and Zoe were the only members of SCC who showed up to school. The three were the talk of Roosevelt High. The kids knew who they were and never disrespected. Jon spent his free time in the hallways with Lynette sometimes in his truck with Kay and Zoe. The school wanted to place Jon in the tenth grade instead of the ninth but Jon refused. Kay and Zoe were his boys and he wanted to graduate with them.

Don stopped by the school at times to pick up a girl for fun. He'd creep on Shawn and was never busted. Shawn wanted to go back to school but Don didn't think it was wise. He hired a tutor for her.

Even though Don and Shawn was a couple, he kept it a secret. When Shawn told him she was pregnant, Don went straight to his mother and brother hoping that they would be just as excited.

"What do you mean you got Shawn pregnant?" Jon asked with a frown.

Before Don could answer Tina jumped in.

"You're only fifteen. You're still a baby. Oh Lord, I knew I should've put my foot down a long time ago."

"Forget it then. I just thought since I was happy y'all be happy," Don said looking from his mother to his brother. "I guess I was wrong."

Don stormed out. Jon was upset at Shawn for not telling him about Don. Things just didn't feel right to him. He went off and confided in someone he trusted.

"What you mean you fucked Shawn?" Kay said.

"It was more than just a fuck," Jon said looking at the ground. "It was something special. I'm telling you," Jon said looking straight at Kay." If I wasn't in love with Lynette, Shawn be that girl."

"I can't believe this shit. So what about the baby?" Kay asked.

"I don't know, I really don't know. Part of me thinks that it's my baby, the other part don't want it to be. She always tried to dog Don out for the way he acted and now they a...c'mon, man."

"I'm a tell you like this," Kay said and placed his hand on Jon's shoulder. "If she didn't tell you that it was yours, don't sweat it. You know that she'd ask you to break-up with Lynette. If I was you I wouldn't trip, just be happy for your brother."

"Yeah," Jon said smiling. "You right."

The indictment of the heavyweight ballers brought a big time drug drought. Prices were so high that it was almost impossible to make a profit. All the small timers were either getting beat by their connects or they were getting robbed by doped-fiends. The only people that were still profiting were ballers pushing keys.

The boys managed to stay afloat by doing out-of state robberies. Profits were down fifteen percent. Because of their reputation as stick-up kids, they were having a hard time finding new connect. Jon went to Bay Bro with no success. Despite the failure Jon never quit looking for an account.

Will and Shine came up during the drought. G stayed in Nashville, Tennessee until things calmed down. While in Nashville, G met a connect that allowed Shine to keep prices the lowest around. Shine and Will were eating well. G wasn't around and the two hung-out tough. Neither had forgotten the SCC.

17

Spring '95 brought plenty suppliers. Those awaiting indictment were indicted. The big ballers left untouched started supplying everyone not affiliated with the SCC. Despite the fear people had of SCC, the boys remained in the business. Their big break came when they met someone just as ruthless.

The twins were outside their house chatting about setting up another place like Pauline's in another part of town. Jon had already scouted and found the perfect building in the right neighborhood. The only thing lacking was the product. The boys needed to find the right supplier. It was then a five-five, honey colored brick-house came out of walking out the twin's basement. Her long black hair dropped past her shoulders. She had hazel eyes and full lips.

"Damn!" Don shouted. "You're a beauty."

The girl gave Don a polite smile and tried to get by. Don blocked her path. "You might be beautiful, but what you doing coming out my house?"

"I went to see Twon."

"Twon…!" The twins shouted at the same time.

"Cut the games. You too beautiful to be hollering at Twon." Don said.

"How you gone diss your man like that?" She asked.

"Nah, it wasn't like that. What's up I'm Jon. This my brother Don. Twon's our man and we'd never intentionally disrespect him."

"Yeah," Don rejoined staring at the girl.

"It's been nice, but I have to go," she said squeezing Don's cheek.

"What's your name?" Jon shouted after her.

"Jackie," she smiled.

"That's Jackie…?" Jon asked with an incredulous look.

"Jackie who?" Don asked.

Jon raced to her black '95 BMW 325I, opened the door and hopped into the passenger seat, startling Jackie.

"What's so urgent?" She asked.

"You're the Jackie that everybody is talking about? The one from Chicago, right?"

"Yeah, that's me. Why, what's up?"

"I'm sure Twon told you that we do a little something but right now we hurting. We need a plug bad and these scare-ass niggas won't sell to us. I'm saying, why don't you hook a brother up?"

Jackie turned the motor off. She liked his straight forwardness. "Give me a call and we'll talk later," she said handing him a business card.

"Thank you," Jon said.

"Which one are you?" She asked starting her car.

"Jon," getting out the car.

G grew homesick and came back to Gary against Shine's wishes. Instead of laying low, he served notice that he was throwing a big welcome home party. The word spread fast.

"Give me five hundred dollars," Trina, a tall, slim, dark skinned girl said to Kay.

"Trina, if you don't get out my face..."

"Oh, you gone give me something," she said putting her hands on her hips and getting in Kay's face. "Or I'm going to tell mama. Don't think I don't know what y'all be out here doing."

"How you gone blackmail me? I'm your brother."

"Look," she said wagging her head. "If you don't give me the money right now I'm a march straight to mama and tell her everything I know."

Kay reached in his pocket. He peeled off five crisp one hundred dollar bills and handed them to her. "Thank you," she said smiling.

"What you need all that money for?" Jon asked.

"I'm going to this party tonight and I gots to be right," she flirted with Jon.

Jon reached in his pocket and gave her two more hundred. "Be careful."

G's party was off the hook. Everybody showed respect, voicing how much they missed him. In Nashville G learned why they called it Cashville. Shine didn't show. He thought G was flossing too much. Shine's little brother Jason was there doing his thing with Trina. G saw the two and went over.

"What's up Jase?" G said looking Trina up and down. "Who's this?"

"I just met her," Jason said shaking G's hand.

"My name's G," he said stepping closer to Trina.

"Trina," she said with attitude.

"This my party, you should be nice to me."

Trina took a step back from G.

"This might be your party, but right now you're disturbing my groove."

Jason busted out laughing and G got pissed. He pulled Jason to the side and whispered in his ear. Trina walked away. Jason followed her.

"You pissed G off," he said catching up.

Trina turned around to face him. "I don't care. He shouldn't be all up in my grill."

"G don't like being dissed. C'mon we got to talk." Jason said leading her upstairs to one of the rooms. They walked inside. Trina's eyes widened with surprise.

"What the fuck is going on?" Trina asked.

"Bitch, shut the fuck up," G said walking over to her. "Who the fuck you think you are? All up in my shit thinking you the shit?" G said getting real close to her. Trina stepped back.

"Look," Trina said backing into a wall. "I...I just ca-came to have a good time. I didn't mean to piss you or nobody off. I'll leave right now if you want."

"Nah, you cool. You came to have a good time so I'm a give you a good time."

G snatched Trina by her hair. She screamed. He led her to the bed and flung her to the mattress.

"Help me! Help me!" Trina screamed at Jason.

"Bitch, shut the fuck up," G said smacking her face a couple times.

He ripped her blouse. Trina fought back but was no match. Jason stood at the door watching in shock. Trina's bra was off and her breasts were exposed. She tried covering them. It was useless, they stuck out like cones. She kicked, screamed, scratched and hit G. He punched her in the face knocking her unconscious. G kept snatching her clothes off until she was butt naked.

G pulled his pants down and rammed his dick inside Trina. He forcefully pumped all the while talking shit to the unconscious girl. He got his nut off then turned to Jason.

"You better get some of this. The bitch tight."

"I'm straight," Jason said unable to hide his disgust.

One of the girls Trina came with became concerned. She had seen Trina walking off with Jason. The girl started roaming the place in search of her friend. She made it upstairs and heard the screams coming from a closed door. The girl slowly walked to the door and opened it enough to see G fucking Trina in the ass before Jason closed it. The girl ran to the nearest phone.

"Y'all better get out here quickly. Trina's getting raped."

She gave Kay the address and went outside to wait. The boys ran every red light and stop sign getting there in ten minutes.

"Where's my sister?" Kay said jumping out his truck with an assault rifle in his hand.

The girl ran into the house and showed them the room where she had seen Trina. Kay pushed her out the way and opened the door. Trina was the only one in there still wearing nothing but one sock. She sat on the bed crying. Blood oozed from her ass. Kay ran over to her.

"Who did this to you?" Kay asked shaking his sister.

"G and Jason," she said between sobs.

Kay got up from the bed seeing only red.

"Get some clothes on her." He told the girl as he passed her. Kay, Jon, Don, Ron, Zoe and Smoke went down in the basement. G and Jason were off in a corner talking when G saw the twins in the crowd.

"We gotta go," G said grabbing Jason by the arm. "It's about to be some shit." The two slipped out the house and quietly into G's truck, getting away.

Kay got frustrated and started shooting people. People were running, ducking, screaming, and fighting trying to get out. Jon followed Kay's lead, shooting anybody he saw and then the rest of the clique followed suit. At the end of the gunfire everybody that couldn't get out of the basement was dead. Kay walked around the eleven unfortunate dead bodies searching for G. Jon ran upstairs and got Trina and her girlfriend.

"Let's go." Don said pulling on Kay's shirt.

They met Jon, Trina and her girlfriend outside. "Hospital or my mama?" Jon asked Kay.

"Hospital," Trina said. Don called Bay Bro and told him to meet them at the hospital.

While Trina was getting examined Bay Bro and the boys

were outside talking about G and Jason.

"I ain't trying to hear that," Kay said pacing back and forth.

There was mixed feelings about striking right back.

"You know they gone be waiting for us to come back out there," Don reasoned with Kay.

"Don's right. You don't want to do anything while you're pissed. Be smart. Let yourself calm down and then handle your business." Bay Bro puffed as he spoke.

"I heard everything y'all said and it's all bullshit. If it was Lynette both you and Jon would be out there right now." Kay said staring at Bay Bro. He turned to Don. "And if it was Jon or Shawn you'd be the same way. I don't need nobody to ride with me. Shit, I'm a soldier."

"I'm with you my brother," Jon said hugging Kay around the neck.

The nurse came out and spoke to Bay Bro. Trina's jaw and nose were broken, she had a cracked rib. And was given stitches for injuries to her vagina and ass. Kay took off running to his truck. Jon was hot on his heels. Kay slowed down when he reached G's street. Jon spotted police and news hounds posted outside G's house.

"Ah fuck it!" Kay said and sped off.

Kay headed straight to Miller projects. It was empty.

"I didn't come out here for nothing all these cribs gone catch it," Kay said.

Jon grimaced but he felt Kay's pain. He was down no matter what.

"Fuck it, they all get it," Jon said loading a new clip into a Glock.

Kay had two assault rifles and four Glocks. He had extra clips for each weapon in the truck. The two loaded the weapons. Kay drove around the projects shooting every house they passed, only stopping to reload.

The two shooting incidents made Gary look like the wild-wild west. Eleven were killed at G's house. Nine dead and fifteen wounded from the projects. Jon read the paper while waiting to visit Trina at the hospital.

"What's up beautiful?" Jon said smiling as he entered the room.

Trina rolled away hiding her face.

Jon walked into the room and sat in the chair.

"Trina," he said in a soft voice. "You are beautiful. I had a crush on you since I was five. Right now things are fucked up but it will get better. You have people who love you and we'll see to it that you get well and they pay."

Trina was facing the window. She was crying and Jon crawled into the bed with Trina. He held her in his arms.

"I know that you're older than me but you're still only seventeen. I need you to promise me, no more house parties and let us know when and where you going clubbing. We all got you."

Trina buried her head in Jon's arm and cried.

For the next couple of weeks Kay and Jon went on a shooting spree limited to the Miller area. The shooting brought extra officers to the projects. They patrolled two to three deep in a car. Jon and Kay were setting the tone for the summer.

Jon and Kay were chilling in the game room with Don, Twon, Zoe and Smoke discussing their plans on expanding and setting up another apartment. "I don't know about 2nd," Smoke said puffing on a blunt. "It's some shady niggas down there."

Jackie had agreed to supply them but they couldn't agree on a location.

"We already got about thirty brothers holding shit down there. So what if niggas wanna trip?" Don said puffing the blunt. "Fuck 'em!" Don said chugging beer.

"I'm with Smoke. I don't like second either. Y'all know some cut-throats down there. They don't like us and don't forget about the brothers off fifth," Twon said sitting his beer on the table. "Y'all know they gone wanna start some shit. Y'all ready for another war?"

"Fuck fifth!" Don said choking on some smoke.

"All I'm saying is that we don't need extra beef when it can be avoided," Twon said as the phone rang. He was the closest to it and picked it up.

"Hello," Twon listened for a minute before saying, "You crazy. SCC don't pay shit!" He slammed the phone down.

"Who was that?" Jon asked.

"Some dude saying it was time to pay our debt," Twon said laughing.

"What's up little men?"

The boys looked up and saw the bouncer from the Savoy. He was wearing a police uniform.

"What's up?" Don said still puffing.

"I think it's time we all sit down and talk. You know? Clear

up a few things."

"A few things like what?" Twon asked.

The police sat down at the table across from Don.

"Well for starters, I'm the one who tipped y'all about the undercover. Second, I let y'all shut down the Savoy. And last, I can bust y'all for all the murders y'all did and even throw a couple bodies on y'all."

"That's bullshit!" Smoke jumping up from the table. "You ain't got shit on us."

"I think you should sit your ass down," the officer said sternly. "I'm Mad Dog and I can do what I want to do."

The boys had heard about Mad Dog and they didn't like the stories. Officer Johnson also known as Mad Dog was corrupt as a politician. He shook all the heavyweights down and even put a couple murders on some innocent people.

"What's the deal?" Jon asked. "How much you want and for what?"

The next hour was spent negotiating prices and services. Mad Dog would get fifty thousand a month for his services. Those included eliminating certain rivals, making evidence and witnesses disappear. He'd feed information on any undercover agents investigating them. The boys hated shakedown but decided it was better to have Mad Dog working with them than against them.

Shine and G were kicking it at his crib watching the NBA playoffs.

"I don't know what's going on with them kids," Shine said rolling a blunt. "It's like they got a death-wish."

G failed to mention the incident with Trina and had told Jason to keep his mouth shut. Shine had no idea of what brought on the shootings and killings.

"I'm telling you man," G said as he sat his drink down. "We should just go and kick-in their door. Get this shit over with quick fast."

G was scared. He heard that Trina was the sister of one of the boys. Shine lit the blunt.

"Them little niggas messing up my money," he said inhaling real deep. "They got the hood hotter than hell."

G took a swallow of Hennessy. "You know I'm a ride whatever you decide," he said.

Jon needed to talk with somebody who knew Mad Dog. Jackie did and he asked her to meet him at his mom's house. They were sitting in Don's room discussing the deal SCC made with Mad Dog.

"I don't trust him. I wanna kill his ass," Jon said.

"Don't think that thought haven't cross my mind," she said sipping orange juice. "It's cool to have somebody on the inside. Just don't trust his ass, that's all. It's best to work his ass than to get worked. Think of it like this, once you have him take care of a nigga, then you got something on him. Just make sure you have him hurry up and slump a muthafucka."

May 23rd Shawn was in labor. The main crew was at the hospital to support Don. Even Tina was there. Don was keeping his cool by telling jokes about when Victoria was in labor and how Bay Bro was going crazy.

"All right boy, it ain't gone be so funny when you gotta change them nasty diapers."

"That's what mama's and grandmama's for," Don said kissing Tina on the cheek.

"Oh no, you didn't," Tina said laughing. "You'll do your share of diaper duty."

The gang sat around until the doctor came out and made an announcement.

"It was a baby boy."

"John Markel Jenkins," Don announced and everybody cheered. Don took Jon to a corner. "It's going to be a good summer," he said.

June came and all those indicted, received their time. No one got over seven years. A majority copped pleas for five years. The government had done a lot of illegal things and violated constitutional rights to get evidence. The news spread throughout Gary. Jon was the most affected.

"Pretty Ricky was telling the truth," Jon said sitting in his truck. "We killed him for nothing."

"We had no way of being certain. We did what was best for all of us," Kay said.

"What was best?" Jon said raising his voice. "The best

thing for us to have done was to believe our boy. I don't know about y'all, but I'm getting tired of all this shit. I don't know what the fuck to do."

"I'm wit'cha," Kay said looking at Jon.

18

Jon, Kay and Zoe passed the ninth grade. School was out and summer was in. Rides and Jewels were being flossed by ballers. Business was going well. Even though some crew members were not in agreement, the boys opened Bobby on Second and Buchanan. This venture was going to need more security and product. Jon knew he'd need Jackie. He went to her home to meet with her.

"Why do you want to double-up?" Jackie asked sitting in her air conditioned living room.

"We're setting up a new spot on Second," Jon said.

"You better slow ya roll. The more houses you open up the more problems you're bound to have."

"Nah, we be alright. The only problem is the brothers off Fifth."

"You know I got your back." Jackie shook her head and smiled.

Jackie's telephone rang.

"Get yourself something to drink. I got to take this," she said walking away with the phone.

Jackie returned a few minutes later.

"I got to make a trip to the Bronx. You wanna tag along?"

"Sure, why not?" Jon said sipping the rest of his orange juice.

Jackie drove and they chit chatted mostly about her. The car ride came to an end outside a house where a group of men stood. Jon's presence seemed to set off a buzz amongst the men.

"You know them?" Jackie asked.

Jon glanced at the men. "Nah," he responded. "But we beefin with this dude Will from out here."

"Will? That nigga a snake. Don't sleep on his ass. I'll make this quick."

Jackie got out the car and looked at the men. "That's my brother and if y'all fuck with him," she said pulling out a 9mm. "I'm a deal with all y'all asses."

She walked off and took care of her business. The men ice-grilling Jon stopped. When he returned to the game room, Jon told the crew what happened. The boys shared a good laugh.

"I'm telling you Shine," Will was saying as he rode in Shine's '95 Cadillac Deville. "We can hit they ass."

Shine and Will sat around talking payback. Shine was bored.

"I'm getting bored waiting. I want to know when and where."

Will smiled. "That's what I'm talking bout. They got a new spot on Second and Buchanan. We do a little stake out and when the time is right, we get they lil' asses."

"They kinda deep now," Shine said and lit a blunt. "We gone need more men."

"Yeah but, we got the projects and the Bronx. We deep."

Shine bobbed his head to Snoop Dogg's *Murder Was The Case.*

"It's going to be a beautiful summer," he said.

Lynette had been thinking of having sex with Jon since Shawn had given birth. She felt changes in her body whenever she and Jon cuddled and kissed. Lynette confided in Victoria.

"It's normal for you to be experiencing those kind a feelings," Victoria said sipping a cup of coffee.

"I want to do it," Lynette said looking down at the kitchen table.

"Just be careful," Victoria grabbed Lynette's hand and smiled.

Jon and Kay were on their way to Miller. They drove by a service station.

"There goes that bitch-ass!" Kay shouted. The truck swerved.

"What? Who?" Jon said regaining control.

"G he's at the gas station."

Jon turned on the next street and doubled back.

"Right there. His bitch ass right there," Kay said pointing.

"Sho' is. We gone kidnap this muthafucka." Jon said.

"Hurry up," Kay said pulling out a chromed .40 caliber. Jon sped up and turned into the gas station.

"What's up now nigga?" Kay said jumping out of the truck pointing his gun before Jon stopped. G turned around and saw the gat in his grill.

Jon quickly came to a stop and hopped out the truck.

"Yeah, what's up rapist? It's your time to feel helpless."

"What y'all talking bout?" G asked. His hands were held high.

Kay smacked G with his gun. G collapsed like a wet sack on the ground. Kay stood over him then spat on him.

"Come on. Let's get his ass in the truck before the police come."

Jon and Kay carried G to the truck. They threw him in the backseat. Kay joined him. Jon jumped into the driver's seat and peeled.

"Search him," Jon said.

Kay elbowed G in the nose and mouth while frisking him. He took a 40 caliber off G.

"Yeah, this nigga was packing all right." Then Kay looked down at G. "We got some big plans for you, special plans. You wanna rape my sister? I'm a show you what it feels like."

"I don't know what you talking bout. I ain't raped nobody."

"You calling my sister a liar?" Kay said hitting G in the head with the gun.

"Nah, nah…" G said holding his head. "It wasn't me but I know who it was. It was one of them young niggas from out there.

I beat his ass real good. That's the truth."

Jon stopped the truck on a deserted street and they dragged G to the ground floor of an abandoned apartment building. They taped G to an old chair and gagged his mouth with duck tape. Then they left.

"This nigga gone feel what it's like to be misused. You seen the way he done Trina?" Kay said and blasted an old *Above The Law*.

"You right Kay. The nigga will pay. I'm with you no matter how far you want to take it."

Kay looked at Jon. "All the way."

Jon and Kay brought back Trina, Don, Ron and Sweets, an old pimp that got strung out on heroin. Sweets spent his time in and out of jail. They got out and Trina looked around.

"Why ya'll bring me here?"

"Come on, let me show you," Jon said hugging her.

They entered the apartment building.

"Oh shit! That's him," Trina screamed.

She ran to G slapping him several times in the face and spitting on him.

"You deserve everything you're gonna get."

Jon snatched the tape from G's mouth. G winced.

"So I guess you beat up that other dude for nothing," Jon said.

"Fuck you nigga. Gimme what you got!" G spat.

"You gone get everything you got coming and then some," Jon said wiping off his face.

"Yeah nigga," Don said walking up to the tied up G. "By

the time we finished with you you'd be wishing you never fucked with us."

"It's time for you to go," Jon said to Trina.

"I ain't gone bleed as much as that bitch bled. You was nice and tight all the way round." G shouted as Trina walked out.

Jon smacked G in his mouth with the butt of his gun. Two of G's front teeth came out.

"Fuck you nigga! Fuck you nigga! I'm a stay and watch everything." Trina shouted. She snatched Jon's gun out of his hand and shot G in the shoulder. He fell with the chair to the floor.

"Now it's time," Jon said.

He unzipped the duffel bag and removed two lead pipes. Jon threw one to Kay and the other to Ron.

"Remember me?" Ron asked walking over to G with the pipe.

Jon lifted the chair upright.

Ron swung with all his might. G's kneecap was crushed. He was screaming loudly. Jon walked over and stuffed a rag in his mouth. He taped G's mouth.

"This is only the beginning," he whispered to G. Jon then turned to Ron and Kay. "The arms."

"Yeah nigga, this for my sister," Kay said then swung the pipe hitting G's forearm. Ron hit G in the bicep area. G screamed, coughed, cried and pissed on himself. They cut the tape and G slithered to the floor.

"You are sure you want to stay for this next part?" Jon asked Trina. She shook her head yes. "All right Sweets, you're up," Jon said smiling.

The boys then circled G and began looking at each other.

"I ain't gone do it," Don said looking around the group.

"Me either," Ron said throwing his hands in the air.

Jon looked around the group and then at Trina. "Come here Trina. I need you to do something."

Trina slowly walked over to the boys. "What's up?" She said with apprehension in her voice.

Jon grabbed her by the shoulders and looked Trina in the eyes. "I need you to pull his pants down. You know how men are."

"Boy," Trina said walking over to G. "Ya'll crazy. All the shit y'all do and y'all scared to do this." Trina squatted down unbuttoned G's pants and pulled his pants and boxers down to his ankles. "You stink." She said looking up at G. "Now who's the bitch?"

Jon walked over to Sweets and gave him a half ounce of heroin.

"You ready?"

Sweets smiled revealing four missing front teeth. "You know I am, baby. Let Sweets take care of his business."

"Sweets gone take real good care of ya," Sweets said smiling.

Sweets rolled G onto his stomach.

"Nah nigga," Jon said pulling out a jar of Vaseline. "You want to fuck with my people. Rape my love ones and this," he was placing the Vaseline in front of G's eyes. "Is only if you're too tight. I want you to feel what Trina felt."

"Handle yo business Sweets," Don said smiling. Sweets pulled his pants down and his dick was already a full eleven inches.

"Give it to his ass," Trina cheered.

Sweets fucked the shit out of G, for seventeen minutes.

"It's time to wrap this up," Jon said walking over to the duffel bag. "We been here too long."

Jon went inside the bag and pulled out wire pliers, a hammer and a bottle of charcoal fluid. Don got the hammer, Kay the wire pliers and Ron the charcoal fluid. Don knocked out G's teeth while Kay was pulling out toe nails. The pain was too much for G to bear. He passed out. Ron squirted fluid on the bottom of G's feet, his hand and face. Jon lit all three areas. G became conscious and wiggled around. After a minute Jon poured water on G.

"Damn! You fucked up." He then turned to the group and said. "I ain't doing it." The others looked at Trina and Jon. "Trina ain't either."

"What's up?" Sweets asked.

"Cut his dick off and stick it in his mouth," Don said coldly.

"Shit, I'll do it. What's in it for me?" Before the boys could say anything Sweets said. "Don't bullshit me. This ain't gone be cheap."

"What do you want? What would be fair?" Jon asked.

"One ounce. A whole ounce," Sweets said.

"Do it good and I'll make it two," Jon said smiling.

Sweets took the knife and in one swing G's dick fell from his body. Jon uncovered G's mouth and Sweets put G's dick in. Jon taped G's mouth. G gagged shaking his head. Jon reached down and grabbed G's chain and they left.

When they returned to the hood, Jon gave Sweets his reward.

"Are y'all sure y'all want to do this?"

"Yeah," Don said looking at the emblem on G's chain. "Let's let it be known."

Jon started the truck and drove off.

Three in the morning Will had just dozed off. His house phone and cell phone started ringing. They wouldn't stop. Finally, a groggy Will picked up his cell phone.

"Yeah..."

"They got him, Will. They finally got him." It was Shine and he was hysterical.

Will didn't comprehend what Shine was saying. "Got who? What are you talking bout?"

"G dead. Them lil' niggas killed him."

Will sat up in his bed.

"Are you sure? When? Where?"

Shine lit a blunt and took two long pulls. "I got his chain and it's covered in blood. The lil' niggas hung it on a phone booth in the projects and folks saw 'em."

Will was now lighting his own blunt. "What you want to do?"

"Tomorrow it's on."

19

The boys sat around the game room playing video games. They were awaiting Don's arrival. Don moved out of his mom's house and into his apartment with Shawn and his son, John. Jon remembered his date with Lynette.

"I'm going to need some people to make the drop-offs and pick-ups today," Jon said.

The boys pretended not to hear Jon. "I know ya'll heard me," Jon said getting up from his chair. "Don't make me pick."

The boys were looking around at each other when Don walked in.

"Don will do it," Zoe said smiling at Don.

"Do what?" Don asked shaking the crew's hand.

"I can't make the rounds today," Jon said.

"Oh yeah Zoe, you tried me like that. I'll tell you what," Don said hugging Zoe. "Me and Zoe got the Bobby." Zoe's laughter faded.

"Kay and Ron got Pauline. I'm out," Jon said throwing up a VL sign.

Jon took Lynette to the Museum of Science and Industry in Chicago. They went on a boat ride in the waters of Lake Michigan then they went to the Navy Pier to eat. They had been spending much time together since Jon started the company. Between that and the dope houses Jon really didn't have much time for anything else. It was a beautiful day and the lovebirds were enjoying themselves.

Meanwhile, Kay, Ron, Don and Zoe packaged everything and headed out.

"We gone meet back here," Don said as they split in pairs.

"I hate this part of the job," Zoe said adjusting his seat.

"How do you think Jon feels? He do this shit everyday, sometimes twice a day," Don said.

"You right, I'm a start helping him out," Zoe said.

"Yeah, me too," Don said.

"Let's get that shit," Will said from inside a van he and Shine were in.

"Not yet," Shine said his eyes on the building. "Too many fiends in there. Let it clear out."

The two sat in a car parked across the street from Bobby.

"Them little nigga's spot sho's pumping," Will said watching a group of fiends leaving.

Shine watched the steady flow of customers and knew the boys were clocking figures. They were definitely doing their thing, Shine thought.

"Maybe we should hold down some shit like this," Shine said reaching for his Tec on the floor. "It could be profitable."

"You must've read my mind," Will said smiling.

"Let's go," Shine said and grabbed extra clips.

The two men were getting out of the van. Shine saw Don pull up in front of the building.

"Hold on, we'll get 'em on they way out." Shine eased back into the van.

"Fuck that! I'm a do they asses now," Will said getting out the van.

"Ahight, fuck it then, let's go." Shine said and dialed a number on his cell phone. "It's time." He said into the phone then hung-up.

Zoe and Don were busy getting the duffel bags from the back of Don's truck. They never saw what was going on around them until it was too late.

"Oh shit!" Zoe yelled reaching for his gun.

Don turned and saw a crowd bum-rushing and immediately jumped into the back of his truck.

"Get in! Get in!" He shouted.

He rushed to get his AK. Will and Shine led the way as crews from the Bronx and Miller projects came busting guns.

Zoe stood outside the truck shooting at Will and Shine.

"Hurry up!" he shouted emptying the clip.

Zoe ducked behind the truck's door as Don fired the AK from the window. Will and Shine's crew ran for cover. Workers from the top two floors started shooting from opened windows. Other workers called for reinforcements. The security teams that were placed at the four corners blocked off both ends of the street and opened fire with AK's.

Kay was driving like a madman with Smoke and five more cars packed with SCC members behind Ron.

"Jon," Ron yelled in his cell phone. "Bobby under attack. We on our way there now."

"I'm going the back-way. I got Lynette with me but I will be there soon."

Jon ended the call and looked at Lynette.

"I'm sorry but we gotta go."

He paid the check and hurried to his truck. Jon was speeding down the expressway he looked at Lynette who was saying nothing. "You alright?" He asked.

Lynette knew their beautiful day was over.

"You really don't have to go. The rest of them can take care of whatever it is."

"I'm sorry but I have to go. Don's in trouble."

"Don, Don, Don, I know that's your brother but you don't have to run every time he calls. He's a big boy."

"What! You don't even know what's going on."

"I don't care what's going on, but I know what ain't going on."

"Whatever, I ain't trying to hear this."

Lynette was determined to make Jon hear something.

"Oh yeah, well since you ain't trying to hear me," she said turning off the radio. "Hear this. It's over. We're through. I ain't got time for your shit."

"Then we through."

Don and Zoe were pinned in the truck under a barrage of gunfire.

"We gotta get out of here," Zoe said ducking down.

"Not yet Zoe. We gotta wait for some help."

With the two hoods combining they were seventy-seven strong and SCC only had sixteen members present. The odds were against them making it to the apartment building. Zoe didn't care about odds. He wanted to get away from the bullets and truck.

"I ain't sitting here too much longer getting shot at."

Zoe looked up and saw his opening. "Come on let's go!"

The cars blocking the North end of the street separated, Kay and the other cars turned onto the street. Six cars led by Kay's truck were slowly driving down the street shooting. Zoe took this as the perfect opportunity to make a run for it and opened his door.

"Nah, wait until they get in front of us so that they can cover us."

Zoe heard Don but jumped out the truck and started running for the apartment building.

"Zoe wait!" Don shouted.

He jumped from the truck firing to provide cover for Zoe. Jon was on the other side making his way forward. Jon reached the front of the apartment building. Zoe was running then he seemed to stumble.

"Got that lil' muthafucka!" Shine said watching Zoe fall.

"I got him," Will said.

Jon ran to Zoe catching him before Zoe hit the ground.

"I got you, I got you," Jon said.

SCC started shooting everywhere as Jon dragged Zoe to the side of the building.

"Zoe, Zoe..." Jon screamed.

Zoe's eyes were as wide as an owl's.

"I fucked up Jon. I should've listened," Zoe said with a weak voice.

"Its cool little brother. We gone get you outta here," Jon said with tears falling. "Just hang in there, just hang in there."

Zoe took a deep breath. "Thank you Jon." He began coughing blood.

Shine gave the signal for the crews to retreat. He and Will made their way back to the van.

"There'll be another time to rob they ass," Shine said as he started the van. "That's for G."

Will nodded his head in agreement. "Rest in peace, folks," he said then turned on the radio.

Don saw the back of Zoe's cream colored Pelle Pelle shirt soaked in blood.

"I told you to wait," Don said in a high pitched tone. Then he began to cry. "I told you to wait."

Jon was in a trance, rocking back and forth with Zoe.

"It's going to be all right." He kept repeating not realizing

Don was there. Don dropped to his knees still crying and staring at the bullet holes in Zoe's back. "Can he make it?" Jon asked looking at Don.

"Make it where?" Don asked confused.

"To the hospital stupid, it's right up the street."

A blank expression enveloped Don's face. He looked down at Zoe and decided not say anything.

"Come on," Don said grabbing Zoe's leg. "Let's go."

The two of them carried Zoe's body to the alley and put him in Jon's truck. Lynette screamed and burst into tears when she saw Zoe.

"What happened?" She managed between sobs.

"Shut the fuck up! You don't care about Zoe or any of them!" Jon said with tears still falling from his eyes. Don was as he drove.

20

It had been a month since Zoe passed away. The boys were traumatized by his death, especially Jon. When the doctor told them Zoe was dead Jon walked out the hospital and went straight to the Bronx shooting at houses, people, even dogs. He left only when he had no more bullets. Jon went to the game room, got more shells and magazines then did the same to the Miller area.

No one had been able to get through to him since Zoe's death, not his mama, Don, Kay, Lynette or Bay Bro, nobody. Jon isolated himself and walked around zombie-like. The crew suffered as a result.

Jackie has been conducting business with Don and Kay. She didn't like the inconsistency. Jon hadn't been to see her or even answered her phone calls. Jackie heard about Zoe's death and how hard Jon took it. It was time Jon stopped grieving, Jackie thought.

She drove all over the city looking for Jon. Finally she

spotted his truck at the beach. Jackie found Jon sitting and staring at the water.

"What's up stranger?" Jackie said sitting next to him. "I haven't seen you in awhile."

Jon kept staring at the water. Jackie wasn't phased.

"So you just gone ignore me, huh?" she said as she nudged Jon. "It's cool though. I can do all the talking." She said picking up a handful of sand. "I want you to listen to me Jon. Zoe's gone. I feel your pain but you've gotta move forward and carry his love and memory. That's what Zoe would want. Instead of sitting here feeling sorry we should be kicking in doors trying to get even." Jackie got up and squatted down in front of Jon. "Where's my little brother? The one who don't take no shit. The one who gets even when you fuck with him. What's up Jon? You want to go take care of this or what?"

"I'm straight," Jon said looking down at the sand.

"That's too bad." She said reaching into her pocket. "Because I got an address."

Jon quickly looked up. "Where at?"

"Let's go," Jackie said leading the way.

They went to the game room. The rest of the boys were there.

"All right," Jackie said walking into the backroom. Jon was by her side. "This shit gone stop. I got this address to Will's baby mama's house and we gone go take care of his ass. Then we gone do Shine."

The boys were quiet and all eyes were focused on Jon not Jackie. "Y'all have invested too much time and energy to let everything fall to pieces."

"Jackie's right, we've all sacrificed a lot to make this happen but none more than Zoe." Jon paused and cleared his throat. "I'm not going to let his death be for nothing."

Jackie looked around the room. The boys' posture, facial expression and mood all changed. Jon was the glue that held them together.

"What we waiting for?" Kay asked embracing Jon.

The boys busied themselves grabbing weapons.

"Whoa." Jackie said in amazement. "All this artillery. We not gone need all that. A couple of guns will do." Jackie hugged Jon. "Welcome back."

Jon kissed Jackie on the cheek. "Thanks…"

Will's baby mama lived in Merrillville with white people on a nice quiet street. There was no sign of Will's rides at the house. Jackie got out and knocked on the front door. A brown skinned woman answered the door. The two women talked and Jackie returned to the BMW. Will just left.

"Fuck it!" Ron said from the backseat. "We wait."

"Yeah, but not out here," Jon said. He got out of the car.

"We going up in there and have that bitch call his ass." Jon said leaning into Smoke's window.

"How we know he gone come?" Smoke asked turning off the car.

"The nigga just left. She can tell him that he forgot something or that she need something. We'll think of something."

"Fuck it." Twon said getting out the car. "Let's do this."

The boys lined up on the side of the house. Jackie knocked on the door again. This time when the woman opened the door the boys rushed. They knocked the woman down.

"What's going on?" She asked from the floor.

Jon stood over the woman and extended his hand.

"Help us and we won't hurt you. The sooner you get Will to come here the sooner we'll be gone," he said.

The woman grabbed Jon's hand and got up from the floor.

"What is this, a robbery?" She asked looking only at Jon. "Will don't keep his money here, I mean maybe twenty, twenty-five thousand but that's it. I get y'all that right now."

"We didn't come her for money," Jon said with a wild look in his eyes. "We came to see Will. He owes us something worth more than money. Either you get him here, or today, you be paying his debt."

The woman's eyes bulged. She tried to run but Jackie's fist caught her.

"Stupid bitch," Jackie said adjusting the rings on her fingers. "Where you think you going?"

The woman looked up at Jackie and started crying. "Why y'all doing this to me? I haven't done nothing. Me and Will not even together. I'm not his woman. Tasha is."

Jon helped the woman to her feet and walked her to a chair.

"It's Will we want. You protecting him because y'all have a child together but Will took a child away from us."

The woman looked shocked. "Will would never do that," she said shaking her head.

"It's true," Jon said standing up. "We'll do whatever we have to get Will." Jon paused. He made sure the woman was looking at him as he continued. "Even use your child." The woman wasted no time calling Will.

"He's on his way," she said hanging up the phone.

"Where's the baby at?" Don asked with a half smile on his face.

"Uh… ah. She um…" The woman was stalling.

"I'm not going to hurt her, I love kids," Don said.

"The baby's in the back sleeping. Please don't wake her."

"How many kids y'all got?" Jackie asked.

The woman looked at Jackie and turned her nose up. "One," she said.

Jackie caught the look. "Bitch, you can lose the attitude before I lose you," Jackie said walking up to the woman. "I thought Will had a boy."

The woman stood up and faced Jackie. "He do got a little boy," the woman said with a smirk on her face. At that very moment Don came into the living room with the infant on his shoulder.

Jackie looked at the little boy and smacked the woman across the face.

"This bitch is setting us up," Jackie said and kicked at the woman barely missing her. The woman scrambled to her feet and the two women squared off with the size advantage going in favor of the woman. She was three inches taller and twenty pounds heavier.

"Yeah bitch," the woman said putting her guard up. "Try that shit now."

Jon hurried to break it up but Jackie held her hand up stopping him. "I don't need no help, little brother. I'm a wreck this bitch."

The woman swung missing badly. Jackie hit her with a quick one-two to upside her head. Jackie caught the woman with a hook to the mouth. The woman stumbled blood came from her mouth. She charged Jackie with her head down and her arms swinging wildly like a madwoman. One of the woman's wild swings caught Jackie in the eye dazing her. The woman wrestled Jackie to the floor. The two women rolled around on the floor biting, kicking, scratching, pulling and tearing each other apart. Jack punched the woman twice in the throat taking all the fight out of her.

"Stupid bitch, look what you did to my clothes." Jackie said lunging. Jon grabbed her.

"Hey beautiful," he said pulling her to the next room. "You won. Now what are we going to do?"

Jackie looked down, her shirt and bra were torn exposing her breasts.

"Can you believe this?" She asked pointing at her breasts.

Jon stared but couldn't help it. Jackie's titties were pointing straight at him. "Boy what you looking at?" She asked pushing Jon.

He took his shirt off exposing an eight-pack, toned chest and arms. "Even now you're beautiful," Jon said handing Jackie his shirt.

"Damn, milk does a body good," Jackie smiled putting on the shirt. She hugged Jon.

"Nice," Jon said gripping Jackie's round ass.

"All right, enough," she said and pulled away. "We can kill

the bitch and kidnap the baby. Kidnap them both. I really don't give a shit."

Jon thought about the options. "We walk," he said after a couple beats.

Jackie gave him a crazy look then shook her head sideways. "Well alright, if that's what you want. I wouldn't."

The two walked back into the living room. "Is Will coming?" Jon asked standing directly in front of the woman.

"No," she said with her ample sized breasts fully exposed.

Jon tightened the grip on his gun while staring at the woman. He wanted to send Will a message. "Come on, we out," he said.

Don gave the woman the little boy. They all left.

Instead of going to his baby mama's aid, Will went to the Bronx. He got two workers and went to the twin's house. They kicked in the front door and searched the house tearing up everything. Will clogged the sinks and toilets up and turned on the water. He walked out the house and lit a blunt thinking about his baby mama and the signal that he told her to use if anybody ever kicked in the door.

She was down for him despite all that he had put her through. The twins went to their mother's home. They found the house flooded. They put their mom in a hotel for the night and bought her a house in South Holland, Illinois the next day.

It had been a month and half since Jon and Lynette broke

up. The two would see each other and not speak. Jon was interacting with the crew and was also running the operation again. Jon was showing Kay everything that must be done and how it should be done.

He thought about Lynette all the time. His pride kept him from apologizing and Jon was always depressed. Lynette tried to apologize but gave up. Two weeks before school started Lynette was stressing that Jon picking one of the many girls that flocked around him.

Lynette called Jon and told him that she was alone and heard a sound outside the house. She asked him to come and check things out for her. Jon hurried out the door.

He pulled up to the house and saw the front door open. Jon cocked his gun and got out the car, cautiously walking to the house. He went inside, closing the door behind him. Jon started searching the house. He opened Lynette's bedroom door. Lynette was on the bed wearing one of his button-up jerseys. Candles lit the room and R. Kelly was on the speaker. She got up from the bed and walked to Jon.

"I'm sorry for the way I acted." Jon was mesmerized by her beauty. "I should've never--"

Lynette placed her index finger over Jon's lip cutting him off.

"Shush," she said softly kissing his lips. Lynette led Jon to the bed and pushed him down. "Tonight's my night." She stripped him of everything he was wearing. Lynette sat on his leg. He could feel her moistness. Lynette kissed Jon from the top of his head. At his navel she paused and looked up at him. Jon wore a look of surprise. She held his dick with one hand and licked around it. Her other hand caressed his washboard stomach.

"Oh shit..." Jon moaned with pleasure.

Lynette sucked as much as she could inside her mouth. Jon held onto the sheets. Lynette worked her head up and down his dick like a pro. Occasionally taking it out and licking its full length. After five minutes Jon exploded in her mouth. She swallowed it. Lynette moved back up to face Jon. He grabbed her and rolled on top.

"My turn," Jon said unbuttoning her shirt.

Kissing her softly on the forehead, he made his way down her body. When he reached her breast Jon took one nipple at a time into his mouth, sucking it like an ice-cream pop. He made his way down to her flat stomach and her pussy. Jon licked at her outer lips before sliding his tongue inside her. Lynette grabbed his head. Jon licked her inner walls. She rubbed his braids.

"Right there. Right there," Lynette said between deep breaths. Jon had found Lynette's magic spot. He licked her clit until her legs stiffened and her toes curled.

Lynette was still breathing heavy after the orgasm.

"I'm ready baby." She said while pulling Jon up and kissing him passionately.

"Are you sure?" Jon asked not wanting to hurt her. "We can wait if you want to." Jon looked at Lynette's green eyes and was about to speak but Lynette beat him to it.

"I don't want to wait," she said.

Lynette ran her nails up and down Jon's back. "Put it in, Jon. Quit playing with me."

Jon grabbed his dick and rubbed it up and down Lynette's

pussy searching for the opening. After a minute the moistness led him to it.

"Aha ouch...ah...ah..." Lynette swallowed hard as Jon penetrated her. He looked down and was about to pull out.

"I'm fine." Lynette said grabbing Jon's ass to stop him from pulling out. Jon slowly slid his dick inside Lynette. When he was all the way in, he kissed Lynette and slowly started moving in and out of her. After a couple of minutes Lynette was moving in rhythm with Jon. "I love you Jon."

"I love you boo..."

21

During the '95-'96 school year Will and Shine put a price on all SCC. The war with the boys had cost them thousands of dollars. Shine wanted the thirsty people to deal with the boys. He wanted to focus on his new love, Renee.

Shine didn't know much about Renee's past. The first time he saw her in Hustlers, he had to have her. Renee knew about the beef he had with Don but never mentioned that she dealt with Don. Will moved his son and Kenya even further into the suburbs and didn't let anyone know where, not even Shine. Will trusted no one in the dope game especially since he and Shine started their own version of the boy's Bobby and Pauline's.

Shine was already supplying Dorie Miller projects he and Will locked it down. The two rented three houses in someone's name and set up shop. The houses were next door to each other making it easy for Will and Shine to protect them. Dorie Miller was the perfect place to put the houses because there was only one entrance.

The houses were doing well but Shine wanted them making the same amount of money he seen Bobby making, if not more. Will was content with sales and thought Shine was being greedy. Will continued to play the background.

Lynette got pregnant the first time she had sex. She was ecstatic about having a baby. Jon was going to be a father. They thought Bay Bro was going to hit the roof but he was cool.

Don was loving family life and spent a lot of time with his son. After Zoe's death, he helped Jon make runs to the apartment buildings but didn't hang out with the crew at the game room like before.

Kay had a high school sweetheart and they often went out with Jon and Lynette. Twon was now in charge of the boy's new apartment building on 36th and Carolina, named Christine. He was happy about his new responsibility and was now pretending to be a big shot.

Ron continued to run Pauline and handled the security matters for the crew. He had found a new love and was now thinking of retiring. Even though things were looking up for them, the boys missed Zoe.

April '96. Victoria was pregnant again. When she told Bay Bro the news he said that it would be a boy. Victoria was trying to have all the fun. Bay Bro took her out every night dancing over in Chicago. He didn't allow Victoria to drink any liquor. That didn't stop Victoria from getting her party on. Victoria was into all the latest styles. She saw a dress in Hustlers that she had to have. Bay Bro didn't shop for clothes in Gary but made an exception for Victoria.

They went to Hustlers. Bay Bro was impressed he found that the store had a lot of hot items. Victoria showed Bay Bro an outfit she wanted him to have.

"Isn't it hot? And it's your colors too," Victoria said pointing at the black and gold outfit.

Bay Bro shook his head. "It's kinda hot, but I don't wear denim suits," he said.

The disappointment was written all over Victoria's face. "But for you," he said kissing Victoria's forehead. "I'll make an exception." Bay Bro took the outfit from the rack and then they went to get the dress.

"I'm wearing this tonight." Victoria held the dress against her body Bay Bro stared.

"I'm glad niggas know who I am," Bay Bro said smiling and whistling. "Whew now that's hot."

Victoria got a couple more dresses and a short set and the two went to the check-out counter. Bay Bro stared at the man behind the counter. His face looked familiar.

"Do I know you?" Bay Bro asked the bald headed man.

The man looked at Bay Bro and froze. Bay Bro stared.

"What's the matter, boo?" Victoria asked looking at Bay Bro.

"It's nothing," Bay Bro said still staring at the man. "Nothing at all." The man told Bay Bro the price.

Victoria had not even looked at the man until she heard

his voice.

"Cash...?" She asked looking at the man.

The man hurried to stuff their items into a bag.

"Excuse me," he said. "I think you're confusing me with someone else."

Victoria and Bay Bro focused on the man.

"It is you Cash, your sorry ass. I know who you are," Victoria said walking around the counter. "Nigga you ain't shit. If I knew this was your store I wouldn't even have shopped here."

Bay Bro grabbed Victoria and pulled her behind him. "Oh yeah nigga, I got sump'n for yo ass."

Bay Bro reached for his gun just as two customers entered the store. Cash rose from under the counter with a .45 pistol. Bay Bro was holding the .357 magnum on Cash. Both men fired.

"No baby, no baby," Victoria said as she held Bay Bro in her arms. "You can't do this to me."

Tears were flowing from Victoria's eyes as she held Bay Bro in her arms.

"Did I get him?"

Bay Bro opened his eyes and looked at his beautiful fiancé. He was trying to get to his feet but couldn't. "Is the nigga dead?"

Victoria looked down and caressed Bay Bro's face.

"Yes baby," she said kissing him all over his face. "You got him."

Cash's bullet hit Bay Bro's shoulder. Cash wasn't that lucky. He was dead.

Victoria helped Bay Bro to his feet. The two customers ran outside and flagged down a police car, telling them what they had witnessed. Bay Bro and Victoria made it to the door only to see the

three squad cars parked outside. Bay Bro looked at the police.

"They're going to arrest me," he said.

"No, it was self-defense. Don't say that." Victoria looked at Bay Bro and started crying again.

"Hey you right, boo, everything will be alright."

The two walked out the store. Bay Bro was arrested and placed in handcuffs while Victoria kicked, screamed and cried.

She called Jon and told him what happened. Jon consoled promising he'd take care of everything. He told Don, Kay and Smoke what Victoria told him.

"What we gone do?"

"Get rid of the witnesses. No witnesses. No conviction."

"How...?" Smoke asked leaning on the table.

"Mad Dog will give us their addresses," Don said.

"Exactly..." Jon pulled out his cell phone. "This the type a shit we bought." Jon dialed Mad Dog's cell phone.

"Yeah," Mad Dog sounded irritated.

"I know you heard what happened at Hustlers," Jon said. He walked to the mini refrigerator. "I need addresses as soon as possible."

Mad Dog had the addresses in his book. He had taken the witnesses' statements. "They got that shit locked away. I ain't got that key. They acting all top secret with this case but," Mad Dog paused to think of a number. "Get fifty thousand dollars and I can pay an informer."

"Done," Jon said not convinced of the reason for the money.

"Give me a couple of hours and I'll let you know," Mad Dog

said smiling.

"It's done," Jon said after hanging up.

The police notified Jossie of Cash's murder. The witnesses reported that Bay Bro was trying to rob the store. Their entrance distracted Bay Bro long enough for Cash to get his gun. Both fired shots. They ran out the store to get help. Jossie listened to the story and knew something wasn't right.

Cash wouldn't jeopardize his life for a couple of dollars. He always reminded her that he had his family to live for. Jossie asked the Officer who killed Cash and he told her. She didn't recognize Bay Bro's real name.

"Is he from 11th," she asked.

"Yes," the officer said.

After the police left Jossie cried hard and long. Her son awoke crying from his sleep. Josie looked into her son's eyes and realized that Cash would always be with her. Jossie held the baby in her arms. Thoughts of revenge coursed through her mind.

Mad Dog called Jon. He agreed to meet in the parking lot of the grocery store behind the stationhouse. Mad Dog met with Jon and gave him the addresses of the witnesses in exchange for the fifty thousand. It was clear they had no trust for each other.

Jon, Don and Kay would handle the two witnesses. The three went to the first address and knocked on the door getting no response. They walked around to the other side of the house. They checked through the windows, she wasn't home and went to the next address. The house was located right outside the hood on 19th and Cleveland. Don knocked on the door and.

"Can I help you?" A young man greeted the boys with a smile.

"Yes," Jon said as he looked down at the piece of paper Mad Dog had given him. "I'm looking for Devon Jones."

"That's me. Do I know you?"

Jon pulled out his gun and aimed it at the man's chest. "Get inside."

The man stumbled backwards into the house, raising his hands into the air. "I didn't do anything," he said backing into the house. "What did I do?"

Don and Kay pulled out their guns and the three boys followed the man inside.

"That bet not be another bitch," a woman shouted walking into the living room. "If it is..." The woman stopped in the middle of her sentence when she saw the three guns.

"Run and I'll shoot yo ass," Jon said pointing at the woman.

"What's going on?" She asked.

"What's your name?" Jon asked lowering the gun.

"Sh-Sh-Shelby..." The woman stuttered.

"You the Shelby Williams from the east side?" Jon asked.

"Yeah, that's me," Shelby exhaled relieved he knew her.

Jon looked back at Don and Kay nodding his head.

"It's them," he said and cocked his gun.

"Wait! Wait! Devon screamed. "The two what?"

"Y'all the two bitches gave the phony statements to the police on my man." Kay cocked his gun.

"No," Shelby pleaded. "We told the truth."

"Well, you know what they say; the truth shall set you free."

Don fired twice hitting her in the chest. The man tried to run but caught bullets from Jon's and Kay's guns in the back.

"Put the mask on!" Jon ordered. He pulled out a Captain America mask. The boys put their masks on and left the house.

At the same time Don, Jon and Kay were taking care of their business, Jackie was at one of her dope houses trying to figure out why her money kept coming up short. She was all up in one of her lieutenant's face. Damon was supposed to be in charge of the house and money.

"Why the fuck is my money not right? When I drop off five thousand worth of product and pick up four thousand cash. Shit, sometime it don't even be that."

Damon was the average height with an average build. He didn't like working for anybody, especially a woman.

"Look Jackie," Damon said backing away. "The money be right. I be counting it. Ain't no shorts or playing with the dough," he said without looking her in the eyes.

"Oh yeah, somebody playing with my money. I got an idea who," she said.

"What do you mean by that?" Damon asked with a screw-face.

"I ain't got all day. Be a man. Tell me the damn truth but if you gone be a lil bitch then you can tuck yo tail between yo legs and get the fuck out."

"That's right bitch!" Damon walked towards Jackie. "I been robbing you ain't..." Damon never saw it coming.

Jackie shot him in the groin. He dropped to his knees screaming in pain. Jackie walked over to him.

"A bitch ain't supposed to have nuts," she said standing over him. "You wanna play with my money and be arrogant about it. Nigga, you know what time it is?"

"You stupid bitch! How you gone shoot me in my dick?"

Jackie pointed the gun at him.

"Wait! Wait!" Damon shouted. "Jackie let's talk. I was wrong and I know I was wrong but this ain't the way. Not for me and you."

Jackie laughed. "Stealing my money was for me and you, right?"

Damon didn't answer. He looked at Jackie wearing a pitiful expression on his face.

"You got anything else to say, Mr. Big-man?" Jackie asked still pointing the gun at Damon's grill. "I know you got something else to say."

"I'm sorry..."

The words had hardly left his mouth. Damon felt the sting of the steel in his chest. She put one more in his head. "Sorry is right."

Jackie rushed out. She called Jon and asked him to meet her at his mom's new house. She needed an alibi. Damon had been down with her from day one. He always had her back. She'd have forgiven him for anything. Stealing was unacceptable. Jackie drove listening to her thoughts. If he didn't act ignorant, he'd be alive.

May 23ʳᵈ, Bay Bro was still locked up. He kept telling the boys that he'd be out soon. If the police came asking questions, Jackie and the boys had each other as alibis. Tina would support them. Jackie was relieved and things went back to normal. It was the grand opening of Debbie's, the boys' new apartment on 5ᵗʰ and Durbin.

They stood in front pitching. Jon's phone rang.

"Hello," Jon said. His face lit up with joy. "I'm on my way." Jon looked at the fellows. "Lynette's in labor. I'm out." Jon ran for his truck. They all followed. The boys headed for the hospital. Six hours later, Lynette delivered a healthy baby girl, named Donita Zoie Jenkins.

The next couple of months went smoothly. There were no fights and shootings. Jon wanted to give up the game. Kay and Ron agreed, Don, Twon and the crew wanted to remain in the streets. Jon didn't want to leave Don in charge of the operation and stuck around a while longer. Kay was riding with Jon no matter what. Ron was slowly easing out.

It was a cool July night. The Savoy was throwing a talent show. Up and coming rappers, singers and dancers were getting their burn. Heavyweight ballers were scouting new talent for

investment. J-Roc was at the Savoy to demonstrate his rap skills. Smoke went for support. People from Concord projects were there, just-in-case.

J-Roc, Smoke and two members from Concord were at the bar drinking Coronas and talking shit. A loud boom thundered through the club. Smoke looked around. The loud sound was heard a couple times. Two Concord members hit the floor.

"Get the fuck down!" J-Roc yelled.

Smoke heard but was too busy looking around to see who was shooting. J-Roc scurried over to Smoke and pulled him down.

"What the fuck...?"

Smoke snatched his arm away from J-Roc. "I'm trying to see who shooting at us."

"Smoke, we gotta get the guns off Chill and Kenny. That's the only way we gone make it outta here alive."

Smoke looked at the two dead boys and shook his head.

"Damn! We..." Smoke slurred. He was drunk. J-Roc took the lead.

J-Roc tried to figure where the shots were coming from. They seemed to be coming from everywhere. Time was running out for them and J-Roc knew it.

"Fuck it! Stay here Smoke. I'm a get the guns."

Smoke shook his head in agreement and moved. J-Roc ran over to Chill and Kenny sliding on the floor next to Kenny. He frantically searched Kenny's body for the gun. The shooters zeroed in on J-Roc. He used Kenny's body for cover and grabbed the .45. J-Roc crawled over to Chill's body and removed the .40 caliber from Chill's waist.

"Smoke." J-Roc said sliding the .40 caliber over to him. "Get the gun."

Smoke picked up the gun.

"Get back over here," Smoke said cocking the gun. "I got you covered."

J-Roc nodded his head. Smoke jumped up shooting his gun wildly, J-Roc jumped up from the floor and hopped over the bar landing next to the bartender. He stuck his head up and saw Smoke getting wet-up. J-Roc didn't know how he was going to make it out. He heard the siren. The police were coming. J-Roc peeked over the counter in time to see Will running out of the club.

J-Roc called the game room and told Kay what happened and that he was on his way. A few minutes later, J-Roc entered the game room. He heard Kay, Jon and Ron talking.

"What's up brothers?" J-Roc greeted them and took a seat.

"What the hell happened?' Ron asked clearly upset.

"Them niggas was everywhere. We couldn't tell where the shots were coming from."

"How did Smoke end up dead?" Ron asked interrupting.

"He was drunk and was standing up like he was bulletproof. I had to pull his ass to the floor. Once he got the gun it was like he felt he was invincible."

Everybody was quiet for a minute and then Don spoke.

"You saw who did it?"

J-Roc looked up from the table. "Damn right. I saw Will running out the club."

Ron jumped up from the table. "It's time for that nigga to pay. I say we hit the Bronx tonight."

Jon had been quietly weighing the options.

"Nah," Jon said looking at Ron. "Hitting the Bronx is only going to kill innocent people. He'll get away. We'll pay for his ass, dead or alive. We gotta start being smart. Everything that happens doesn't need a violent response right away. Look at Bay Bro if he'd waited till Cash left the store, he wouldn't be in jail. We on some other shit now."

The next day a phone call was made to the Gary Police Department.

"I have info on some killings." The anonymous male voice said.

"Who's calling?" the dispatcher asked.

"Listen, I'm not telling you my name. I'll tell you this. There are two twins riding around in a burgundy Cadillac with guns used in murders. If you act now you can catch them going up Broadway."

"How do you know this, sir?"

"I'm trying to do a good deed and you give me the third degree. I'm telling you, they got guns and a couple keys of crack. Now do your job."

The phone went dead and the dispatcher relayed every detail of the conversation. The detective ran out of the precinct leaving the dispatcher bewildered.

Don and Jon were on their way to pick up a cake for Bay Bro's homecoming. Don had to get another vehicle after his was shot up the day Zoe got killed. He wanted a Cadillac. The twins were talking about retaliation against Will. Jon was explaining his position when lights flashed behind them.

"Ain't this a bitch," Don said pulling over to the side. "I've been driving for four years without a license. And as soon as I get one, I get pulled over."

A second police car pulled in front of the Cadillac and then a detective's car pulled behind the first police car.

The detective walked to the Cadillac, gun in hand. "Step out of the car!" The white detective ordered Don.

"We haven't done anything wrong. I ain't stepping out of shit," Don said reclining in the driver seat.

Three more police cars pulled up. The officers jumped out with guns drawn.

"Something ain't right," Jon said as he watched other officers approaching. "This ain't no traffic stop."

"We were tipped off that y'all carrying illegal guns and drugs," the detective said raising his gun at Don. "Now get out of the car!"

Reluctantly the two boys got out of the car. The police found two guns inside the car and an AK in the trunk. They didn't find any drugs.

"The guns are all we need to lock y'all up for a long time. Let's see if the SCC can get y'all out."

Jon shook his head and gave a chuckle. Don laughed hysterically. The boys were taken in and finger printed and photographed. They were transported to the Lake County Juvenile Center.

Their arrest sent shockwaves through all the hoods. Tina stayed on the phone with the police station, the juvenile center and different attorneys. Kay called all the SCC members and told them that he would be in charge until the twins were out. Twon disagreed with Kay. He felt he was the closest to Jackie. Kay pointed out that Twon was never around. A vote was taken and Kay won unanimously.

Bay Bro consoled Lynette. He called Tina and offered his lawyer to the boys. Things weren't the same without Jon. Bay Bro called Goldie to have breakfast at their favorite spot on Chicago's south side. He got into his truck and headed for the highway and was busy searching for a CD. He never saw the white station wagon tailing. Bay Bro pulled into a gas station to fill-up.

He went inside the station to pay for the gas. Bay Bro saw a young woman parked at the pump behind him in a white station wagon. She had a baby in the front seat but there was something familiar about the station wagon. He dismissed the woman and went to pump his gas. The woman walked up behind him.

"Bay Bro," she said.

"Yeah," Bay Bro said turning around.

The woman pulled out a .380 from her sweatshirt.

"This is for my brother Doug and my husband Cash."

Bay Bro felt seven shots ripping his chest and stomach. He fell to the ground. The woman stood over him.

"Payback is a motherfucker, ain't it?"

Jossie turned and got back in her car. She pulled off rubbing her baby's head. "It's over now," she said.

News of Bay Bro's death hit unexpectedly like a sucker-punch. Half of Chicago and some of Gary wanted revenge but there were no witnesses and no one had a clue. Victoria and Lynette bonded even more after Bay Bro's death. Lynette was pregnant again and turned to Victoria. Shawn too was pregnant. She kept trying with no success, to reach out to Tina. Shawn cried to Don on the phone about how she felt. Don talked with mom asking her to try and get to know Shawn. Jon also asked Lynette to spend some time with Shawn and for the kids to grow up around one another.

Jon took Bay Bro's death the hardest. He withdrew from everyone, including Don. When the twins stepped foot into their section, respect was immediately shown. There were no problems until after Bay Bro's death. Jon beat up two inmates and broke a guard's jaw. He was locked down for the incident. As soon as he was let out, Jon beat up couple more boys.

Don let his brother vent. He was amazed to see how two years of boxing made Jon nice with his hands. Jon had used the isolation to reflect on his life. He realized he wanted to walk away from SCC and the streets.

With the twins out the picture, it was the collective effort of Kay, Twon and Ron that kept SCC afloat. Cliques were applying pressure attempting to take over the territory. The crew of Shine and Will were eating plenty. Their prosperity had a lot to do with Twon wanting sole leadership. After losing the vote, he began encouraging SCC members to side with him. This caused confusion.

Shine wanted all of the buildings. Kay wasn't relinquishing the reigns of the crew to Twon and started distancing himself. He wanted no part of equal leadership. He watched Jon use equal leadership to assume full control. J-Roc stepped up to fill the void

that Twon's absence created.

Don and Jon were labeled as drug dealing murderers by the Gary Police Department. The state recommended rehab. Despite the vigorous argument from their attorney, Don and Jon were sent to High Plains Youth Center in Phoenix, Arizona for twenty-four months.

The place was located in the middle of nowhere. There were nine hundred youths housed in the facility. Their ages ranged from ten to twenty-one. Six hundred of the delinquents were affiliated with the Crips organization. There were no other Vice Lords at the time of the twin's arrival. The facility had a small number of white kids and about two hundred Latinos.

The guards were huge bodybuilders. They were known to body-slam inmates who got out of line. The center was set up for offenders to attend one of the three groups. There were violent offenders, sex offenders and drug abuse offenders. Sixty percent of the population was sex offenders. The groups were mandatory and were classes.

Jon was given an IQ test on arrival. With a score of 186, he shocked the teacher. The teacher tested Jon again. This time his score was 188. Jon excelled, exceeding even the teacher's expectations. He was a few credits short of getting his diploma and decided to pursue it. Jon tutored some of the kids.

Jon became a fitness buff. He lifted weights and pounded the heavy bag. Jon quit eating red meat. He didn't like playing sports and kept to himself. It was clear that he wasn't trying to make new friends.

The teacher liked Jon and did everything he could to help him. He petitioned the court for Jon to get an early release. The court's response was if Jon graduated, passed the SAT or ACT, stayed out of trouble and was accepted by a college, he'd be released early. Jon was overjoyed by the news and thanked the teacher everyday. Jon graduated at the age of seventeen and the teacher quickly set up the mandatory test. Jon aced it. He applied to Black colleges and decided on Grambling State University in Grambling, Louisiana. He'd serve eleven months of his sentence, if he could stay out of trouble.

Don was given the same IQ test. He scored well-above average. Don was a drop-out and didn't have high school credits. He'd have to wait until he was eighteen to take the GED. Classes didn't appeal to him. He did what was required of him to stay in good graces.

Don was the same hot-head. He stayed in arguments with the other boys and fought at least twice a week. Don played sports all the time with the other kids and his cockiness always came out. Basketball was the reason Don and the Crips weren't getting along. They were always sending someone to fight him. Don welcomed the challenge and easily handled whoever the Crips sent. He had quit eating red meat but didn't lift weights.

Both boys worked in the kitchen. They'd pick the easiest jobs then sit kicking it until they had to leave. Don got cool with a female supervisor. Not long after, Jon played look-out while Don fucked the broad in a kitchen closet. Don was loving the youth center.

The boys were also on the State basketball team together. The team had players form California, Philly, New York and Carolina. All of the boys on the State team had game and they were one of the teams vying for the first place. The coach of the state team had played college ball at UCLA and also played a couple seasons in the CBA.

The twins spent time with each other's children during family visits. Tina, Shawn, Lynette and the twin's kids visited twice a month. Shawn had a boy, named Don Jr. Lynette had a boy named Jon Jr. The two infant were born three days apart. Lynette gave birth first.

On visits everyone got along and the kids all looked like they came from the same parents. Jon enjoyed spending time with his family and enjoyed even more holding his kids in his arms. Don also loved the time spent with his family but was always trying to figure a way to get pussy from Shawn.

Two weeks before Jon was set to leave all hell broke loose. The twins were at work in the kitchen when a Crip came through the line and disrespected Jon. Jon let the comment slide but Don didn't. He went into the cafeteria and used a food tray to smack the Crip. Don then stomped the boy. The other Crips jumped up from their seats and bum-rushed Don.

Jon had followed his brother into the cafeteria and once the other Crips jumped, Jon ran to his brother's aid. Although outnumbered the twins brawled for twenty minutes. The officers quickly got things under control. Jon's early release was in doubt but his teacher pulled strings and the incident was never put in his file. Two weeks later Jon was out.

He was in Gary for a month. Jon and Kay were sitting in Kay's car.

"I'm no longer down, Kay," Jon said.

"What…?"

"I want out of the game…the street life, all that," Jon said. Kay stared in surprise at him.

"You through with SCC…?"

"Kay, come with me to Louisiana."

Kay thought for a moment then spoke. "I can't man, you know Don gon' need help running things. Maybe later on…"

"Ahight…"

Jon spent time with his family. He'd take Shawn and his nephews to the beach and other places. Jon hung out with Jackie who was happy to see him. She was sad to hear that he had retired. Jon packed up and left for college. Lynette and the kids left with him.

Don was depressed when Jon left the center. He fought everyday with any Crip. A couple of weeks later, Don calmed down and started lifting weights. He liked the feel that he got from lifting not to mention the look. Don passed his GED and spent more time in the kitchen with the supervisor he was seeing.

A couple months after Jon left two boys from Indiana came to High Plains and one of them was from Gary. Juan was from Gary and knew of Don. Juan was from the Glen Park area and wasn't affiliated. Juice was a Vice Lord from Michigan City. He was rugged, jet black, with big nose and large. Juice loved lifting weights. He and Don quickly became cool. The three were inseparable until Don left.

22

The summer and fall of 1998 brought back new life and old memories to the city of Gary. Don was back and spent his first couple of days with Kay catching-up. He was highly upset to find that only the Pauline remained after all the hard work. Kay had done his best. Kay explained Twon's behavior and told Don about the confusion Twon started. Don was uninterested. Kay told Don that he was leaving and going to Louisiana with Jon.

"Be cool and stay safe," Don said.

It was clear that Don had changed and it wasn't for the better. Jon came back in the summer and spent time with his brother. The brothers greeted each other. Don immediately pulled Jon to the side. They had a private talk.

"What' up baby brother?" Don asked hugging Jon.

"I'm your only brother," Jon said embracing Don.

"That's what I'm talking bout," Don said smiling. "You my

only brother and you leave me hanging like this."

"What are you talking about?" Jon asked with his head cocked sideways.

"We've been in this together since day one. You go down to Arizona and let a teacher poison you. You always had my back. I'm asking you to come back. Together we can take this city over," Don said smiling.

"You my brother and I love you. But there is no way I'm coming back. I've had enough. I just wanna spend my life happy and worry-free. You can do what you want to with your life but I know how I'm going to spend mine."

Don looked at his brother and shook his head. "So sad. They done turned my brother into a pussy."

Jon grabbed Don by his shirt and snatched him out of his chair and up against a wall.

"I ain't no pussy," Jon said between clenched teeth.

Both boys had grown to be six-five but Don was a little heavier because he had hit the weights hard-body. Even with the size in Don's favor he knew that there was no way he could beat Jon. Jon released his grip on Don and walked out.

Shine and Will damn-near owned all the drug sales going down in the city. Will held his spot in the background, while Shine was up front, soaking up all the glory. Success got to this head. He'd ride around giving middle fingers to everyone. Shine threw blunt butts at females and had people kissing his six point star ring like he was King.

He got a wake-up call when he heard Don was out. Shine called a meeting of his entire crew and told them to stay alert. Don wanted the apartment buildings they took from them. Shine also put a million dollar hit on Don's head. He wasn't taking Don lightly and started getting chauffeured around with bodyguards by his side at all times.

Don spoke with Twon about his problem.

"So what's your beef with Kay?" Don asked as they sat in the game room.

"I ain't got no beef with that fool. I'm just tired of being treated like I'm a peon, that's all."

"Ahight, so straighten up and be my second in command," Don said.

That was music to Twon's ears. He got his act together and joined Don. Together they'd be even bigger than Shine and Will.

Next on Don's list was Goldie.

"Did y'all ever find out who shot Bay Bro?" Don asked.

Goldie seemed a lot older. He had picked up about twenty pounds and was graying. Goldie's pain was all over his face at the mere mention of Bay bro's name.

"Nah, the muthafucka got away to tell about it. But if I ever find out."

"I hear you on that one. Goldie, this is what I need to talk with you about. It's been six years since I took my oath and I put in hella work."

"You want some rank," Goldie said with a smile.

"Yeah," Don said grinning. "I think it's long overdue."

Goldie nodded in agreement. "You know Bay Bro was going

to bless y'all with something when y'all got out. Since he ain't here, it would be my pleasure to bless you with everything I can. Call some peoples to witness."

Don pulled out his cell phone and called everybody in his crew. J-Roc was the first to arrive, followed by Twon and some other SCC members. Goldie blessed Don with the most rank that he could and gave him a promise of more if he stayed on the right path. Don was official now and he wanted everybody to know it.

Jon and Kay were back in Louisiana. Don planned a hit on all the apartment buildings to see which was the most vulnerable. He found Debbie to be the weakest but Don still didn't have the manpower to go up against Shine.

Twon cleaned up and was around everyday supervising. J-Roc was on the rise. He had Concord projects on lock and plenty of soldiers to go to war. Don had J-Roc by his side. He was still missing a valuable piece in the dangerous game he was playing.

When the middle of September rolled around Don still hadn't gained control of any of the other apartment buildings. Shine was the man and it showed in his numbers. Don was standing in front of the game room when a car pulled up.

"What's up brother?" Juice greeted Don stepping out of the cab.

Don looked at his man and smiled. "When yo ass get out?"

Juice paid the cab driver and gave Don a hug. "Today..." Doug laughed and the two walked inside.

"You know that I ain't no problem getting with your team but I ain't got no family up here."

Don put his hand over his heart.

"I'm offended. All the shit we been through together in Arizona and you don't consider me family." Don shook his head and took a swallow of beer. "I got you. You ain't got to worry about nothing."

Juice smiled and grabbed a beer of his own.

"It's on then. Let's get that money, Don."

Juice started putting in work for the crew immediately. Juice was feared by a lot of people. In a matter of days Juice's name was known by all the major dealers. He went on a robbery spree that put a huge dent in a lot of suppliers' pockets. Don sat back and watched his man tear the city apart. Juice grew in wealth, respect and fame, so did Don.

It was Juice who Don now turned to for advice. He consulted with him instead of Twon. Juice was doing too many reckless things to last long in the game. Twon played his position when Don was ready to initiate his takeover.

The Debbie was at the top of Don's list and he sat in a borrowed truck with Juice, J-Roc and Twon. They were parked across the street from the Debbie waiting for the pick-up and drop-off. Don thought it'd be right to take the Debbie back the same way Shine and Will took Zoe.

He positioned four teams on the corners to take out the security that were in the cars. Two more stolen vans filled with SCC members waited on the next block for the signal. Two hours later, a Caprice Classic pulled up. The driver got out and went to the trunk pulling out big duffel bags.

"Let's move." Don said grabbing the SK and exiting the truck.

Don, Twon J-Ron and Juice ran up on the two men. All were firing SK's. The driver was dropped and the passenger never made it out of car. The security teams that were parked on the corners heard the shots. Before any of them could start the cars, bullets riddled all four. Two cars tried to get away but the SCC members ran behind them shooting. The cars turned down Durbin heading straight towards each other. Don fired into the cars.

Workers in the apartments shot from the windows. Juice, J-Roc and Twon let off bullets causing the workers to duck. Don and crew approached the apartment building. They were joined by the other crew members parked on the next block.

Juice went to the basement door and tried to kick it in having no luck. Don remembered the iron-bar that was used for keeping robbers out.

"It won't do any good Juice." He laughed looking up at the apartment building. "The doors not gone give like that. We gone have to shoot the doors off."

Juice, Twon and a couple more members cocked their guns and were about to shoot. "Hold it. I got another idea," Don said looking at Juice. "It's gone give them niggas a chance to escape with their lives."

"Nah, fuck that," Twon said slamming his hat on the ground. "Them niggas didn't give Zoe a chance. Fuck that!"

Twon's anger left Don with no choice.

"Fuck it then." Don said throwing his hands in the air. "Blow these bitches off the hinges. Let's get this shit over with."

Don split the crew up into three groups. Juice took some to the top floor. J-Roc had the middle floor. Don and Twon covered the basement. The three groups blew the doors off the hinges and

killed the workers that were inside as they all tried to run out the backdoors.

SSC regained control of the Debbie but had time to celebrate, they heard police sirens.

"Grab all the money and the dope you can find in the apartments," Don said.

Twon searched the basement apartment. Don went out to the Caprice and grabbed the two duffel bags. The SCC members hurried back to the stolen vehicles and were out before the police got there. Don smiled to himself. The Debbie was only the beginning.

Shine received calls about the apartment building from several workers. The way Don took back the building surprised Shine. He had underestimated Don's strength and numbers. Shine called Will. The two of them needed to sit down immediately.

"So what happened?" Will asked lighting a blunt.

They were sitting in Shine's living room. Renee was in the bedroom at the back of the house.

"Them niggas hit us hard," Shine said sipping Hennessey.

"What you wanna do now? We gone strike or what?"

Shine took the blunt from Will. He pulled long and hard on it thinking about the next move.

"Nah, they got that," Shine said coughing. "We not gone throw anything away over one apartment building. We gone put extra security on the other buildings and just let everybody know that they got to stay alert."

Will shook his head disagreeing with Shine. "That ain't the way to handle this." Will said as he sat on the couch. "Letting them think they got away with this is only gone strengthen them. Niggas gone start joining them thinking that they the winning team. And with more security on the apartments, it ain't gone matter cause they gone be deep enough to takeover anyone they want."

Shine sat back feeling the effect of the weed.

"We don't need any heat right now. Shit's smooth and we on top. We the winning team. Fuck what other niggas think, we on top. Anyway," Shine said leaning forward. "The crib on Buchanan is where our money at. We straight."

One month later, with SCC membership growing, Don and J-roc made an agreement so that SCC and Concord became one. Don and J-Roc had equal say in all matters. The Concord members were only concerned with making money for themselves. Don and J-Roc started making plans taking back over the Bobby. They were all set to strike when war broke out between Concord and the Bronx.

Soldiers from the two hoods were killing each other everyday. J-Roc got tired of the war. He wanted to put an end to it once and for all. J-Roc asked Don to gather everyone. He wanted to hit the Bronx hard one time ending the feud. Don agreed and the two started making plans.

Don and J-Roc had put together their master plan to take down the Bronx. It would take place on Thursday. This was Sunday and there was a concert at the Savoy. No Limit Soldiers were in town and everyone was going to be there.

Since Smoke was killed, the Savoy was forced to increase security in order to keep open. Weapons of any kind were banned from the club. The owner got rid of Mad Dog and two metal detectors were installed at the front door.

These precautions helped in the decline of violent incidents. Neighborhoods, cliques, crews and organizations had to find areas in the parking lot where they could park in groups. Rivals had to get run for their gun hoping that you were parked closer to the club than your enemy. There was police stationed inside the parking lot. This was the type of security that the No Limit Soldiers received.

Nine o'clock that night the concert kicked off. SCC made their entrance at ten-thirty. Silkk The Shocker and Mystikal were performing, *It Ain't My Fault*. Heated words and deadly glares were exchanged between Concord members and people from the Bronx when the groups bumped into each other.

The females in the club were passing Don their numbers and kissing him all over his face. Don was enjoying himself. J-Roc couldn't relax because the Bronx member kept their eyes on him. J-roc didn't have his gun and this made him real uneasy. The concert continued and Master P was now performing his old hit, *Ice Cream Man*. A member from the Bronx was walking by SCC and bumped into a member from Concord.

"What's yo problem?" The Concord member asked.

The man from the Bronx looked around the whole SCC crew and laughed.

"You joking right?"

Don walked over to the man and swung knocking the man to the floor.

"Who the joke on now, muthafucka?" Don asked stomping on the man. SCC members spat on the unconscious man. Seconds later every Bronx member in the club came to their homeboy's aid.

The Bronx didn't have enough size or members to deal with SCC and some of the members knew it. They quietly made their way to the exits planning an ambush. Don noticed the small number of Bronx members.

"Get some people out in the parking lot," Don said to J-Roc.

J-Roc immediately ordered ten members to post up in the parking lot. Don and some SCC members continued to punish the already beaten and bloody Bronx member, helpless on the floor. The security guards made their way over to SCC and escorted them out the club. The security guards knew of the rep Don and J-Roc had.

SCC crew made their way to the parking lot. At the same time way a convoy of cars and trucks were pulling into the lot. The group made it halfway to their cars. Suddenly, gunfire erupted.

"Get down!" "Get down!" Don shouted jumping behind a car.

J-Roc followed Don and the other SCC members scrambled to find cover.

"Gotta be them Bronx niggas," J-Roc said.

"Yeah, it's them all right," Don said peeking around the car's bumper. "Fuck Thursday, it's going down tonight."

The Bronx boys were still shooting in their direction and the SCC members weren't firing back.

"You think them little niggas left us hanging?" Don asked.

"I trust my little soldiers with my life," J-Roc said shaking his head.

Don peeked around the bumper again and saw the cars and trucks that had just come into the parking lot headed in their direction. Assault rifles were hanging out the windows.

"I see you trusted them with my life too," Don said with sarcasm.

The cars and trucks were moving at a slow pace. They were two aisles away from Don and J-Roc. Don was about to slide under the car but heard more gunfire followed by tires screeching.

"I told you!" J-Roc shouted with a smile. "My soldiers coming..."

Don used the opportunity to make a run for it. The SCC members and the Bronx exchanged gunfire. Don, J-Roc and the others scampered to their section of the parking lot.

"It's on now," Don said pulling out an AR15 equipped with scope from the trunk of his Cadillac. "This shit will end tonight."

"Damn! I see you been holding out on a nigga," J-Roc said.

"We need some brothers to circle round back and come up behind them niggas. Try and bring they ass in," Don said.

J-Roc picked five youngsters and gave them their orders. The youngsters grabbed extra clips to their AK's and took off.

The Bronx boys were still shooting and more cars were pulling into the lot.

"Damn! They gotta have the whole hood out here," J-Roc said.

"The more the merrier," Don said.

He took a deep breath and pulled the trigger. One by one Don dropped six Bronx boys causing the rest to get low. The five youngsters dispatched by J-Roc had made their way behind the Bronx boys. Once in position, their AK's started spitting rounds.

J-Roc took fifteen SCC members and attacked the Bronx boys frontally. Don stayed in his position sniping at heads. Neither side was backing down. Both cliques held their positions and their gats bark. No one seemed to care that members of both sides were dropping. It was all out war and the participants had a death wish.

Police cars flew into the parking lot five minutes into the shootout. The police station there now had back-up and ran out of the mini station with guns blazing.

"Watch this," Don said aiming at an officer. He squeezed and shot two police officers in the head. Don hit three in the chest. Members of his crew that were close by laughed. "This shit is better than any video game I've ever played," Don said peering through the scope for another victim.

The Bronx and SCC turned their gun-fires on the police. They were seriously out-gunned and officers ducked behind their squad cars trying to find cover. The crews were delighted at getting payback.

"Shouldn't we get outta here now?" A SCC member asked Don.

"Nah, we straight, all 'em muthafuckas can get it tonight!" Don said hearing the sirens approaching. He took aim and fired, barely missing a police officer's head.

J-Roc and his crew were giving it to the police. The Bronx members that were in the trucks started circling the police cars letting off shots from their assault rifles as they drove by.

By the time the back-up arrived, three officers were dead and seven injured. The city, state and county police were there as helicopters hovered above. A barrage of bullets met the Gary SWAT team. The driver lost control changing directions. The added police

had the Bronx boys running into the nearby woods.

J-Roc and his crew pulled back to where Don and the rest of SCC were positioned.

"I think it's time for us to bounce too," J-Roc said.

"Not yet Roc," Don said scanning the parking lot for targets. "We can take 'em."

"You tripping now, Don" J-Roc said signaling for everybody to come in. "Let's go, Don. It's time to be out." J-Roc pulled Don by the back of his shirt.

"All right, okay. Can't a nigga have some fun with these cops? They do it to us." Don said laughing. "Let me cause a little distraction." He aimed the rifle and shot the gas tank of two squad cars. Don shot the gas tanks on six more before fleeing into the woods.

Newspaper reporters and camera crews were arriving just as Don, J-Roc and the others ran off.

The body count was high, thirteen Bronx boys, nine SCC members and five police officers killed. Another twelve officers seriously injured. No arrests were made. The mayor of the city was infuriated. The mayor requested help. The National Guard was brought in and an eight pm curfew was established by the state. The jails immediately became overcrowded as more federal agents were brought in.

Dozens of arrests were being made every day with the feds able to snatch any case they wanted to prosecute. A majority of the arrests were crack-heads. The feds used them to set-up their suppliers. It was an effective method proved. Snitching, which was normally unheard of, became in vogue. The violence ended and the murder rate declined. Law and order returned to Gary.

23

Winter '99 got off to a slow start. The feds were still looking for arrests so the hustlers up played the cribs. Money was there but the big drug dealers were hesitant to sell drugs. The heavyweights were waiting out the crusade by the feds. SCC no longer sold keys. The profits came from the apartment buildings. Don and J-Roc threw stripper parties every weekend to keep crew members happy.

Shine was griped about things but still sold weights to whoever called. Will wanted no parts of the operation and left Shine. Will continued to operate the Bobby and the Dorie Miller project houses. Shine's greed and carelessness caused Will to think about retiring.

Ron was used to the way Jon did business and didn't like the way Don handled his. Don was power tripping, wanting to control everything around him. Ron used his fiancé as the excuse to exit the drug game. They planned on marrying in March during

Jon's spring break. Jon was to be the best man.

Twon sat back watching Juice play his position and now it was J-Roc. Twon had believed Don. He wanted to be the right-hand man but after a couple months Twon felt like he was no longer needed. Twon started distancing himself away from SCC again. He was thinking about leaving for good. Twon had made a lot of money with SCC and had a little crew on the side. It was just his time to do his thing. He just didn't know how Don would take it.

March rolled around bringing Jon, Kay, Lynette and the kids back to Gary.

"What's up brothers?" Jon said walking up behind Don, Ron, Twon, J-Roc and Juice. Everybody turned around to see Jon and Kay standing there.

"Oh shit! Y'all people's here." J-Roc shouted.

"I wouldn't have missed this moment for the world," Jon smiled and said.

Hugs were exchanged and greetings were made. They all walked into the game room.

"Where Lynette and the kids at...?" Don asked.

"She went straight to Victoria's. We gone go by moms later," Jon said sitting in his favorite chair.

"That's cool, but I'd like to see my niece and nephew. They got big," Don said.

"We're here for two weeks," Jon said looking around at the changes to the game room. "You'll have plenty of time to spoil them."

The seven men sat around for the next two hours laughing, joking and playing catch up. With the exception of Juice, it felt like old times to all.

March 12th Ron was married in a private ceremony at 20th Century Baptist Church. Later that night Jackie gave Jon a welcome home party at the Crystal Palace in East Chicago. The club was packed with SCC members. G.D's. from East Chicago were also present and as the night went on more blue rags started to surface. Juice noticed the strange faces. He turned to Don.

"Who all these niggas with the blue shit...?"

Don looked around the club. He noticed the growing number of unfamiliar faces.

"I don't know," Don said throwing a shot of Hennessy down his throat. "But if the niggas get outta line we gone deal with they asses."

SCC was strapped. Jon was on the dance floor with Jackie having a good time. Kay sat at the bar with Twon. It wasn't long before the two gangs bumped heads.

"Yo, let me get a dance," a GD said to Jon.

Jackie paid the dark-skinned man no mind. She continued to dance.

"I know you heard me," the man said hitting a nerve with Jackie.

"Nigga, can't you take a hint," she said walking up to the man. "I ignored yo ass to save you some embarrassment but if you gotta hear it, no."

The whole club heard and laughed.

"Fuck you bitch!" He said and walked away. "You ain't all that and if you disrespect me again I'm a beat yo ass."

Jackie hurried to the bar got a 9mm out of her purse and walked up behind the man. She hit him hard in the back of his head with the gun.

"Do you know me nigga?" Jackie asked striking the man again. The man stumbled forward fighting to stay on his feet. "Nah nigga," Jackie said swinging the gun again this time missing the man. The man managed to turn around seeing that it was a woman who had hit him, pissed him off. Jackie swung again. This time the man grabbed her arm and punched her in the eye. She fell back releasing the gun. The gun fell and he reached for it. He never made it. Jon hit him in the temple knocking him out. The G.D's saw this and huddled.

"What the fuck's yo problem?" A light-skinned G.D. said.

"Yeah nigga, what's yo problem?" another chimed in.

Jon ignored them, picked up the gun and walked over to Jackie.

"You all right?" he asked holding Jackie by her chin.

"Yeah, he just lucky," she answered laughing.

The G.D. who had been knocked down, stumbled over to his boys and got a gun. He turned and fired. Jon threw Jackie to the ground, jumped on top of her and aimed Jackie's 9mm. He fired hitting the man twice in the chest.

Juice, J-Roc, Don and Twon pulled out their guns and started shooting at the G.D.'s. Kay jumped behind the bar, he didn't have a gun. G.D.'s started shooting back. The two gangs exchanged gunfire. The G.D.'s kept shooting while backing out the club. The gunfire ceased. Juice glanced up at Don.

"I'm shot," he said.

"Where...?" Don asked looking at Juice. He didn't see the blood.

"In my back," Juice said.

"I got you brother," Don said.

He turned to everybody.

"Juice got hit. We gotta go to the hospital," Don shouted.

The club emptied early, everybody was running to their rides. Don took Juice to Michigan City where the police wouldn't ask questions. All the while he drove Don kept wondering how Juice got shot in the back.

In the days that followed no one could figure out how Juice was shot in his back, when all the G.D.'s were to the front of them. Juice thought that Twon had set him up. Don didn't believe and defended Twon. They agreed it was someone from the crew and they had to keep their eyes open. After three days, Juice was released from the hospital and wanted to jump right back into action. The feds had slowed down arresting everybody. It was a good sign for Don to make his move.

"Yo Shine, they got it," Will said into his phone.

Shine was at home with Renee watching college basketball.

"Got what? Wha' you talking bout?" Shine asked lying in bed, his head in Renee's lap.

"Don," Will said lighting a blunt. "They got the apartment building back. The nigga cleaned house about twenty minutes ago."

Shine sat up in his bed and put his hand on his head.

"That's some bullshit. We can't afford to lose that building,"

Shine said getting out of bed. "That's a lot of money we'll be losing." There was along pause.

"Well, what you wanna do?" Will asked breaking the silence.

"We gotta get it back. That was our biggest moneymaking project. I ain't gone let them niggas profit off our shit. Fuck that! I'll burn the muthafucka down first."

Will smoked a blunt and listened to Shine. Although they'd be losing a lot of money, Will didn't want the building back.

"I hear what you saying," Will said pouring a glass of Hennessy. "Warring over that building will only make it hot for whoever gets it. The feds already watching and we don't need them in our life."

Shine thought what Will said made sense but his pride couldn't deal with SCC taking something from him again, especially Don. "How you think we should handle this?" Shine asked.

"Just let it go," Will responded. .

"We'll let it go," Shine said in a low voice. Will was shocked but got off the phone.

As soon as Shine hung up the phone, he called four of his trusted soldiers and they headed to Second Av. Shine parked two streets over. Everybody grabbed two five-gallon cans of gasoline as they exited the truck. Shine's plan was to sneak in and out without being seen. They crept along the alleys undetected and made it to the back of the Bobby. Shine and crew hurried to pour gasoline all around the building and stood on one side ready to light the match. Shine gave the signal and the four men kicked in the basement windows pouring gas through the apartment windows. Shine lit the gasoline taking a couple seconds to admire his work before running off. Bobby burned for two hours before firefighters put the fire out. All the workers managed to make it out unharmed. When Don heard the news, he was dead-set on revenge.

24

According to the calendar it was officially Spring but the weather was saying something different. It was still chilly and people stayed inside waiting for the weather to break. Don was checking out a new apartment building down on Second. He had plans to get even with Shine but was focused on his family.

Shawn was two months pregnant and nagged Don all the time about spending more time at home. His oldest son was quiet but smart, while his other boy stayed in something messy. Whenever Don was around he would spoil his children giving them whatever they wanted and all his attention.

Shine heard Will's dissent about burning down the building. He paid it no mind. To appease Will, Shine told him that all future decisions would be fully discussed. Shine felt that he was on top of the world.

When Juan was released from the youth center, he went to see Don.

"What's up nigga?" Don greeted Juan. "They let clean-ass Don-Juan out?"

Juan smiled giving Don a hug.

"Man, they didn't want to let a brother go," Juan said lighting a cigarette. "But after the state told 'em they wasn't gone pay they ass no more." Juan inhaled.

"So when did yo ass get out?" Don said fanning some smoke away.

"My fault," Juan said blowing the cigarette smoke behind him. "I got out yesterday. You know a nigga had to get some pussy all day first." Juan smiled. Both laughed and shook hands.

"Yeah, I feel you on that one." Don said. "So what you plan on doing?" He asked in a serious tone.

"Get that gwap," Juan said.

"How you plan on doing that?" Don asked.

"Shit, I been scrambling all my life. By any means necessary. I'm a get that."

Don smiled and grabbed Juan by the shoulders.

"You came to the right one. We don't play no games down here. Look, stay low and keep yo ass outta trouble and I got you."

In the days that followed Don spent a lot of time with Juan taking him shopping for clothes, jewelry and bought him a car. He also showed him their dope spots, introduced him to different people and had long talks with him at his house. After days of grooming Juan was ready for the streets.

"I'm telling you," Juice said as he and Don were getting fitted for Jon's wedding.

"I don't like that nigga."

"He all right," Don said looking at his reflection in the store mirror. "You just mad because he took that kitchen broad from you," Don said smiling. "Let that shit go. He crew now."

"It ain't nothing like that," Juice said as he was getting measured. "Dude's a snake. I seen his kind before. I'm telling you, bringing him in is bad news."

"Why you telling me this shit now? I'm saying, it's only been over a month."

"I told you a while ago that I didn't like that nigga but I didn't push it because I didn't want you thinking that I was acting like a broad, all jealous and shit. I know you gone do what you gone do, Don. All I'm saying is watch that nigga."

"Damn I hope you wrong. I don't need any drama before Jon's wedding. Do you know the nigga hate Gary so much that he was going to elope?" Don looked at Juice with intensity in his eyes. "Look, I need you to watch that nigga until after the wedding. Just in case you right. I can't have nothing going wrong. If the nigga slip, we gone deal with his ass in the worst way."

Juice knew how much Jon's happiness meant to Don and respected that.

"Don't worry bout a thing. I'll hold you down. Now you plan that wedding, Mr. Wedding Planner." They both laughed.

May came Jon, Lynette, the kids and Kay returned to Gary. This time Kay brought his high school sweetheart with him. Don insisted that things be different this time and went about making plans for the wedding.

"Are you nervous?" Don asked Jon once they were alone in the church.

"Negro please," Jon retorted with a half smile. "For what...?

This the love of my life we talking about. I had an idea that this would happen when I was in seventh grade."

Don nodded his head agreeing with Jon. "That's not what I'm talking bout," Don said straightening Jon's tie. "You know how people always say that they were nervous right before their wedding even if they were a hundred percent sure. They'd still be nervous."

"You need to quit smoking all that weed. Cause you either tripping or thinking about getting married yourself?"

Don gave Jon a sly smile and looked at the floor. "You bullshittin...?" Jon said smiling.

"I've been thinking about it for awhile now. You know I'm getting old and this street shit ain't what's happening no more. I'm proud of you. I've always been proud of you. I see you, Ron, Kay doing y'all thing and I'm jealous. I'm out here fighting over streets and buildings that ain't even mines. I must be crazy."

"Nah, brother you ain't crazy," Jon said hugging Don. "You just now realizing that there's more to life than the streets. It's a big step for you even thinking about it. But look at it this way." Jon laughed. "If all else fails, you got a future as a wedding planner." The two brothers joked until the wedding started.

Shine heard about Jon and Lynette's wedding. He knew that every member of SCC would be present for the special occasion and saw this opportunity as a chance to put an end to their feud once and for all. He asked Will to come by. Shine hoped that he'd be open minded and back the decision.

"What's up folks?" Will greeted sitting on the front porch.

"Shit, I can't call it," Shine said sipping a beer. "You know them niggas having a wedding today."

"Don't even think about doing nothing stupid," Will said pointing his index finger at Shine. "That'd be the worst mistake you can make. Trust me on this one."

Shine slowly moved Will's finger away from him.

"Why should I trust you on this one? I mean, you was the one against burning down the apartment building. Acting all scared and shit talking bout the police and a war. I did it and ain't shit happen so why should I listen to you now?" Shine slurred.

Will hoped Shine wasn't too drunk to listen to reason.

"Do you know whose wedding it is today?" Will asked.

"It don't matter who wedding it is because they all gone be up in there. We can hit 'em up quick and hard and it's all over with," Shine said opening another bottle of Corona.

"It's Jon's wedding. You mess with the wedding and Jon is gonna take charge of SCC again.," Will said grabbing a beer. He continued to persuade Shine showing him that without Jon the SCC is disorganized.

"All right," Shine said. He didn't want to deal with Jon again. "We'll just sit her and get fucked-up. Maybe we'll hit the club later or sump'n."

"Now Folks, you know I'm down with that," Will said pulling out a blunt. The two sat on Shine's porch smoking and drinking the day away.

The wedding went according to plan. Don and Kay both played the best man role. Victoria was maid of honor. Ron and his new bride were in attendance along with Tina, Jackie, Shawn, Juice, J-Roc, Juan and five other SCC members. Jon wanted to keep the wedding small.

The reception was held in a club Don recently bought. Affectionately named Zoe's, the club was in the hood located at the corner of Eleventh and Harrison. No one knew that Don had bought the club which made things go a whole lot smoother. All of SCC were either in the club or outside the club on security detail. Don went all out getting the R&B group, Next to perform their hit song, *Wifey*. A local group, G.I.B. shared the billing.

The club erupted when the DJ played *Here and Now* by Luther Vandross. Kay dropped to a knee and proposed. The party lasted all night long and everyone had a good time. Jon and Lynette left early for their honeymoon in the Bahamas. The kids were left in the care of Tina and Victoria.

Six days after Jon's wedding Jackie was on her way to meet Don. She was pulled over by the police and arrested on an attempted murder warrant. Jackie was photographed, finger printed, strip searched and harassed for three hours before given her phone call. Jackie called Don who told her he was on his way. She was sitting in the drunk-tank eyeing the dope fiends and prostitutes. Mad Dog was supposed to make the warrant disappear months ago, Jackie thought. Instead of taking care of his business, he played her.

Thinking about it made her even more pissed. She couldn't stop the flow of images popping into her head. Mad Dog lying to her face, assuring her that he had destroyed the warrant then her being stripped and searched. She vowed to make the crooked officer pay.

Don showed up and Jackie was released on a nine thousand five hundred dollars cash bond. She placed a call to Mad Dog from her cell phone and had Don drop her off at home.

An hour later, Mad Dog showed up. Jackie had showered and relaxed smoking a joint.

"What's up beautiful?" Mad Dog said entering the house.

"Nothing much," Jackie said in a normal tone. "I think we need to sit down and work a few things out."

Mad Dog leaned back in the living room chair. "What, business bad?" He asked.

Jackie sat down on the couch. "Business ain't bad but you bad business," she said.

Mad Dog looked confused. "Whoa, wait a minute. I don't know where that's coming from?" he shifted nervously in his seat.

"Oh, you ain't heard?" She asked getting up. "Let met tell you what I'm talking bout. You lied to me."

"What...?"

"You lied about the warrant," she said pacing in front of him.

Mad Dog's eyes was big as saucers. "I can explain," he said and sat up. "I did do it. I took care of it, just like I said I would. Someone made another one."

"Bullshit!" Jackie said looking down at Mad Dog. "You just gone lie to my face like that, right?"

"It ain't like that," he pleaded.

Jackie walked to the dining room table. "Our contract's null and void."

Jackie picked up an envelope from the dining room table.

She turned around to find a .357 Magnum aimed at her.

"What the fuck is you doing?"

"You know I can't trust you like that," Mad Dog said getting to his feet. "Now let me see both your hands."

Jackie put both her hands out in front of her, holding the envelope in her right hand.

"This your last payment," she said waving the envelope in front of her. "Now put that gun away. We don't do business like that."

"My fault," Mad Dog said and tucked the gun back in his holster. "It's an occupational hazard. You can't trust no one," he said smiling. Mad Dog sat back down in his chair and Jackie tossed him the envelope.

"What the fuck is this?" Mad Dog asked pulling writing paper out of the envelope. "This some kind of joke, right?"

"Ha, ha, you right, this is a joke," Jackie said.

Don came walking from a back room pointing two 9mm's at Mad Dog.

"The jokes on you," Jackie added.

Mad Dog wanted to reach for his pistol but knew he'd be dead before he could get it out.

"Hold up, wait one fucking minute here. I can make it right. I'm asking for one more chance," Mad Dog said.

Don laughed and looked at Jackie.

"The nigga sound like Biggie now... should've been more like TLC *Ain't 2 Proud 2 Beg*." Don clowned.

"C'mon, Mad Dog, I know dogs like you know how to beg real good. C'mon, be a good boy and beg." Jackie laughed.

Mad Dog became enraged. He couldn't hold back his anger.

"Who the fuck y'all think y'all talking to? Don't you know? I'm Mad Dog," he said beating his chest. "I got killers on my team, too. Shit, ya'll better recognize."

"Recognize that muthafucka," Don said as he fired.

Mad Dog winced and grabbed his stomach wound.

Jackie grabbed one of the 9's from Don.

"This is for the bullshit you put me through and for all the niggas you fucked over."

"Fuck you bitch!" Mad Dog shouted as he reached for his gun.

It never made it out of the holster. Don and Jackie both fired at the same time.

"Let's burn the piece a shit!" Jackie said.

Jackie sat in her truck while Don was inside the house pouring gasoline over everything. He lit a piece of newspaper and threw it inside. Jackie and Don watched the flames. After five minutes Jackie was satisfied.

"He might as well get used to fire since his ass gone burn in hell." Jackie said as they pulled off.

Jackie kept a low profile. Juan's true colors started to surface. His appearance took a hit. He started looking like a bum. Juan became arrogant, forgetful, disrespectful, and lazy. He was either late for meetings or was falling asleep. Don, Juice and J-Roc discussed Juan's behavior and concluded that Juan had to be

messing with drugs. Juice was sure that Juan was sitting in his car smoking weed one night as he and Don pulled up.

Don got out and tapped on the window. Juan ignored him. Don angrily snatched the car door open.

"I don't know what the fuck your problem is. But you don't ignore me."

Juan looked at Don and started laughing. "You look funny as shit," Juan said pointing.

"That nigga high as a muthafucka. I don't know what the fuck he high on but he definitely high," Juice said.

Don took the joint from Juan and hit it.

"This nigga wet," Don said holding up the joint. "I took yo ass in and you repay me by smoking water. Don pulled out his gun and smacked Juan in the head. "Nigga, don't ever show yo face around here again," Don said walking off.

"You making a big mistake. That nigga know too much," Juice said pulling out his gun. "We gotta kill him."

Don looked back at Juan and laughed. "Fuck him! Let him try sump'n stupid. We'll deal with his ass."

Don and Juice walked off leaving Juan unconscious in the car.

The SCC thrived. They opened up another apartment building on Second and Garfield, called Gina. Juan hooked up with his man, Terry, from his neighborhood and the two plotted a quick come-up. Juan had paid close attention to the amount of money SCC made but didn't know where they kept it. Terry figured the money was close to Don. The plan was set and the two men headed to Don' house knowing that he wouldn't be there.

Juan and Terry waited outside Don's house. They rang the doorbell. Shawn peered out the window and wondered why Juan was there. Don had told her about Juan and instructed her to call him if he ever showed up.

"What's up Shawn?" Juan said as he looked at her through the window. "I need to talk to Don."

Shawn had never seen Terry before and was a little nervous. "He ain't here," she said closing the curtain.

Juan looked around. There was no one outside. He kicked-in the door. The two men ran in the house. Juan grabbed Shawn and Terry closed the door behind them.

"What's up Shawn?" Juan said smiling.

"What the fuck you doing? Don ain't gone like this," Shawn said trying to wiggle free.

"Fuck Don!" Juan shouted. "I don't give a fuck about him. Where the money at?"

"What money?"

Juan flung Shawn across the room against a wall. "Oh, you wanna play games," Juan said walking over to Shawn.

Her two sons came running out of their bedroom.

"Mama, mama," Don Jr. said while John tried to shield.

Shawn wrapped her arms around the two boys and stared coldly at Juan.

"Why are you doing this? You know that Don don't keep his money here. If you leave now I won't tell him it was you."

"Yeah, I bet." Juan laughed. "Then where do you keep the money?"

"In the bank," Shawn said.

"C'mon, we wasting time," Terry said.

"Gimme a minute," Juan said staring at Shawn and her two boys.

"Come here!" Juan said snatching Don Jr. "You wanna play this game?" Juan pulled out his gun. "All right, let's play."

"Ain't no money here," Shawn said when she saw Juan's gun.

Juan didn't say anything he just shoved his gun inside Don Jr's mouth busting his lips and chipping four of his teeth. The boy started crying. John jumped up causing Juan to smack him in his head with the gun. John dropped unconscious to the floor and Juan pointed the gun at Shawn.

"I came her for some money. I ain't leaving without it. I know y'all got a safe in here."

"Yeah, yeah," Shawn said nodding her head. "It's in the bedroom."

Juan turned looking at Terry and smiled. "To the bedroom we go."

Shawn got up from the floor and led them to the bedroom. She turned the dial to the safe.

"It ain't that much in here. I'm telling you, he keeps the money in the bank."

"Shut up!" Juan yelled and pushed Shawn in the back of her head. When Juan heard the click, he pushed Shawn to the side and opened the safe. He pulled three diamond necklaces, four diamond watches, three bracelets, a .380 and one hundred and sixty five thousand dollars.

"Where the rest of the money at...?" Juan shouted.

"That's all that's here. I keep telling you, he keeps his

money in the bank."

Terry counted the money. "C'mon man, this better than nothing," he said.

Juan looked at everything he pulled out.

"Fuck it, let's be out."

The two men were walking out of the bedroom and Shawn sighed in relief. Juan turned around.

"Oh, you think this shit funny?" He asked snatching her up and throwing her on the bed. "Is this bitch laughing at us?"

Terry stood in the doorway looking at the front door now opened.

"C'mon man, we ain't got time fo' this shit. Somebody done came up in here…"

"I'm a teach this bitch a lesson first," Juan said ripping at Shawn's clothes.

"I ain't with this shit." Terry said and walked away.

"Where the fuck you going, nigga…?" Juan asked.

He jumped up from the bed his gun in hand. Terry reached for his gun but Juan shot him twice in the chest.

"Another time," Juan said waving the smoking gun at Shawn. "I'll see you real soon." Juan gathered up everything he took out of the safe and left.

Shawn immediately called Don. He made it home in record time. Juice was by his side. They ran into the house with guns drawn. Shawn and the kids were huddled together on the kid's bedroom floor.

"You alright…?" Don asked and tried to hug Shawn.

"Get away from me!" Shawn screamed. "This your fault! You the reason this shit happened."

Don looked around then at Shawn, John and Don Jr. He examined the three of them Don noticed a scar on John's head and blood coming from Don Jr's mouth.

"That nigga is a dead muthafucka," he said.

Juice nodded in agreement. He wanted to say I told you so, but didn't.

"Let's get them outta here. They can't stay here tonight," Juice said.

"Yeah, you right. We'll take 'em to the hotel," Don said looking at his injured family. Shawn sat on the floor rocking her two sons in her arms.

"I ain't going no where with you," she said with a hateful look on her face.

"C'mon baby, we gotta get y'all outta here."

Shawn stood. "Me and the kids are leaving but not with you," she said determinedly.

Don couldn't believe his ears. "Y'all ain't going nowhere," Don said snatching Don Jr. "We'll talk later." Don gave Don Jr. to Juice and grabbed John and walked away. Shawn crying, followed them.

Don and Juice spent half the night looking for Juan coming up empty. Don went to the hotel where Shawn and the kids were. Shawn had gave the kids a bath and put them to sleep. She was in the tub when Don walked in.

"Are you alright?" He asked.

"I can't do this anymore," Shawn said sitting up in the tub. "You're never around and people know that. That's how Juan had the balls to come to our home. Our home Don…"

Don rubbed Shawn's shoulders. "You're right. Give me one month and I'm done. My birthday party will be a retirement party." Don kissed Shawn on the lips. "I love you and you and my family is more important to me than the streets. You're my life. Just give me one more month."

"Hold me, hon." She said reaching out to Don. They embraced.

25

After Mad Dog was killed, Jackie played the crib. She conducted all her business from her house in the Miller area. Jackie used a driver whenever she needed to go out. The police wanted to question her about Mad Dog's murder. When they pulled Mad Dog's charred body from Jackie's house, it was unrecognizable. The police found out it was Mad Dog through his dental records.

Jackie grew bored and one evening she went cruising in her Denali. She drove out to the beach. Jackie bumped into a few of her friends they invited her to a birthday party at a popular night spot. She had forgotten how much she missed partying and headed to the club.

She was pulled over by the police. The patrolman ran Jackie's ID and found the outstanding warrants for her arrest. He called for back-up. Jackie was arrested and questioned about Mad Dog's murder. Jackie refused to say anything.

The news of Jackie's arrest hit the streets. Kay called Jon

and told him everything, including what Juan had done. Jon and Lynette had decided to extend their honeymoon an extra month but Jon cut it short. It was time for him and Lynette to go.

Jon, Don, Kay, Juice and J-Roc sat around one of the tables in the game room discussing everything. Jon heard everything and sat back thinking what course to take. All eyes were on him. It was just like old times.

"All right," Jon said as he looked around the table. "First thing's first, Jackie. We need to give her an alibi putting her out of the city when Mad Dog was killed. Now the only thing I can come up with is my honeymoon."

"I'm not following," Juice said.

Jon sat up in his chair and spoke. "This is what we have to do. First we gotta find someone greedy person at the airline ticket place and then Don can fly down and pay off one of them hotel clerks."

"Why me...?" Don asked.

"If you would've talked some sense into her then we wouldn't be having this discussion. Plus, you are the one who was down there with her. It gives both of y'all alibis. We need to get on top of that tomorrow." Jon rest his elbows on the table. "Now that bitch-ass nigga...The nigga is a dead and stinking. He don't mess with my family and think everything's cool. SOS my niggas, shoot on sight. If you can wound him and let him know why he about to die, cool. If you can't, just kill him. I'm personally putting up a half mill on the nig's head. Anyone can collect. Put the word out."

The five men discussed other issues. Don must've asked Jon to come back to the circle every ten minutes. Jon declined with a smile every time.

July Fourth and Jackie's alibi was airtight. The state's attorney prolonged her imminent release, he was aware that she was missed on the streets. Jackie's attorney was the best in Northwest Indiana and assured her that she didn't have anything to worry about.

"Their case won't make it to trial." He said to Jackie.

Jon visited her every week in the county jail. Kay spent time with his family in Gary. After Trina's rape the two became close but Trina grew closer to Jon than anyone else.

Jon, Kay and Trina were in the mall looking for some outfits to wear to the concert. They were walking by the Cinnabon Shop, Trina pointed inside.

"There go Jason right there."

"Jason who…?" Kay asked peeking in.

Trina looked at him and rolled her eyes. "That nigga helped rape me," she said before walking in his direction.

"Wait a minute," Jon said softly holding Trina by her wrist. "We gone do this the right way. You and Kay go get the truck. I'm a bring him out."

Kay and Trina walked off while Jon waited on Jason to come out. He walked out with a tall woman on his side laughing and joking.

"Do you know what today is?" Jon asked Jason from behind.

"Tuesday," Jason said turning around.

Jason saw who was standing behind him and all the blood rushed from his face.

"Nah nigga," Jon said pulling out his gun. "It's a good day

to die."

"What's going on? What he do to you?" The woman asked.

"Shut up and walk," Jon said looking around.

"I ain't going nowhere," the woman said raising her voice. "Don't you know who my brother is?"

"I don't give a fuck who your brother is. If you keep getting loud, I'm a kill yo ass right here. Now," Jon said nudging Jason with his gun. "Let's go."

"He knows and it don't matter, Michelle. This is a big misunderstanding so don't get yo self killed over nothing because he'll kill you."

Michelle's eyes widened and they walked through the mall doors. Kay was double parked right in front. Jon, Jason and Michelle got into the truck and Kay pulled off. Trina turned around and spit in Jason's face.

"Bitch, what's yo problem?" Michelle asked.

"Shut the fuck up!" Jon said patting Jason down. Michelle watched. Jason was clean.

"You think Don want in on this?" Jon asked Kay.

Kay smiled as he looked in the rear view mirror. "You know he do. Call him up."

Jon called Don explaining the situation and asked for a good place to meet up at. Don told him an abandoned house on Second was perfect.

Jon got off the phone and told Kay their destination.

"What's going on? What have we done to y'all?" Michelle asked.

Trina turned around saying. "Your lil' boyfriend's a rapist.

Now your ass bout to be feel it," Trina said.

"My brother ain't no rapist. He ain't got to take no pussy from no bitch."

"Who you calling a bitch, bitch?"

"Y'all two cut it out. Kay, I think you better drive faster," Jon said. He glanced at Michelle. "Your brother and G raped my sister up there and now its payback time."

"But I didn't do anything," Jason pleaded and Jon hit him in the mouth with the gun.

"No more talking," Jon said looking around the truck. "Turn the radio up!"

By the time Kay pulled up Don had everything set up. He even had ol' Sweets with him. Everybody walked inside the house and Jason continue his plea.

"Y'all got it wrong. I ain't no rapist. I tried to stop G…"

"Yeah nig, sure," Don said walking to Jon.

"Nah, I'm telling y'all, y'all making a mistake. Ask her."

Trina didn't need to be asked anything because she spoke up. "Nigga you lying. Both of y'all raped me. Don't get scared now nigga."

"My brother ain't no rapist. If he say he didn't rape her then he didn't do it. Y'all making a mistake. Please, just let us go."

"That ain't gone happen. At least not yet," Don laughed.

Jon, Don and Kay huddled while Trina and Sweets kept watch on Jason and Michelle.

"All right," Jon said walking back to Jason and Michelle. "Let's get down to business." He smacked Jason with the gun so hard that Jason fell on Michelle. They both hit the floor.

"Please, please don't do this," Michelle pleaded, tears rolling down her face. "Let us go."

Michelle held Jason's head in her lap. Don and Kay walked over to them holding two sledge hammers. They both swung crushing Jason's leg. Jason and Michelle both screamed.

"Get the duct-tape," Jon said.

Trina retrieved the tape and ran over to Jon. He taped both of their mouths shut and the beating commenced. No one touched Michelle, they focused on Jason. The three beat him with baseball bats and brass knuckles until they thought he couldn't take anymore. Next Sweets pulled Jason's pants and boxers down, greased him up and started humping away. Michelle sat helpless with tears in her eyes watching the violation. Sweets was finished with Jason, it was Michelle's turn.

Don ripped Michelle's clothes off. Kay and Jon burned spoons. Michelle was stark naked and the two men held burning spoons to her nipples. She screamed and kicked. Don brought a broomstick, greased it and shoved as much of it inside Michelle's pussy. When he thought no more could fit Don shoved harder.

Trina turned her head. Sweets was busy keeping Jason's face pointed in Michelle's direction. Kay wanted Jason to feel the pain he had felt. Don was through violating Michelle. Kay broke bottles and cut Michelle all over her body, from her head down to her feet.

"You ready for extra Sweets?" Jon asked picking up a Rambo knife.

"You know I is," Sweets said revealing his toothless smile.

Jon gave Sweets the knife and Sweets went to work. He

cut off Jason's dick and put it in his mouth then they all left.

Michelle waited until she heard the vehicles pull off before she struggled with putting on her shirt and pants. Jason was on the floor. Michelle was too weak to walk. She crawled out the front door in search of help. A lady driving down the street saw Michelle and stopped. Michelle had enough strength to tell the woman that Jason was in the house needing help before she passed out. Michelle woke up in the hospital. Shine was by her side crying like a baby.

"Shine," Michelle said weakly. "Jay, Jason."

"I know, who did this to you and Jason?"

Michelle shook her head slowly from side to side. Shine was determined to know and asked again.

"Come on baby." He said massaging her head. "I need to know, who did this?"

"Twins…"

Shine jumped up from the chair and headed out of the hospital. Will was standing in the waiting area and ran after Shine.

"What's up Folks?" He asked.

Shine stopped and turned to look at Will. "It was the lil' niggas. They killed my brother and fucked up my sister for life." With tears running down his face Shine continued. "This is beyond personal now. I want they whole family dead."

"I'm with you. Let's put an end to this shit."

Shine put a million dollar contract on Don and Jon and a price on all their family members' head. When Michelle regained her strength, Shine told her that Jason died before the ambulance made it to the hospital. He wanted to know everything Jon and Don said and who else was involved. Michelle told him about Trina, Sweets and Kay. Shine knew that his brother didn't rape anyone. He wouldn't put it past G. Shine put a price on the heads of Trina, Kay and Sweets.

Jon knew blood would be shed over the incident. He wanted his wife and kids safe. Lynette wouldn't go back to Louisiana without him. Jon packed up and they headed back down south with Kay and his fiancée following.

"Don you should bring your family and come down with us," Jon said to his brother.

"I ain't running from no man," Don said.

"Watch your back, and call me if anything goes down brother."

Jon convinced his mom and Victoria to come down and visit.

The seventeenth of July, a week before Don's self proclaimed retirement party. Juice, J-Roc and Shawn were the only people who knew Don was retiring. Juice and J-Roc were slotted to take control over the mob. Shawn was planning her getaway from Don. She was thinking the two of them needed to go on a trip alone, without the kids or anyone else.

She borrowed Don's Denali that morning to go make travel

plans for a getaway. It would be a surprise to Don. They could leave the day after his birthday. She wanted to visit Jamaica. Shawn visited a friend and arranged babysitting services. Shawn went mall shopping for Don's birthday gift.

Shawn pulled into the drive-thru of a fast food restaurant. On her way through, three men were parked and getting out their car.

"Wait," one of the men said. "That's that nigga right there?"

All three men looked at Don's truck. "Yeah that's him. Shine got a million dollar price tag on that nigga head," another said.

The driver reached under his seat and pulled out a Desert Eagle.

"Whoa, what the fuck you doing?" One man asked.

"Shit, I'm a collect. I ain't scared of that nigga. Y'all with me or what?" The driver said while checking his clip.

The other two men pulled out their guns.

"Let's go get this money." The men exited the car, guns drawn.

Shawn was busy singing Juvenile's *Back That Ass Up.* She wasn't paying attention to the men walking in her direction. The girl brought her order to the window and she let the window down. Because of the dark tint covering the windows, the men couldn't see inside the truck.

They opened fire when the window came down. The first couple shots didn't hit the truck. Just as the girl held the bag out of the window, a bullet hit the bag. The girl dropped the food and ducked inside.

Shawn quickly realized that the shooting was right in front of her. Shawn tried to reverse but the car behind her wouldn't budge. The men got closer and had a better aim. Bullets ripped through the Denali's windows and Shawn ducked down screaming and crying. The shooting stopped. Shawn looked out and saw the men changing clips.

She pressed the gas and the truck passed the three men. The driver changed his clip and was again shooting. Shawn caught one bullet in her neck and another on in the side of her head. The truck crashed into a parked car. The three men ran up on the vehicle, shooting as they approached. Once they made it to the truck the three men shot their guns inside the truck before looking in.

"Oh shit!" The passenger shouted as he saw Shawn's lifeless body slumped over. "That's his broad. We gotta get the fuck up outta here."

The three men ran back to their car and tried to pull away but police had blocked their exits and more police were coming.

The driver looked around. There was nowhere else to go.

"What ya'll want to do?" He asked.

"We dead either way, I'm a take my chances right now. I'm a run," one said.

The police were now squatted on the opposite side of their cars waiting with guns drawn. "Fuck it!" The driver reloaded his weapon. "On three, one, two, three…"

The three men jumped out of the car with their guns blazing heading for the back of the restaurant. They didn't have a chance. The police mowed all three down. The scene was taped off and the coroner was called to get the bodies. Don was devastated.

Jon, Kay and Victoria went back to Gary for Shawn's funeral while Lynette and Kay's fiancée stayed in Louisiana. The funeral was the day before the twin's birthday, Lynette wanted to go but Jon wouldn't let her. He knew that things were unstable in Gary and didn't want his wife and kids involved in the hostility. Jon tried to talk Victoria out of going back but she refused.

Eleventh Avenue wasn't the same when Jon and Kay returned. No one was out hustling and very few people were even standing outside. It looked like fear had been put in everyone's heart.

"How you holding up?" Jon asked looking at his depressed brother.

"I'm holding," Don said feebly.

"The dudes that did it, was they plugged in with Shine?" Kay asked sitting down. Don gave a faint laugh saying. "The niggas was trying to collect on a reward. Shine put a million dollar on us including our family." Don put his head inside his hands. "I don't know what I'm gonna do. I was going to retire tomorrow. This was supposed to be my last official day as head."

"You still can retire," Jon said walking over to his brother. "Shawn would want you to honor your promise and get out while you can."

"How can I? They took my baby from me. I can't let that shit ride. I can't leave now without getting my revenge. I'm staying in for Shawn."

"You have to use your head, Don. If you go out there and get yourself killed who gone be your kids parents. You won't be doing them justice if you get killed. Come back with us and lay low for awhile. Let niggas think you ran off and get relaxed, then pop up on the scene and handle yo business." Kay said touching Don's shoulder. "And I'm a ride with you."

"Me too," Jon said rubbing Don's back.

"I'm a think about. I'll let ya'll know,' Don said with a sigh.

All SCC was in attendance at Shawn's funeral. It seemed like anyone who knew her attended the funeral. Don was having a hard time keeping it together. Tina and Jon greeted the guests. Twon, Kay, Juice and J-Roc tried comforting Don. He was too emotional to speak. Twon, Kay, Jon and Tina spoke highly of Shawn and told the guest a few funny stories. Tina spoke of the intimate moments they shared, Don was able to laugh. The ceremony progressed to the grave site. Don couldn't keep it together no longer and broke down. He stayed an hour after everyone else had left while Jon, Kay, Twon, Tina, Juice and J-Roc waited in their cars. A Lincoln pulled up and Goldie got out.

"I just heard," he said giving Don a hug. "What can I do?" Don hugged the old-timer and cried.

Shine took the news of Shawn's death bad. When he put the hit out on the twins and everybody associated with them he didn't calculate on Shawn being one of the casualties. He went into depression. There wasn't anything that anyone could do or say, not Michelle, Will or Renee. Shine blamed Don for not protecting Shawn. The only thing keeping Shine going was a determination to see Don buried. His hatred for Don was even deeper now fueled by

Shawn's death. He didn't want to accept responsibility for Shawn's death. Shine put the whole incident on Don and promised that he'd make Don suffer.

July twenty-fourth was the twin's birthday. Jon was ready to go. The city seemed dead. There was no life on the street and everything was calm. Jon and Kay went to see Don who was already packed up.

"I see you decided to leave with us," Jon said hugging his brother. "You doing the right thing by your kids."

"Yeah, I thought about what Kay said and I'm a do it his way," Don said looking at a picture of him and Shawn. "You better believe that this shit ain't over till that muthafucka, Shine gets it in the worst way. I'll lay low for awhile but when I come back." Don put the picture down and looked at Jon and Kay. "Revenge will be mine," he said.

Jon was just happy to get his brother out of the city.

"We got a long ride," he said and picked up some luggage. "We better get going." They packed up Jon's navigator and headed for the highway leaving Tina behind. She refused to leave Gary.

26

Each passing day saw Don growing even more restless. He had been down in Louisiana for three months and a day didn't go by without him thinking of Shine. Don bought a house on the same block as Jon and Kay, close to the university. He spent most of his time in his backyard swimming pool meditating while Lynette babysat John and Don Jr. She took them all over the city, showing them the sites.

Grambling offered no attractions to appease Don's spirit. It was too small, clean and quiet for his liking. There were parties going down at one of the frat houses but Don wasn't into partying and meeting people. His focus was on getting revenge.

Three days before Halloween, Don went to see his brother. The two sat around Jon's swimming pool while their kids played inside the house.

"I'm telling you Jon, now is the time for me to strike," Don said lounging and sipping Corona. "I heard them niggas done

went to sleep by now. They vulnerable, they slipping, I gotta take advantage."

Jon had prayed that this day would never come. "Man, you straight down here. You ain't got to worry about a thing. No bullets, no wars, no killing, nothing…"

"This for the birds," Don said and sat up in his chair. "You know me better than anyone and you know that I can't live my life knowing that bitch-ass, Shine still breathing. He killed my loved one and all I do is fantasize about killing his ass with the most pain."

Jon hoped that the change of environment and the whole college scene would have helped ease Don's pain. He had to admit to, he wouldn't have let it go either.

"I don't want you to go back," Jon said standing up. "But if you think now is the perfect time then go handle take care of BI. But," Jon said pointing at Don. "If you need me, call me. I ain't forgot how to get down for my crown," Jon said smiling.

"I know you ain't," Don said getting up from his chair. "Look lil' brother, I'm a leave the kids down here with you and Lynette until shit's over with. I can think better knowing they safe. Don't worry, I got this, I got it." Don hugged Jon. "I was so close. I love you."

Don went back. He had been in the city for two days. Only Juice and J-Roc knew he was back. Will and Shine had let their guards down. Will more than Shine. The talk round town was that Shine ran Don off. People were saying that Jon was the real leader and Don was a pretender. Someone even had the balls to spray paint: *Chicken Shit*, on the side of the game room. With all the talk of Don being coward, no one tried to war with SCC. Not one robbery or an attempt was made on any of the apartment buildings. This was mainly because everyone assumed J-Roc was in charge with the unpredictable Juice at his side. Shine figured SCC's demise would happen naturally. Shine knew their supplier and without her they'd eventually fade.

Don had left Juice in charge of keeping tabs on Shine and Will. Shine had been hard to follow because no one knew where he stayed. He wasn't hanging out in the streets like before. When the rumors started circulating that Don had left, Will relaxed. He became so comfortable when there was no retaliation from Don, he started hanging even more in the streets. Will started back going to club flossing his wealth. He made it easy for Juice to find out where he lived.

Juice followed him after a night out on the club. Will led Juice right to his house. Juice passed the information to Don and told him about a lead on Juan's hide-out. Don sat in the cut and watched Will for a couple of days in the hopes he'd lead him to Shine. Don had already waited over three months to get his revenge, a couple more days wasn't going to matter.

While Don waited on Will to slip, he paid a visit to the county. It had been months since he last saw Jackie and didn't want her thinking he had forgotten about her.

"What's up stranger?" Don said into the phone.

Jackie still looked beautiful.

"What's up with you?" Jackie smiled. "Why you didn't tell me you were coming back? Hold up," she said pointing at Don through the glass. "Ain't you supposed to be in school?"

Don laughed realizing Jackie thought he was Jon.

"Oh so Jon is the only twin that loves you. I'm hurt," Don said his hand covering his heart. Tears started streaming down her

face and Jackie was unable to speak. "Hey," Don said smiling. "I'm all right. As you can see, I'm still standing."

Jackie managed to control her tears. "I heard about Shawn. I'm sorry. I wish I could've been there for you."

"It's all right," Don said looking at the floor. "He'll pay."

Jackie sensed that Don was still mourning and changed the subject.

"I got some good news, I'm outta here the first of the year," she said smiling.

"Why so long?" Don asked looking at her.

"Them damn holidays. Hey, it still sounds better than sixty years."

"I hear you," Don said smiling.

They chat about other things. Before they knew it, the visit was over.

"You take care, Don," Jackie said.

Don blew her a goodbye kiss and left. In his mind, Will was going to die that night.

He was parked across the street from club Genesis, smoking a blunt. Don was waiting for Will to come out the club. Don puffed thinking about all the good times he and Shawn had and even some of the funny bad ones. The more he reminisced, the angrier he became. Don called Jon down in Louisiana.

"What's up brother?" Don said when Jon pick up the phone.

"These bad ass kids," Jon said laughing. "They about to drive me up a wall."

Don shared the laugh. He knew Don Jr. was tearing up

Jon's house. "You can handle that. All you gotta do is use some of that psychology shit on them."

Jon laughed even harder. It felt good to hear Don joking again.

"This psychology shit must only work on white kids because these kids here ain't hearing it."

Don laughed. "Oh yeah, Jackie said she'll be out the first of the year."

"That's cool. So you went to see her?"

"Yeah," Don said. Will strolled out. "I was checking in, but I gotta go. It's that time. You know what I'm saying?"

"Be careful, brother," Jon said knowing what Don meant. "I love you."

"I love you too, Jon," Don said starting his car. "I'll be in touch."

"You do that," Jon said hanging up.

Don turned off his cell phone and looked at Will. "It's on."

Will was feeling real good walking leisurely to a navy blue Lexus. He wore a smile on his face. Will had just received some brains in the club. If his girl wasn't home waiting, Will would've headed straight to the telly with a few girls from the club. His rep as a big-time hustler had spread, but didn't let the streets interfere with his family life. He went home every night and kept the promise he hade to wifey and son, lil' Will.

Will stopped at a liquor store to get a bottle of Dom Perignon for wifey. He wanted her mood to match his. He didn't see the beat up Chevy behind him. Will parked in the lot outside the liquor store. Don kept driving. Will lit a blunt in the empty lot and listened to the lyrics of Hove's: *Jigga My Nigga*.

He was singing the chorus when a gun came smashing through the driver's side window startling him. Will looked up. Don was there holding a Glock to his head.

"What's up now, nigga?" Don said, a sinister smirk on his face.

Will was speechless. Don reached inside the car and unlocked the door.

"Get the fuck out!" Don said backing away.

Will got out of the car, leaving his gun under the seat.

"You got me," Will said looking around. "Now what?"

Don swung the gun at Will's head putting a gash above his eye.

"I don't want yo ass," Don said watching Will falling to the ground. "Where the fuck is Shine at? All you gotta do is tell me where Shine at."

Will's head was spinning. He was having a hard time focusing.

"I don't know," Will said trying to get to his feet. "The nigga's been missing."

"What the fuck you mean; missing?" Don asked.

Will gave up on trying to stand and decided to sit on the ground.

"When Shawn died he disappeared."

Don kicked Will in the head. "Y'all killed her. Don't sit up here and play word games with me. I'm not in the mood."

Will's head hit the door of his car.

"If you gone kill me just kill me," Will said holding his head. "If not, do whatever you gone do." Will wasn't going to give up

Shine's whereabouts. Don shook his head as he looked at Will. "What?" Will asked.

"I guess you got down with the wrong team," Don said before shooting Will in the head and chest. He then rifled through Will's pockets, taking money and snatching jewelry. "It's gotta look like a robbery," Don said. He spat on Will's carcass and walked away.

Will's murder was big news in the drug community. Every big-time drug dealer wanted to know who had the balls to do Will. Shine had gotten the call on his cell and couldn't believe it. Don was the first name that popped into his mind. Michelle explained that it was a robbery. Shine quickly dismissed Don as a suspect. After hanging up, Shine thought about all the stick-up kids with enough heart to kill Will. He came up empty every time.

Outside of SCC he couldn't think of one person who would risk going to war with him. Shine sat in his Florida beach house contemplating attending the funeral and decided against it. He had started to get over Shawn's death and wanted to clear his mind by the time he returned to Gary. He continued to focus on healing himself.

Don was going crazy. It had been three weeks since he killed Will and Shine still hadn't surfaced. Shine didn't attend Will's funeral. Don was getting tried of playing the shadows but didn't want to expose himself too soon. Don sat in his apartment when the phone rang.

"What up?" Don said pouring a drink.

"I got this nigga," Juice said and smacked Juan in the back of his head with his gun.

"Got who?" Don asked.

"Juan…"

"Where ya'll at?" Don asked and sat his drink down. Juice gave him the address. Don was out of his apartment before Juice could finish.

By the time Don walked into Juan's house carrying a baseball bat, Juice had already worked Juan over real good. Juan was sitting in a chair with the whole left side of his face bruised, bloody and swollen.

"I left the other side for you," Juice greeted smiling.

Don walked in front of Juan and looked at him.

"Please Don," Juan begged reaching out to Don. "Don't kill me. It's these drugs man, I can't help it. You know I wouldn't play you like that."

Don backed away from Juan and looked at Juice.

"Is this nigga wet?" He asked.

"Nah, I think I caught him on his way to go cop."

"Good," Don said before he swung the baseball bat hitting Juan in the ribs.

Juan fell to the floor doubled over in pain yelling and gasping for air.

"Please Don," he screamed gasping for breath.

"I brought you into my fam. You piece a shit, betrayed me. You tried to rape my wife." He swung catching Juan in the back. "Who was with you?" Don bellowed cocking the bat. "Who the fuck was with you?"

Juan was on the floor crying when his roommate walked in.

"What the fuck is going on?" The roommate asked.

"Pain," Don said turning to face the roommate.

He turned and tried to run. Juice hit him in the back of the head with a .44 Desert Eagle. He crashed to the floor.

"Two for the price of one," Juice said.

Juice tied up Juan's roommate. Don continued to punish Juan. After Don inflicted more pain.

"Who was with you? Who was the other nigga?" He asked again.

Juan laughed and winced from the pain.

"You don't know?" He asked between swollen lips. "I ain't saying shit!" Juan spat blood on the floor as Don watched with the bat in hand.

"All right," Don said walking away. "You wanna be tough, go out like a soldier. We'll see."

Don went out of the house and returned a few minutes later with a gasoline can. Without saying anything, Don poured gasoline all over Juan as he crawled on the floor.

"We about to see just how tough you really are," Don said pulling out matches. "One last chance before you go up in flames," Don said producing a stick. "Who was the other nigga?"

"All right, all right," Juan shouted putting his hands up. "It was Terry."

"Good," Don said with a smile on his face. "We getting somewhere. Who the fuck is Terry?"

"I'm sorry dog. I can't go out like this." Juan had tears in his eyes. Don turned and looked at the roommate.

"Mr. Squeaky Clean...?" Don asked snatching the gag off. "Thought you going to get off easy, huh?"

"Nah dog, it wasn't me..." the roommate said looking up at Don with eyes wide as deer's.

"Now you wanna lie...?"

Don swung the bat splitting the man's forehead. Terry was out cold but Don kept swinging with all his might. Juice grabbed him.

"He's history," he said looking down at the blood pouring from Terry's head and face. "Let's get this shit over with."

"You right," Don said walking back over to Juan. "Thought I forgot you...?" Don looked down at Juan. "Since we was boys I'm a give you a choice. How you want it?"

"Shoot me. Pump one in my head." Juan knew that his fate was sealed and wanted the quickest way out.

"Hell no...!" Don shouted. He pulled out the matches tearing one off. "This is for my kids." He lit the whole book of matches and tossed it on Juan. "Let's get the fuck outta here." Don picked up his bat and walked out.

Word came around that Shine was back for two days. He sent fear through his crew criticizing their inability to protect one another. Shine executed his best bodyguard. Four other members were killed for not stepping up after Will's murder. They'd let profits suffer. He had the whole crew stressed, fearing who'd be next.

Shine dangled a two million dollar reward for the name of Will's killer.

He had a new outlook on the business. While away Shine learned you have to befriend the enemy to achieve your goal sometimes. He planned on making it where even his enemies would want to collect.

Don went back to Louisiana for a week to spend Christmas with his kids. He was in Gary by New Year's Eve. Don didn't want to deal with the sneaking around any longer and decided to come out of hiding.

He along with Juice, J-roc and a few other SCC members sat in the game room laughing and joking. Twon walked in and was surprised to see Don sitting in the room.

"This truly is a surprise to see Don here with us," Twon said smiling at. "When did you come back?"

Don got up from his chair and hugged Twon.

"I been in and out taking care of a few things. I just got back today."

"That's fo' sho." Juice laughed.

Twon looked at Juice and then at Don. "So you've been coming back and forth and didn't let me know?" Twon asked with a scowl.

"It ain't nothing," Don said sitting back down. "I just had to see a few people, that's all."

"Yeah, I must not be as important to you as I thought," Twon said and looked at Juice.

"C'mon Twon, you know we brothers."

"Yeah, we brothers," Twon said with a light smile. "Everything's cool," he said before sitting down. "Fill me in."

The two spent the rest of the night talking about everything, even Will and Juan. Things were back to normal. Don set out to be even larger than before.

December 31, 1999 Don spent the whole day with his crew tripping, telling old war stories. At ten o'clock in the night he wanted to bring in the new year with his family, not his clique. His mom was the only real family in the Gary area. Don drove out to the house to celebrate the new millennium with her and never noticed the blue Cutlass tailing.

"You got my money...?" A voice barked.

"Who the fuck is this?" Shine asked looking at his phone.

The person on the other end only wanted the reward. "Names ain't important. The only thing important is Don killed Will. He back in Gary."

Shine was all ears now.

"How do you know? How the fuck can I trust you when you won't even tell me your name?"

The caller on the other end was anxious. "Look, I know where he at. Either you gone pay me or not...?"

"Alright..." Shine said sitting up. "Where he at?"

"My money...?"

"Hell nah. Fuck that!" Shine said jumping up from the couch. "It don't work like that, for all I know you can be trying to beat me. I'm a business man. If it checks out I'm a pay you."

"Give me half now and I'll give you the address. After you see him or whatever you give me the rest."

Shine thought for a few seconds. "If you fuck me," he said as he searched for a pen and paper. "You know I'm a kill you...?"

The caller didn't want to come out of the situation empty handed. He had someone parked two blocks from Tina's house ready to get the reward. The caller gave Shine Tina's address and warned Shine that if he tried anything shady, Don and the rest of the SCC crew would be alerted. The caller hung up and Shine ran out the door to get the money.

Don had been at his mom's house for an hour and a half. The two sat around playing cards and Playstation. They were watching a Chicago Bulls basketball game when Don turned to Tina.

"Can I ask you a question?" He asked turning the volume to the television down. Tina sat her bag of microwave popcorn down. "You know that when you spoke at Shawn's funeral it really caught me off guard. At first I thought you just making stuff up to look good but then I realized you was telling the truth. I never knew y'all had got close. How long was y'all cool? I mean, how did it happen?"

Don looked up at his mother. She was smiling.

"If you must know, when you was in Arizona," Tina said her hands in her lap. "She was having a hard time with the kids and being alone. So we talked one day and I realized that I had misjudged her. We started talking everyday and she started spending nights over here with the kids. And I guess somewhere in our conversations she grew on me," Tina said nudging her son.

Don hugged his mama and kissed her cheek. "Thank you."

Tina had tears in her eyes as she hugged her son back.

"I love you."

"I love you too."

Tina got up from the couch straightening her Chicago Bulls jersey.

"Let me go get us some more snacks," she said before walking away.

"You ain't got no leftover pies and cakes?" Don asked smiling. "You know I got a sweet tooth."

Before Tina could respond her front door was kicked-in. The men charged in, shooting. Don yanked Tina by the arm pulling her down to the floor and then pulled out his Glock shooting anyone in sight. Don only had seventeen shots and no extra clips. He made sure every bullet counted. Don killed and wounded twelve perpetrators. They kept storming the house.

"Ma," Don said as he looked at Tina. "You got a gun in the house?"

Tina was on the floor crying.

"No, you know I don't like guns." Tina then looked at her son's eyes. "They're going to kill us, ain't they?" She asked shuddering in fear.

Don looked around the couch. He saw the men still charging in.

"I'm sorry ma, I shouldn't never come here. This my fault."

Tina hugged her son. "I love you."

She stood and immediately caught a bullet to her right shoulder. Another went in her stomach. Tina dropped to the floor and Don jumped up from behind the couch shooting his last couple shots and hitting no one. The men hit Don once in the chest. The bullet didn't kill him. They rushed into the house and surrounded Tina and Don.

"Well, well, well," Shine said. He stood over Don. "It looks like your luck done run out."

"We gotta make this quick," One of the men said giving Shine an ax. "You know them crackers gone be here real quick."

Shine took the ax and looked at Don. "You get off easy but you still gone suffer." Shine said kicking Don in the mouth.

Don spat blood on Shine's shoes. "Nigga fuck you! Gimme your best…"

Shine smiled at Don and then looked at Tina. "Before I kill you," Shine said signaling for his men to get Tina. "You gone watch her die…"

Don said nothing. Him and his mother were dead anyway. He didn't want to give Shine the satisfaction of hearing him beg.

"Hold her down!" Shine shouted tossing the ax back over his shoulder. "And make sure the nigga watch. This is for Jason. Blood for blood nigga…"

Shine lowered the ax with all his might. Tina's neck gave, Shine had to swing three more times before her head was completely severed. Shine picked up the head and put it right in Don's face.

"She look familiar," Shine laughed. The rest of his crew laughed. Don tried to attack Shine but had no energy. Shine dropped Tina's head and hit Don four times in the face causing his legs to give out. "Drop him." Shine said turning to get the ax. Don fell to the floor and reached into his pocket. He pulled out a switchblade and hid it.

"I hear sirens," a man said running into the living room. "They'll be here any minute."

"We on our way," Shine said standing over Don. "This for Shawn, G and everybody else…" Shine raised the ax.

"You know Shawn wanted me to tell you something," Don

whispered.

"What you suppose to tell me?" Shine asked putting the ax down.

Don mumbled in a lower voice and Shine bent so that he could hear Don clearly. Don felt Shine was close enough.

"Shawn hated your guts."

He lunged and the knife went through Shine's jaw. He jumped back.

"Fuck this shit!" Shine said, blood leaking from the hole in his face. "Let's go." The men walked out. Shine turned around and pulled out his gun. "You know I wasn't gonna leave without saying goodbye to your ass."

Shine shot Don in both legs and arms, once in the stomach and emptied the rest of his clip into Don's face.

"Survive that, bitch!" Shine spat on Don's body and left.

Juice notified Jon about the murders of his mother and brother. Jon, Kay and the rest of the family were there in less than ten hours. Jon wanted to see the bodies immediately. Juice told him that it'd do no good, but Jon insisted. Juice gave him the information of the hospital.

After a lot of talking and bribing Jon was finally allowed to see his mother's and brother's body. The sight of seeing what was done to his brother made Jon nauseous. The shock of seeing his mother's severed head made Jon threw up. When he was finished regurgitating, Jon knelt and cried.

"This is my fault. I should've never left you alone. I broke my oath to you and I'm sorry. I'm back now and people will pay. I promise you. In 2000, everyday will be a good day to die..."

BIOGRAPHY

I am known as Bay Bay and was raised in the small city of Gary, Indiana. Famous for being the hometown of Michael Jackson and his family, the place got slept on. Gary is not a tourist attraction. It's more what you see on The Corner – straight slums. In 2003, Gary was rated the worst city to live in the US, but growing up there was both dangerous and fun.

Despite dropping out of school in the ninth grade and being involved in the system since the age of thirteen, I believed in myself. In '92 I received my GED and an Associate's Degree in '98. It was when I took a break from school that drama from my past caught up to me. Now the feds have me in custody.

There are a lot of things that pushed me into the writing field. I remember being twenty-one and a tutor in prison. The person I tutored was a wiz at getting grants for the system. She would type proposals and ask me and another tutor to proofread for her. She always encouraged me to write a book. Then I arrived in Virginia and a former roommate, Terrance Stokely, was writing a book. He would always ask me to spell certain words he had problems with. Then I got in trouble and was sent to confinement. Isolated, I read a couple of HIP Hop fiction books and was inspired to write one.

A stepson and three bad boys along with my beautiful wife provide me with the inspiration I need. Through my writings I can show my boys a better way.

I write about the two things I know: the streets and the penitentiary. The drama is from the city I grew up in. My hood is real, the peoples are real and I'm trying to make sense of all the violence.

WOMAN'S CRY
AUTHOR // VANESSA MARTIR
ISBN: 0975945386 // $14.95

A GOOD DAY TO DIE
AUTHOR // JAMES HENDRICKS
ISBN: 0975945327 // $14.95

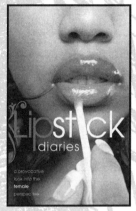

LIP STICK DIARIES
AUTHOR // VARIOUS FEMALE AUTHORS
ISBN: 0975945319 // $14.95

**IF IT AIN'T ONE
THING ITS ANOTHER**
AUTHOR // SHARRON DOYLE
ISBN: 0975945316X // $14.95

Augustus Publishing exposes talented
writers by bringing stories of unparalleled
breadth, depth, and vision to the book
market. We publish quality works of fiction
in the category of **Hip Hop** literature.

**Our stories express the widest possible
range of the urban experience...**

ORDERFORM

AUGUSTUS
PUBLISHING

Make All Checks Payable To: **Augustus Publishing** 33 Indian Road Ny, Ny 10034
Shipping Charges: Ground One Book $4.95 / Each Additional Book $1.00

Titles	Price	Qty	Total
Ghetto Girls (Special Edition) / Anthony Whyte ISBN: 0975945319	14.95		
Ghetto Girls Too / Anthony Whyte ISBN: 0975945300	14.95		
Ghetto Girls 3: Soo Hood / Anthony Whyte ISBN: 0975945351	14.95		
The Blue Circle / Keisha Seignious ISBN: 0975945335	14.95		
Booty Call *69 / Erick S Gray ISBN: 0975945343	14.95		
If It Ain't One Thing - It's Another / Sharron Doyle ISBN: 097594536X	14.95		
It Can Happen In A Minute / S.m. Johnson ISBN: 0975945378	14.95		
Woman's Cry: Llantó de la mujer / Vanessa Mártir ISBN: 0975945386	14.95		
A Good Day To Die / James Hendricks ISBN: 0975945327	14.95		
Lip Stick Diaries / Various Female Authors ISBN: 0975945394	14.95		
Subtotal			
Shipping			
8.625% Tax			
Total			

Name
Company
Address
City   State   Zip
Phone   Fax
Email

Augustuspublishing.com / Info@augustuspublishing.com